THE ADEARIAN CHRONICLES
BOOK ONE—THE OATH

THE ADEARIAN CHRONICLES
BOOK ONE—THE OATH

SHANNON M. HARRIS

SAPPHIRE BOOKS

SALINAS, CALIFORNIA

The Adearian Chronicles Book One- The Oath
Copyright © 2016 by **Shannon M. Harris.** All rights reserved.

ISBN - 978-1-943353-17-0

Editor - Kaycee Hawn and Heather Flournoy
Book Designer - LJ Reynolds
Cover Designer - Michelle Brodeur

Sapphire Books Publishing, LLC
Salinas, CA 93912
www.sapphirebooks.com

Printed in the United States of America
First Edition – February 2016

This and other Sapphire Books titles can be found at
www.sapphirebooks.com

Dedication

To Papa
A remarkable man, who will forever be missed

Acknowledgments

To say this has been a solitary endeavor is an understatement. It truly does take a village. First and foremost, a huge thank you goes out to Chris and everyone at Sapphire books, who took a chance on an unknown author. Because, without you, known of this would be possible.

To Dj and Mom for being first readers and there when I needed someone to bounce ideas off of.

Where would we be without our beta readers. Thank you Candi, Aschlie, and Dian for your insight and input. These characters and the story are better because of you.

To Michelle for the awesome cover; it's exactly what I wanted.

To Heather and Kaycee, thank you, for your outstanding editing talents. This is by far a better manuscript than the original.

And to the readers; thank you for choosing this book to pick up and read with all of the countless choices at your fingertips. I am grateful you chose mine.

Somewhere outside of Klate
Four years before the Festival of the Goddess

Lanis's fingers twitched on her knife, every nerve in her body on alert. Her target, a local merchant, stood some twenty yards away, talking with four men. The rush of the catch never failed to excite her. The forest around her was dense and a perfect spot for waiting. She inhaled as a cool breeze swept over her, bringing a smile to her lips. It was a welcomed change to the excessive heat that always tagged along behind her.

She leaned into a tree. She was a mercenary for the Ramden Council in Trit, a small village on the outskirts of the Windark Forest. Chosen at a young age, she embraced the change while her parents balked at the idea, but no one said no to the Council. Refusing any requests, in essence, would be seen as a betrayal to their people. When she turned fourteen and she and the Council both realized the depth of her ability, everything changed. Her ability not only allowed her to blend with her surroundings, but to disappear into them completely. It set her apart from the other Ramdens who had the ability to blend, but not disappear. Once a proper blend occurred, she couldn't be spotted. She understood the depth of her gift and took great care with the knowledge the gift itself brought.

She prided herself that each successful mission led to the continued safety of her people. Although she stood apart because of her ability, she never received any special treatment from the Council. All ten mercenaries working for the Council had different strengths and weaknesses. The ability to blend set them apart, but they were also trained fighters. Even though her ability tended to get her sent on the more challenging missions, she didn't see herself any different from any of the other mercenaries. She stayed active, and kept her black hair cut neat above her shoulders. Many people told her that her best feature was her smile. She disagreed and thought her best feature was her eyes— they were her father's blue.

Questioning the Council about her missions never entered her mind because they never gave her a reason to. She trusted them completely and would use any means necessary to complete every task they gave her. Sometimes weeks passed before she reached her target. This time, to her good fortune, she'd only followed the merchant for three days. As she watched, he shook the men's hands, and then led his horse and cart down a small path. There were several marked camps along the way, making it easy to follow him. She pushed away from the tree, the wind rushing through her hair as she kept a discreet distance for several miles.

She crept along the tree line, watching from a distance as he set up camp. A short time later, he sat down on what looked to be a seat carved into a fallen tree. Settling in against the tree, she blended. When the sun started to set, she pulled up her hood and moved in closer. The shadows would keep her somewhat shielded, but there was still enough light to see. She took several deep breaths when he turned his face away from her, then entered camp, and blended with a tree.

He whipped back around, eyes darting back and forth. "Anyone there?" he called out, hand gripping his sword tightly. After a few tense minutes, he laid his sword across his lap, eyes still on alert. She didn't blame him—bandits lined these forests. Most merchants hired a sorcerer to keep them safe. It was odd he hadn't, especially in this part of the forest. Steadying her hand, she stepped away from the tree and hurled the knife deep into his chest. He grunted, eyes wide, and reached for the knife while falling off the log. Lanis walked to him and knelt on the ground next to his body. He gasped, blood leaking from the side of his mouth, and reached for her.

She grasped his hand and pushed her hood back, revealing her face. "The Ramden Council sent me. My name is Lanis and I am your executioner." The surprise in his eyes only gave her pause for a moment. She held his hand until the life dulled from him. She reached over and closed his eyes then stood and retrieved her knife from his chest. The Council had gifted it to her and she would never part with it. She eyed the horse and cart. Normally she wouldn't give a second thought about any given mission, but something felt off. Untying the horse, she patted its rear, sending it off into the forest. She watched until she lost sight of it. She reached for the ropes on the cart, her fingers fumbling as she untied all six pieces of rope holding the cover on top of it. She wiped her hands on her pants, grabbed the cover, and ripped it off. Her heart sank as she looked at the contents: blankets. There had to be more. She rummaged through the rest of the cart, but only found more blankets. This didn't make any sense. She shook off her doubts that the Council would send her on a useless mission and settled her nerves. To question the Council was nearly unheard of, but she wouldn't be the first. She grabbed a blanket, unfolded it, and laid it over the merchant's body.

Not taking time to rest, she started walking toward home. In a few weeks' time, she would turn twenty-seven. She loved her people, but a part of her wondered what it would be like to meet a woman and settle down, making a life together. Being a mercenary made that dream impossible at the moment. She hoped, in the future, that would change. She walked all night, pausing for a bite to eat when the sun emerged over the trees. She had a biscuit halfway to her mouth when a familiar sound caught her attention. Putting her things away, she stood when she heard it again.

A woman's screams.

Getting involved in other people's problems wasn't on her agenda today, but when she heard the screams for a third time, she couldn't ignore them. Pulling her hood up and slipping her bag over her head to rest on her hip, she headed in the direction of the sound. Spotting movement in the distance, she slowed her pace, and peeked around a large boulder.

A woman lay squirming on the ground. A giant of a man straddled her, his hands wrapped around her throat. The woman clawed at his arms, leaving angry red streaks. Lanis uncurled her whip from around her waist and let it slide down her leg. When he reached down to undo the front of his black pants, she stepped from the tree and flicked her wrist. The whip cut through the air and wrapped around his hand. She pulled, sending him sideways into the ground. The woman jerked her head toward her, eyes wide. Lanis twisted her hand, drew the whip to her, and curled it back around her waist.

The man stood, cradling his hand against his chest. "Fella, this doesn't concern you. Turn back now and I'll forget this ever happened."

"I don't think so." He looked twice as big as she first suspected. There would be no turning back now.

"We'll see about that," he said, grabbing his sword from the ground, and quicker than the assassin expected, he advanced.

Lanis stepped back, pulling her knife.

He stepped to her right and swung out.

Barely missing the blade, she jumped back, her heel catching on a root, and she fell. Her hood slipped off as she landed on her back, the vile man landing on top of her, straddling her waist. Gasping, she cursed her bad luck as his stench made her stomach turn and she bit back the bile that rose in her throat.

"A woman," he spat. Her knife fell from her grasp as he grabbed her arms and forced them over her head. "I've got a better fate for you. One worse than death."

She wiggled, trying to gain leverage.

He picked up her knife and tapped her on the nose.

Her stomach dropped and her heart pounded.

"Such a pretty face. I bet many men and woman have been tested by your beauty. What will you do when I take that away from you?" He grinned down at her.

Lanis's chest tightened as she struggled beneath him, screaming as the blade dug into the skin beside her left eye. She closed her eyes against the blood blurring her vision, crying out as the blade pierced the skin near her nose, down her cheek, and past her chin.

"Open your eyes!" he screamed. She opened them in time to see him throw her knife to her right. She bit her lip when he stood, anger building inside of her. He stood there, smiling and gloating, never imaging what she was capable of doing to him. The pain in her face vanished as her hatred for him took hold. She would enjoy killing him.

"That's going to be a nice scar." He snickered. "Who will want you now? Next time think before you interfere in other people's business."

"Honey," the woman said. "Are you all right?"

Lanis took advantage of his lapse in judgment when he turned to address the woman. She lifted her legs and kicked out, sending him falling back. Jumping up, she grabbed her knife and ran. She needed to put distance between herself and them. After a few minutes of running, she stopped and blended with the nearest tree. The blend wouldn't be easy because of the pain, but it would have to be enough. The element of surprise would be her only way out of this. It didn't take long to hear his approaching footsteps. Only hearing one set, she kept her ears open for the woman. He walked past her, sword in hand, and stopped, turning in circles.

"Where did she go?" He turned toward where she stood.

She stepped away from the tree. "I'm right here."

His eyes grew wide as he took several steps away from her. "How? You weren't there a second ago," he said, pointing to the tree behind her.

She smiled at the fear in his eyes and for every step he took back, she took one forward.

"Who are you?"

"Your executioner." She would enjoy this.

"Please," he begged, dropping to his knees. Letting his sword fall to the ground, he clasped his hands in front of him as he realized who and what she was – a Ramden Council assassin. "This has all been a misunderstanding. I didn't know what you were."

"And what am I?" Bending down, she picked up his sword.

"Please don't kill me. I'll do anything. Please."

His fear disgusted her. She kept her gaze on him even when she heard the woman approaching. Leaning forward, she whispered in his ear. "You asked what I was."

"Yes." His voice trembled.

"I am your worst nightmare."

His body shook. "Please. I don't want to die."

Lanis wiped at her face, cringing at the amount of blood on her arm. "Do you think I wanted this scar?" She turned the sword in her hand before plunging it into his chest. She pulled it out slowly and tossed it on the ground. The woman screamed, falling on the ground, and cradled his body in her arms.

"What have you done?"

"What have I done? I've saved both of our lives. From him."

"You killed my husband." She held him close. "If it's the last thing I do, I will hunt you down and kill you."

She had nerve. "You can try, but you won't like the outcome." Lanis walked backward, never taking her eyes off the woman. When she was a good twenty feet away, she turned and ran for home. She ran until her legs started to tremble. Bent over, gasping for breath, she watched the blood drip from her face, making a puddle at her feet. Touching the wound, she winced at the depth. How would the Council react? She broke protocol and didn't know how that would affect her future.

She should have never interfered.

How could she be a mercenary with such a

distinctive mark on her face? The Ramden people employed healers, but none near powerful enough to make the cut disappear. She rose up and took several deep breaths, looking back the way she came. She should have killed the woman too.

⚏ ⚏ ⚏ ⚏

Adearian
Present Day
Inside the Windark Forest
Three Months before the Festival of the Goddess

Lanis jolted awake, hitting her head on the side of the carriage. She rubbed it as she looked out the window. By the way the sun peeked through the trees, she saw midday approached. She didn't relish the unknown, but that was exactly what she was getting ready to walk into. Although, at this point in her life, she was used to expecting the unexpected. She was a bit surprised three nights ago when Anya handed her a sealed letter embossed with the seal of Trit. Her first instinct was that something had happened to her parents, but she quickly dismissed that idea. The Council would never send a formal letter for such matters. The Council requested her presence as soon as possible. It was rare for a Protector to leave their charge, but Anya insisted that she go, explaining that in certain circumstances a Protector could leave and give their duties, temporarily, to another. After discussing matters late into the night, Lanis left the Central Temple and found a solider she knew to be reliable. He was humble and agreed to take over her Protector duties until she returned. Running her hand through her hair, she leaned back in the carriage seat. If her estimates were correct, she would soon be back in Trit and facing the people who dismissed her.

Four years ago, the Council, specifically Elder Helt, pulled her from missions, informing her the scar would hinder her success. Such a complete dismissal after everything she gave them hurt her deeply. She took a few months off, and then helped tend her parents' farm. She valued their time together, but couldn't shake the restlessness that settled inside her. One night while she walked the shores of the Tynuck Sea, a man approached her. She listened as he explained who he was and what he wanted. He was High Priestess Anya's Protector and he wanted her to accept the Protector's Mask and take his place. High Priestess Anya was the leader of Goddess Nia's people in Malora.

She would have laughed if not for the look on his face. He didn't give her a choice; he expected her to say yes, and she did. She loved her parents, but couldn't pass up this opportunity. He told her that she need only remember two things: one, never leave the High Priestess's side; and two, never reveal her face to anyone. She broke the second rule three years ago and the first one three days ago.

To receive the mask of a Protector was an honor and a privilege. There were only five masks in existence. The legend was that Kilin and Arut, the God and Goddess of the heavens, were fed up with their five children always bickering and fighting. Kilin sent all five of his children - Shara, Acker, Feine, Novak, and Nia - to Adearian, a small planet he created for this very purpose. Each child inhabited a different area of Adearian. Shara picked land high on cliffs and named it Hadmore. Novak settled in the mountainous region to the west of Hadmore, giving it the name Laramore. Nia picked a small piece of land far away from her siblings that bordered the water and named it Malora. Being the youngest and never getting along with his siblings, Feine chose a cluster of islands off of Hadmore's border and named them Pona. Acker didn't choose a specific area, but chose to roam the land.

Each child also held different abilities. Shara's gifts were geared toward everything having to do with magic. Acker could manipulate weather patterns and summon the land to do his bidding. Feine was a master with animals. Novak's gifts were strength and protection. Because Nia's gift was so different from her siblings, they tended to laugh and ridicule her. She was the Goddess of health and well-being.

Kilin also created a race of people who he spread out all over Adearian so they could choose freely which child they wanted to serve. To a select few of their worshippers, the children gave their gifts. As the population grew, Arut worried someone would find a way to harm her children. Kilin agreed and crafted five masks from Nunik, a rare metal only found within the deepest parts of the earth. It was said only the Gods possessed the power to locate and excavate the metal. Each child gave the mask to someone worthy enough to wear it, as their Protector. Each mask was unique to the child and, once put on, completely transformed the wearer. The Protector was recognized as neither man nor woman. Each was given a long sword, with that particular God's crest cut into the metal of the blade in order to protect their charge. The blade of the sword was also crafted from Nunik. The gifts of a Protector and what they were capable of wasn't completely known. The only thing known was that the mask prolonged the Protector's life and in some ways made them immortal. When the children returned to their parents, the Protector was put in charge of keeping the High Priest or Priestess of the five Gods safe at any cost.

Each time Lanis put on the mask, it took a part of her away. Every sense was heightened to an extreme level. The urge to protect her charge overcame everything else. She would willingly lay down her life for Anya, mask or no mask. The first time she laid eyes on her, for a split second, her heart stopped beating. Her beauty wasn't all that left her breathless; she felt a connection to her. For the first time in her life, she found what she always wanted. It wasn't love at first sight, but it was close. She also knew she could never act on her feelings. She was a Protector and Anya, a High Priestess. Three years ago, all that changed. After being Protector for one year, she made a crucial mistake.

When Anya visited Nia's temple, no one, including her Protector, was allowed inside. On this particular day, Lanis slipped off her mask to see the room through her own eyes, if only for a few seconds.

"I am pleasantly surprised," Anya said from behind her.

Lanis spun around. Stupid! She hadn't even heard the temple door open. Anya leaned against the door, staring at her. Her blond hair hung around her shoulders and her green eyes sparkled. The smile on her face lit up the entire hallway. Lanis took a step back and lifted the mask.

"No. Wait," Anya said, hand outstretched.

She lowered the mask. "I'm sorry. I..."

Anya shook her head. The smile never left her face. "In all my years as High Priestess, I've never seen your face. I wasn't expecting someone so young, someone near my own age."

How would she get out of this? She could ignore her and put the mask on, but she didn't want to do that. "You're not supposed to see me and the mask is never to leave my face." She swallowed hard, clutching the mask in her hands. In all her years as a mercenary, she had stood face-to-face with many different types of people, but standing in front of Anya left her flustered.

"Why take it off then?" Anya pushed away from the door and stopped a few feet from her.

"For a few minutes a day, I like to see the world through my own eyes. Even if it is only a stone wall," she said, pointing to the walls that lined the hallway.

"Well, when we're in this part of the temple or alone, please fill free to take it off. I won't tell." She winked.

"I don't think that's a good idea." In fact, it was a terrible idea.

"Why? I can understand your reasons. There is nothing quite like seeing the world without blinders on, or in your case, a mask. Some people never realize what they are really seeing. Nature, and all she does, is a magical thing. Some nights when I'm looking out my window, it takes my breath away."

"I know, I watch you." She instantly regretted the words as soon as they left her mouth.

"Really?" Anya smirked.

"You know what I mean." Could this get any more embarrassing?

Anya laughed. "I do. If I may ask, what's it like wearing the mask?"

She didn't see any harm in answering her questions. "It takes over all my senses. I see only what is important to the situation. When we're alone, I look at all possibilities of how someone could gain entrance. I also feel the presence of magic. I don't know how, but I know when things around you have changed. I like having the means to protect you." She shrugged. "But I don't like not being myself."

Anya took a seat by the wall and patted the one next to her. "Why were you chosen?"

Lanis kept her distance. "I don't know why I was chosen. I took the position because I needed a purpose. The Ramden Council released me of my mercenary duties because of my scar. I broke protocol, and in a way I was punished for it." She rubbed her neck. "Don't get me wrong. I wouldn't trade the years I gave them for anything, and I loved being able to help my parents with their farm, but as time went on, I knew something was missing."

Anya pointed around them. "And now you've found it."

"And now I've found it." Lanis nodded. They were both quiet, verging on an uncomfortable silence when Anya reached her hand out. Lanis grasped it.

"You can call me Anya."

"I'm Lanis."

Their relationship started then and grew with each day that passed. Anya never ceased to amaze her with her zest for life. Lanis understood the toll being High Priestess took on her, but she also knew the woman that lay beyond the role. She found the one thing she always wanted, but didn't dare ever to hope for—someone to share her life with, and in the most unlikely of places. Their relationship was confined to the temple, which made it difficult at times to be alone, but she wouldn't change a thing about the way her life turned out. She would do anything if it meant keeping Anya safe. To lose the one person who loved her without boundaries was unthinkable. By showing Anya her face, she could have put both their lives in danger. Anya, however, waved off her concerns.

She only hoped that whatever happened in Trit wouldn't pull her away from her Protector duties. Her commitment was to Anya and keeping her safe. She glanced out the window when the carriage veered to the right, taking the familiar road to Trit. After what seemed like a lifetime, she spied the large cluster of rocks indicating the entrance to the village. It was too late to turn back now. Heart pounding, she said a silent prayer as the carriage rolled to a stop. She climbed out and stared at the entrance to the Council house. The building was nothing special—four plain walls and a thatched roof. What lay beyond the walls held the potential to tear her life apart. Entering through the doors used to bring a sense of honor, but now it would only bring dread. She wiped her hands on her pants and, taking her time, walked up the four steps. She stopped at the doors and inhaled; the familiar scent of dirt and the wildflowers that lined the road put her at ease. She gripped the handle and opened the door.

⁂

It never dawned on High Priestess Anya how miserable sleeping alone would be until she actually had to. Lanis should be back tomorrow, or at the latest, the next day. Her life changed for the better the day she saw Lanis without her mask on. Seeing the person behind the mask was a shock and a surprise, and her heart literally skipped a beat. A part of her shifted that day. It wasn't unwelcome, but it was unexpected. Denying the pull toward Lanis would have been like denying the air she breathed. In her position, she couldn't, and wouldn't, doubt her decisions. Nia was her first priority, and to the best of her knowledge, Lanis had accepted that. At least, she hoped she had. When Lanis was called to Trit, the Oracle had been specific in her instructions and what would be expected of Lanis. Even loving Lanis as much as she did, given the choice, she would do everything the exact same way.

The Oracle came to be five hundred years ago after Danath's betrayal. High Priest Wiltor did away with the position of Prophesier after Danath, Prophesier of Nia, allowed his brother Damrek, the creator of the Ramden people, to copy a prophecy he received. To allow another to read or even see a sacred prophecy was blasphemy and punishable by death. To ensure such a betrayal never happened again, High Priest Wiltor chose one from among the Prophesiers and gave him the title Oracle. From that day, the Oracle was confined to the Central Temple.

The Central Temple stood the tallest of the five temples built into one side of the Tynuck Mountains. Made entirely of glass, it was often referred to as the Hall of Windows. Danath's fate had been sealed beyond those panes of glass. The Central Temple was also where the High Priestess and her four personal advisers lived and conducted temple business. On some days, like today, Anya wished High Priest Wiltor had also done away with the position of personal adviser. Her mind and focus weren't in the morning meeting.

The faint sounds of someone talking briefly registered, but she tuned them out. After talking with the Oracle about what needed to occur with Lanis, she set a plan in motion with the Ramden Council. If her actions ruined their relationship, it would devastate her. Living without Lanis wasn't an option. She bit her cheek while watching the birds fluttering outside the window. On top of dealing with Lanis, she recently came into the knowledge that one of her four personal advisers had betrayed her, and ultimately Nia. She couldn't pinpoint which one or the depth of the betrayal, but she would.

"High Priestess Anya."

Keeping her face void of any emotion, she slowly turned from the window and faced her advisers. Surely she hadn't missed something important and considering Merek had been talking, she most likely hadn't. He tended to speak if only for the sake of talking. Sweeping her gaze around the table, the depth of the betrayal hit her full force. She should be able to trust them. She didn't, not fully, and not with her life. "Yes." She wiped the hair back from her eyes.

Merek frowned. "I am finished."

"Very good." She straightened in her seat, giving them her full attention. "As everyone is well aware, the reading of the last prophecy ever written by Danath is coming up shortly."

"How could we forget?" Hensley muttered, straightening the papers in front of him.

Anya ignored his remarks. His frustration was evident, as was everyone else's. Getting everything in order for the reading took a lot of time and effort. "As I was saying. Everyone is well aware tradition dictates the reigning High Priest or Priestess is to read the Prophecy from the balcony of the Central Temple.

When Danath wrote the Prophecy, he stated it was to be read in Hadmore, or more importantly for us today, their capital, Manight. Tradition is tradition, though we have never shied away from change. I would like your views on the matter. Miriam, we will start with you." All of her advisers knew she didn't need their approval, though it went a long way in improving relations. Politics were everywhere. She didn't like the game; she just knew how to play it. From the start, Miriam had supported her. Not because she believed in or even liked her, but because of her faith in Nia. Miriam felt her position held her to a higher standard than Nia's followers.

"High Priestess." Miriam nodded. "I fear no answer will be the right one. Everyone here knows my views on temple matters." She fidgeted in her seat. "We are in uncharted waters. I agree someone from the temple should go. I'm not sure it should be you, though. Five hundred years is a long time for a Prophecy to gather dust. Never in the history of Malora has a High Priest or Priestess traveled to read a Prophecy. No." She shook her head. "You should not be the one to go. The stakes are too high. No one ever mentions it, but the Holders members have grown considerably in the last few years. We know what they are capable of doing. Your life is too precious and invaluable to all of Nia's followers. Others would willingly take your place."

Anya's breath caught, the passion in Miriam's voice surprising her. The pleading didn't sound like her at all and to mention the Holders was odd as well. From the startled looks on the other three advisers' faces, they couldn't believe she had mentioned them either. Five hundred years ago, after Danath confessed his betrayal to High Priest Wiltor, Damrek unleashed his magic upon Adearian. Cities and villages were leveled and thousands were killed. After the blast, High Priest Wiltor sent seven of his finest guards to investigate the blast and to find Damrek. Instead of Damrek, the men found a cave and inside, on a table set against the wall, seven small books. Nestled in the front of each book was a sphere. The first page of each book instructed each man where to go and what to do. Six of the men heeded the instructions and gave themselves the name Holders of the Spheres. The seventh man went straight to High Priest Wiltor and told him everything they found. Not long after his confession, the seventh man disappeared. High Priest Wiltor secured the book in Nia's temple, but the sphere was lost to time.

Anya leaned forward, clasping her hands together on top of the table. Lately, the Holders' numbers had grown two-fold. She understood their need to believe in something, even if their truths were lies. The majority were harmless, but in recent years, a small number had banded together and formed a more radical group. Through a number of sources, she confirmed that a high-ranking member of the group had found five of the seven spheres. A remarkable feat, considering the spheres were spread all over Adearian. Miriam's concerns were relevant; however, she didn't agree with them. "Thank you, Miriam." Kerrison, the complete opposite of Miriam, was also the most vocal about her not becoming High Priestess. In the end, she backed down, but Anya never knew why. Looking at Kerrison now confirmed they had both came a long way together. "Kerrison."

Kerrison bowed her head. "High Priestess. I don't know why anyone has to travel to Manight. What's stopping Queen Abigail from coming to us?"

She waved her hands in front of her. "It's…"

Hensley slammed his fist on the table. "The Prophecy is to be read in Manight as stated in the scrolls. Some of us don't so easily push aside doctrine," he said, glaring at her.

Anya stiffened. Her advisers, in recent meetings, seemed to be getting more volatile. "Hensley."

He sighed. "Yes, High Priestess."

"Do not sigh at me and do not interrupt my meeting. I will not put up with your insolence. Do I make myself clear?"

He bowed his head, locking eyes with her. "My apologies, High Priestess."

She nodded, acknowledging his words. On countless occasions, her other three advisers reflected their opinions as to why he shouldn't have been chosen, and in the same breath, questioning both her and Hensley's competence. As the youngest of her advisers, he still had a lot to learn. He kept his dark hair cut short and his green eyes always held a hint of mischief. His heart was always humble in dealing with the people of Malora and his clothes and attitude reflected that. Everyone was a work in progress, though some felt they'd already arrived. "Kerrison, continue."

"All I meant," she said, glaring at Hensley, "is that times are different now. Over the years, things have changed considerably. High Priest Wiltor understood. He blocked the city from outsiders after Damrek's incident. Hadmore sealed its borders with shields to keep magic out. Things started changing that day and have continued to change. We are not the same Malora as five hundred years ago. The roads are more dangerous now. None of you can tell me any differently." She pointed to her chest. "I am the only one of us who travels regularly outside the city. I have seen firsthand the depravity of so many. While I'm sure, High Priestess," she said, looking behind Anya, "your Protector is up to the task of protecting you, what of the people who travel with you or those caught in the middle? There are some who would like nothing more than to see you dead." She glanced at Miriam. "Just like Miriam, I hear things. You are the most beloved of any High Priest or Priestess to lead Nia's people. You have a great responsibility to her followers and with that comes great power. Some people believe you carry a sphere with you. It is rumor, but it is enough of one that certain people would stop at nothing to retrieve it. Queen Abigail should come to us for the reading. I see no reason to make a spectacle out of it, and that's what the festival will do. The stakes are too high."

Anya agreed with a lot of her points, but the fact remained the Prophecy was never meant to be read in Malora. "Kerrison, I appreciate your concern, but Hensley is right. The Prophecy must be read in Hadmore, or more specifically for us, Manight."

"Why Manight?" Kerrison asked.

"What?" Miriam said.

"Why Manight? The scrolls specially state Hadmore. Manight wasn't in existence then. So why does it have to be read in Manight?"

"Where else would it be read?" Hensley said.

"I think because Manight is the capital and the festival will be going on that the Prophecy should be read there," Anya said. "That is the only reason. There isn't anything stating that I couldn't, say, read it in Biclin, one of the smaller towns on Manight's border." In her last meeting with the Oracle, she plainly stated that Anya couldn't be in or around Malora for the reading of the Prophecy. She just didn't tell her where she would be. "Hensley."

He bowed his head. "High Priestess, the Prophecy should be read in Manight, and," he said, running his hand through his hair, "I can't believe I'm going to say this, but I agree with both Miriam and Kerrison. You should not be the one to go. If something happened to Queen Abigail, her successor would be her daughter, Princess Jalen. But if something happened to you, it would not be so simple. We need you here; this is where you belong."

Anya ran her finger along the tabletop. Hensley always thought about the overall picture. It comforted her knowing his concern lay with the people of Malora rather than with her. Stilling her finger, she turned her eyes to Merek. Even though Kerrison was the oldest, Merek held the position of personal adviser the longest. He wore his long white hair down and kept his face cleanly shaven. He never hesitated when he wanted something, and at times, his arrogance got the best of him. They disagreed often and the only reason she kept him around was because the previous High Priest thought so highly of him. He didn't like her and that was fine with her—she didn't care for him either. The thought of him being a traitor didn't set well with her, but she couldn't stomach the idea that any of them were. Although she knew what he would say, she asked anyway. "Merek?"

He grinned, spreading his hands on top of the table. "It is not for us to change tradition or the scrolls. We are merely caretakers of what came before us. The Prophecy must be read in Manight and you must be the one to read it. Time does not change what has already been written five hundred years ago. You have your Protector; what more protection do you need? No harm has ever come to a traveling leader of any of the Gods. Why would it start now, with you?" He smirked. "I know I speak for everyone when I say whoever you choose in your place will carry out all of your duties until your safe return."

They had all been vying for the position for months. She didn't know whom she would choose. At times, she wasn't sure she could wait for the answer. For the first time since becoming High Priestess, she was ready for this entire episode to be over. "Thank you, Merek."

"If I could, High Priestess," Miriam said.

Anya nodded for her to continue.

"I know we've never had any real trouble with the other Gods' followers. But has anyone taken into consideration the majority of Manight worships Shara? Which is odd considering she is the Goddess of magic and Manight is a non-magical society?" She frowned before continuing. "Will that have any repercussions on any of this? We know that in most parts of Adearian people frown on Nia. Not for who she is, but for which she stands for. She is seen as weak and naïve, because she is the Goddess of health and well-being. Although when anyone is hurt, the first person they turn to is a healer. Who's to say a radical won't take it upon themselves to avenge their God or Goddess by harming our High Priestess?"

Over the years, a few problems surfaced with the worshippers of other faiths, but were dealt with swiftly. Although, among the different Gods and worshippers, there stood an underlying acceptance. They were all vastly different in their beliefs though they held similar qualities. Since Nia and Novak were twins, their followers tended to gravitate toward each other. Feine's followers only lived on the Pona islands. No one knew much about him or them because they rarely let outsiders onto their lands. The majority of Shara's followers lived in Hadmore and Candor. God Acker tended to live off the land and his followers were scattered all over Adearian. She didn't foresee any problems in traveling to Manight. Her relationship with Tothos, First Priest to Shara, was in good standing. "There are always those who feel it is within their power and duty to do the will of their God. I have been assured that no harm will come to me and the people who travel with me once I enter Hadmore. Queen Abigail cannot, nor would she, guarantee my safety outside the country. Although I have never met her, she seems, by all that I've heard, quite capable of keeping her word. I am sure my Protector and my guards will make sure I arrive safely. I trust that they can."

"I agree," Miriam said. "I am still not sure you should be the one to go but I don't see any trouble once you reach Hadmore. I believe Queen Abigail would never allow any harm to come to you and that is something she can guarantee inside her borders. She is competent and has far more power than some give her credit for."

Hensley leaned forward, placing his elbows on the table. "I would not want Queen Abigail as an enemy. If she says you are safe inside their borders, you will be. She is well known for keeping her people and her country from harm. Not unlike it is here. Some see her as a ruthless leader and others as a savior. But, I fear, if any sort of confrontation were to occur and she had to choose, she wouldn't hesitate to save her people over any of us, including you, High Priestess. We have to be prepared for that. We should also take into account they have been fighting at the Brown Pass for the past one hundred and fifty years. Her first priority is, and will always be, her people. She is a people's Queen."

"Hensley, I agree, but at the same time," Kerrison chimed in, "Queen Abigail knows the Prophecy is to be read in Manight. She may not agree with it, but she would never hinder tradition. Since they are still fighting at the Brown Pass and the Berrocka would never allow anyone to cross through Vashta, travelers will have to go through Manight's main port. I am certain that will cause quite a problem for her. The Festival of the Goddess is their annual tribute to Shara and for that to intertwine with the reading is going to bring in a lot of outsiders. This isn't the best outcome for her, but she is accepting it. I believe she would take your life into account, High Priestess, along with her people."

"Yes. That is why she was informed of the Prophecy a few years ago," Anya said.

"I still don't agree with that decision," Miriam said.

"I know." Anya sighed. "It couldn't be avoided." Their constant pettiness grated on her nerves. She only asked their opinion to keep them involved. She pushed up from her chair and stood. "That will be all for now. I will see everyone at the afternoon meeting. Dismissed." She gathered her papers. Goddess willing, Lanis would be home tomorrow. Nodding at her Protector, she headed toward the door, whirling around when a hand reached toward her. "What?" She stepped back. Her Protector held Merek's offending hand in a firm grip. Merek grimaced, trying unsuccessfully to pry his hand away. Hensley, Miriam, and Kerrison took a step away from them. She ignored the pounding in her head and spoke. "I hope you weren't going to touch me." No one was allowed to touch her without her permission. It went against all of Nia's laws. Magic could transfer too many things. She clutched the papers in her hands. "Sometimes you forget your place." The other three looked as stunned as she felt. "You may be my personal advisers, but I am your High Priestess. If any of you ever try something like this, I will replace all of you." She took several deep breaths. "Merek, what do you have to say?"

"I…" He fell to his knees when the Protector squeezed his hand tighter.

"Weren't you the one talking about not changing the scrolls? You know the laws. For your safety and mine." She touched her Protector's arm, never taking her eyes off Merek. "Let him go." Merek stood after the Protector released him, rubbing his arm. He should have been grateful; if it had been Lanis, he would already be dead.

Merek bowed. "I am sorry, High Priestess. It will not happen again. I only wished for a word with you."

To her ears, he didn't sound the least bit sorry. "No, it won't, because next time I won't stop my Protector." She pointed at the door. "You three can leave."

"Thank you," he said, when the others had left.

"Make this quick."

He smiled. "May we sit?"

"I am not giving you that much time."

"Of course." He smiled. "It has come to my attention through certain sources that Councilman Ramus of Queen Abigail's court is a member of the

Holders of the Spheres."

Tapping her foot, she glared at him. Accusing someone of being a member was a serious accusation. After the Prophecy reading, she would start the process to get rid of him. "And you didn't think to share this information with the Council."

"I didn't feel it would serve any purpose to do so."

She would have questioned how Queen Abigail didn't know she had a traitor among her people, but she also had one. "If I am to believe you, I have to know how you discovered this information. I cannot take only your word for it, and the next time you have this type of information, it will be brought up in Council." In order to deal with the Councilman appropriately, she would have to go through the proper channels.

"I have proof." He pulled out a small piece of sealed parchment from within his robes and handed it to her Protector.

Anya accepted it from her Protector, heart pounding at the seal, and opened it. Keeping her expression neutral, she spoke. "You can leave."

"Very well." He smirked and left.

Walking across the room to a door set back in the corner, she addressed the guard on the other side. "Have someone bring Elson Bri to the downstairs meeting room." He nodded and left. She sat down at her desk and opened the note. Only one line and a signature.

Councilman Ramus of Queen Abigail's court is a member of the Holders of the Spheres.
High Priest Lantor

She folded the note and slid it into her pocket. Of all the leaders, she and Lantor got along the best.

He served Novak, God of strength and protection. She trusted him as much as she trusted her Council, but she knew him to be a fair leader and she trusted his faith in his God. He stood against the Holders of the Spheres, as she did. She didn't know how Merek acquired the information, but she knew the note to be authentic because of the seal. She now had one more thing to take care of before she left for Manight. She hoped Lanis's day was going more smoothly than hers.

⁂

Lanis stepped into the Council house and entered into a small, square room. The guard stationed at the doors nodded and pointed behind him. "She's expecting you."

She, not they. Normally, the entire Council would be present for such a meeting. "She" could only mean one person—Elder Helt. Lanis opened the door and walked into the room. Her steps faltered when she saw only two women seated at the head table. Elder Helt and someone she instantly recognized, Priestess Tion, from Nia's temple in Malora. In order for a Priestess to be present, Anya had to have sanctioned this meeting. It also meant—whatever Anya wanted from her—she obviously couldn't come out and simply ask her for it. Keeping her anxiety in check, she walked down the long middle aisle and stopped before the head table. "Elder Helt."

"Lanis, I am glad you made it so quickly."

Lanis quelled her anger. "Didn't really have much of a choice."

Elder Helt pointed to the four seats positioned in front of the long table. "Please have a seat."

Lanis sat in the seat directly in front of Elder Helt, ignoring the Priestess. She cringed when her Elder pulled a single sheet of paper from within the desk and slid it in her direction. Without a word, Lanis leaned forward and ran her finger along the paper, her gaze never straying from Helt's. After an uncomfortable silence, she dropped her eyes to the paper and read the only line written.

The Council requests your participation.

Signing would bind her to the Council and in turn bind her to whatever Anya needed her for. After signing, she slid the paper back to Helt, who proceeded to push it in front of Priestess Tion, confirming Lanis's suspicions. By going through the Ramden Council, Anya had guaranteed Lanis's participation. For Lanis, saying no to the Council wasn't an option, and Anya knew that.

The Ramden people came into existence five hundred years before when Damrek, a rebel and self-taught sorcerer, unleashed his magic upon Adearian. It was written that a group of six people survived near the blast site. No one could come out of an attack of that nature unscathed, and they didn't. One day Ramden, the namesake of the group, leaned against a building and disappeared, only to reappear a moment later. When one of the women in the group gave birth, brown streaks covered the baby's torso. Though the streaks didn't carry any ill effects, they were a distinct marker for the Ramden people. Not long after the baby's birth, the group concentrated on finding out all aspects of their ability. Over the years, the ability to blend became easier to accomplish and became stronger in their offspring. There were hits and misses along the way, but they soon learned what could, and couldn't, be done. At the time, the only person they told of their gift was the High Priest of Malora. As leader of Nia's followers, High Priest Wiltor assured them he would only pass on the information to his successor. As with all things, however, rumors started.

Lanis knew the stories about her people—the lies and the truth. Ignorant outsiders who were blindsided by their own fear had killed too many of her people. Everyone thought they knew the Ramden people's secrets, but sadly, the majority never came close to knowing the full truth. Unlike most, the Ramden people didn't see what happened to them as a curse—they embraced the change with courage and hope. But at times, like now, the Council over-stepped their responsibilities. Lanis knew of others they had manipulated; she just never expected it to happen to her. It was an unfamiliar and unwelcome feeling.

"Lanis, this is Priestess Tion." Elder Helt pointed to the woman beside her. "She has traveled a long way to meet you."

Wordlessly, Tion slid another piece of paper across the table toward her. Lanis didn't bother looking at it, she just signed it and handed it back. Whatever they wanted from her, she already sealed her fate by signing the first piece. The second piece, at least to her, didn't matter.

"Lanis," Tion said. "I am very glad to meet you. I am afraid that I cannot give you any information regarding your oath. Once we reach Malora, High Priestess Anya will inform you of your mission. We leave in the morning." Not waiting for a reply, she stood up and walked out the back door, followed by her two guards.

Caught between irritation and frustration, Lanis

was standing when Elder Helt spoke.

"It's good to see you Lanis. You look well."

Slowly sitting back down, she addressed her Elder. "I am. Being dismissed from my duties was the best thing that could have happened to me." Time had not dulled her anger toward the woman in front of her. "Although, considering where I'm sitting, we never really leave behind who we are, do we?"

Exhaling, Helt placed both her hands on the table. "You know as well as I do neither one of us had a choice in the matter. You do not say no to Nia's High Priestess, ever. It's not the way things work."

"Everyone has someone to be accountable to."

Helt nodded in agreement and relaxed into her seat. "Exactly. I am glad you understand."

Lanis glared at her and pointed between them. "I don't understand. You are the only person besides High Priestess Anya that knows who I really am and yet you still went through with this." She brushed her hand in the air. "Whatever this is."

"You are the only one she wanted." She bit her lip and stood. "It would be in your best interest to be here early tomorrow morning."

Pushing to her feet, Lanis watched Helt walk out the back door. She always knew her gift would be a hindrance one day, and today it was. Anya should have never tricked her into coming here. She couldn't believe she was back after everything that happened. Scanning the room, her unease was suppressed a little at the familiarity of it all. Everything looked the same, from the rows of stone-carved seats, to the dark wood that lined the walls. The familiar smell of dirt and salty air that swirled inside the room stung her eyes. Sidestepping the chairs, she headed toward the far corner of the room. Her footsteps slowed as her eyes locked onto the names etched into the wood on the wall. She scanned the names, her eyes stopping when she found hers. Some of the tension that had settled on her when she stepped inside vanished when she saw her name didn't have a black mark through it. A black mark would have indicated she was given a dishonorable dismissal. The Council must have thought her actions on that fateful day were justified. Taking one last look around, she vowed never to return. These were her people, but she had too much to live for than to go on more foolish and countless missions for people she didn't believe in anymore.

After leaving the Council house, she headed toward her parents' farm. Walking the well-known streets didn't bring her the peace it once had. The only bright spot of this trip would be seeing her parents. Turning left when she reached a side road, she walked the dirt path leading to her family home. A smile split her lips when she spied the chicken coop she and her father had built one summer long ago. Her steps hastened of their own accord, and she didn't realize how much she missed it until everything came into view. Her excitement quickly vanished when she noticed her parents' carriage wasn't in its usual place beside the barn. She rounded the corner of the house and stopped short, almost running into Gordon, the farm's foreman. "Gordon."

"My goodness," he said, pulling her into a hug, then pushing her to arm's length. "It's good to see you. It's been too long. How are you, Lanis?" He slapped her on the back.

"I'm okay. I'm actually only in town for one night." Her heart dropped when a frown graced his face. "They're not here, are they?"

"No." He ran his hand through his shaggy gray hair. "They left a few days ago. Went to the cabin." He shrugged. "Can't blame them. The cabin is beautiful this time of year."

"It is. Thanks, Gordon." She stepped around him to enter the house, but stopped when he addressed her.

"You have a safe trip."

"I will, thanks." She entered through the back door, stopping mid-step as the cinnamon her mother hung around the house hit her full force. The memory of helping her mother hang all the satchels flooded her mind. Closing the door, she slumped against it and buried her face in her hands. As a child, she had asked her mother why cinnamon, and the look on her mother's face was heartbreaking. She explained it was a tradition that passed from parent to child and from generation to generation, but along the way, it had all but vanished. When their people were first created, one of the woman, of the original six, had hung cinnamon in her house as a sign of who they were. So, even in the darkest of times, the Ramden people would still have a way to identify each other, without others realizing the significance. It was a sign of their heritage, but sadly, only a select few still practiced it. Her mother had told her that one day she would understand, and her hope was that she would continue the practice. When she was growing up, she scoffed at the idea, because it seemed so out of date, but now she had Anya and they were making a life together. All of her life, she associated being Ramden with what she could do, but being Protector, she had ceased to use her ability. In time, she came to realize that being Ramden wasn't about what she could do; it was about who she was. In a way, it made her stronger. When everything that you believe in was stripped away, it made that person dig deeper and find their true self. She was Ramden and it was time she accepted that wholeheartedly. She rubbed her hands down her face and pushed away from the door. The familiarity of tradition of those long gone and of her own mother would be a memory she would not soon forget. When she got home, she would ask Anya if she could hang some satchels in their room.

She walked from room to room, but nothing had changed. Her parents were creatures of habit. Entering into her old bedroom, she knelt on the floor and looked under the bed. The pack was right where she left it. Reaching under the bed, she grasped the familiar handle, her fingers curling around the leather, and pulled it out. Not bothering to wipe the dust off, she dumped the contents on the floor. Pushing back against the wall, she eyed the items laid out before her. The two weapons on the floor had saved her life on countless occasions. Drawing the whip to her side, she ran her finger along the wrapped leather. Her Papa had given it to her when she had started her training. Looking at it now, she couldn't believe she had left it behind. One of her most prized possessions, hidden beneath a bed for four years. Standing, she gripped the handle of the whip and wrapped it around her waist. She reached down and picked up the knife, unsheathing it in the process. The polished blade didn't bother her as much as she expected it to. Even though the knife had, at the time, taken away everything she held dear, it had also lead her on the path to where her life was now. The hate she had built up for it over the years vanished as her hand tightened around the handle, and the realization that without it she would never have met Anya was at the forefront of her mind. It should scare her how right the weapons felt, but it didn't; they were a part of her. She sheathed the knife and slipped it into her boot.

She picked up the remaining two items and the vial her Grandma had given her when she was younger and put them into her pack. Sitting on the bed, she fingered the rabbit pendant that lay in the palm of her hand. Her parents gave it to her for her tenth birthday. Untangling the chain, she slipped it around her neck, and secured the clasp. Without a second thought, she swung her legs onto the bed and lay back. It was still early, but morning would come quickly. She closed her eyes and drifted off.

❧ ❧ ❧ ❧

Lanis sat back against the carriage seat, watching the trees fly by outside her window. Kicking her legs out in front of her and crossing her arms, she settled into her seat. Even though she had gone to bed early, she had still tossed all night. Deep down, she knew that whatever Anya needed her for wouldn't involve staying in Malora, and further meant she would be sleeping alone for an unspecified amount of time. She sighed, noticing for the first time how dark the shadows were through the trees. Night was fast approaching.

"I was beginning to think you were going to sleep the day away," Tion said.

"Sorry, it wasn't my intention to fall asleep again."

"I am sure you have a lot on your mind. Remember, Nia never gives us more than we can handle." Tion patted her knee. "Lanis, give your cares to her." Her hand stilled when Lanis tensed. "What's wrong?"

Lanis drowned out the sounds inside the carriage and focused her attention on the ones surrounding them. Her ears quickly picked up a slight disturbance that continued to build. The rhythmic thumping synced with the beating of her heart. Hoofbeats. By her estimates, at least three horses followed them. When the guard beside her stiffened, he confirmed her fears. Considering the road they traveled was strictly for the use of the Central Temple, it seemed rather unlikely that the riders were fellow travelers. She reached down and pulled her knife, eyes darting up when Tion squeezed her knee.

"What's going on?"

"Priestess," the guard said. "We are being followed. Please stay in your seat. We will take care of everything."

Lanis clutched the knife handle, grateful when Tion let go of her knee and sat back in her seat. To her, the guard sounded more confident than he looked. Pulling her bag from under her seat, she slipped it over her head and through her arm, where it came to rest on her side. She swung her head toward the window when movement caught her eye. The nose of a massive horse kept darting in and out of her line of sight. She blinked, catching a glimpse of the rider. He was a blur of black against the night. She leaned forward into the window to catch a better glance of horse and rider when the carriage started gaining speed, throwing her back into her seat. She inhaled deeply, getting her bearings, never taking her eyes off the window when the rider came back into view. The rider smiled at her and reached for the carriage door.

Gripping her seat, she lifted her legs and kicked

the door, sending it flying off its hinges and into the horse. She hoped the rest of the carriage wasn't built as poorly as the door. Her hands grasped the seat as the carriage swerved. She threw her leg out as Tion fell onto the floor, in an attempt to keep her from falling out the opening. Gritting her teeth, her fingers dug into the cushion until the carriage righted itself. While the guard helped Tion up, Lanis grabbed hold of Tion's seat and hopped across the aisle, landing beside her. Her gaze darted to the front of the carriage as shouts echoed outside. Ignoring the Priestess's gasp, she watched one of the riders gallop to the front of the carriage, pull his sword, and with one swing, sever the driver's head, sending his body falling into the horses.

"Brace yourself," Lanis shouted, grabbing Tion and wrapping her arms tightly around her. She tensed her muscles when the carriage tilted, trying and failing to prepare herself for the impact when it crashed into the ground. Her scream pierced the air as her body smacked into the side of the carriage, the flesh ripping from her back as they raced down the dirt road. She bit her lip when it swung sharply, slammed into a tree, and came to an abrupt stop. She gulped in deep breaths, gasping, trying to control the pain. The tingling in her shoulders and the fire racing up her back let her know that at the moment, she was still alive. She closed her eyes and counted backward from ten, pushing back as much of the pain as possible.

Her eyes flew open.

If the riders wanted them dead, they would be coming for them. She shook Tion, who still lay against her, and motioned for her to move. The carriage, to her relief, only sustained minor damage. The guard, however, hadn't fared so well. His limp body lay against her side. Tion placed her hand on his leg and bowed her head.

Lanis took a deep, steadying, breath. "I'm pretty sure he doesn't need your prayers, but we do." The hurt in Tion's eyes lasted only an instant before she nodded, then bowed her head again. Lanis ignored her low murmurs as she braced one hand behind her and gripped the side of the carriage with the other. She pushed to her knees and bent over, gasping for breath as pain exploded behind her eyes. She pounded her fists silently in front of her and bit her lip to keep from screaming out loud. Closing her eyes, she swallowed the bile that rose in her throat. She had to focus.

"Lanis, your back!"

She opened her eyes and reached behind her, swiping her hand across her back. Her hand came back covered in bits of skin, pebbles, and blood. She wiped her hand on her pants, then reached inside the guard's bag and pulled his cape out. After tying the cape securely around her back, she looked at Tion. Her skin was flushed and her tunic was torn, but Lanis didn't see any visible signs of distress. "Are you all right?"

"Yes, I guess you cushioned my fall." She rubbed her arms.

Lanis nodded. Of all the things that could have happened to them, this wasn't at the top of her list. It didn't make any sense. Why them? Why now? No matter the outcome or what awaited them, the one thing they couldn't do was stay inside the carriage. "They should have already come for us. I'm going to check things out. When I scream for you to run, run. Don't stop for anything, or anyone. Run to Malora. I'll catch up with you."

Tion nodded. "Okay, I know not to argue with

a solider, but what about you? You are still only one woman. We don't know how many are out there."

Lanis shrugged. "I don't have a choice. Besides," she said, grabbing the door handle above her head. "I do have an advantage." The riders would hear the door opening long before they saw her, but it was the only way out. She prayed they weren't waiting for them right outside the carriage. Taking a deep breath, she pushed the door open and pulled herself up and out of the carriage. Blending, she hugged the side of the carriage and said a silent prayer when her eyes locked onto the riders. They stood a good hundred or so feet away from her, talking and laughing. The three men never once looked her way. Now, she knew, it was a trap, or at the very least, they were confident enough in their abilities to wait it out. Sliding down the side of the carriage, she crouched, stilling her movements when one of the riders looked her way. Even though she knew he couldn't see her, the panicked feeling that he might sent chills down her spine. The rider's eyes darted around the area before he turned back to the other two.

All three men stood at least a foot taller than her and were twice as wide. Their black uniforms were unfamiliar to her and the gray insignia stitched onto each of their sleeves was as well. She stood and leaned back on the tree the carriage rested against. Closing her eyes and breathing deeply, she pushed the pain to a faraway place. This wasn't a fight she was looking forward to, but one that she would have to follow through with. Opening her eyes, she blinked, and pushed back farther into the tree, deepening her blend. One of the riders stood in front of her, smiling. When he grinned, she stabbed out, plunging her knife deep into his chest.

His eyes widened, and he stumbled back, falling backward onto the ground.

"Run!" she screamed, stepping away from the tree. Out of the corner of her eye, she spied Tion run into the woods and an instant later one of the remaining men jumped on his horse and took off after her.

The third man sauntered up to her, stopping ten feet away, sword drawn in front of him. The sword wasn't like anything she'd ever seen before. The blade was at least five feet in length and polished until it shone in the growing moonlight. The jagged edge along the double blade would cut her in half. His hands gripped a dark polished hilt that was lined with a design she couldn't decipher.

His lips curled into a grin.

Without taking her eyes off him, she reached down and pulled her knife from the dead man's chest.

The third man laughed and winked at her, taking a step forward.

Lanis uncurled her whip, letting the twisted leather rest by her boot.

"You really think you'll beat me with a whip?" His hand twitched on his sword.

The knots in her stomach grew with each beat of her heart. Flicking her wrist, the whip cut through the air, curling and tightening around the sword blade. She pulled, sending it flying onto the ground behind her.

In two steps, he was at her. She dropped her whip, spun on the ball of her foot, blocked his first blow, and ducked his second.

She swung her knife, grazing his arm, but fell backward when his fist connected with her head, the

                    Shannon M. Harris

knife dropping from her grasp. She scrambled to get up, but fell to her knees, coming face-to-face with his black leather boots. He knelt next to her and tapped his finger on the toe of his boots. She could make out his outline, but everything else was still out of focus. She blinked and noticed his sword on the ground in front of her.

He lifted his finger from his boot and ran it down her cheek. "If it were up to me, you would already be dead." He stood up, reared his leg back, and kicked her in the stomach.

She braced herself, but the air was still knocked from her as she landed on her stomach. Clawing at the ground, she gasped for breath as pain ripped through her chest. As he reached for her, she grabbed the sword hilt, holding tight to it when he lifted her up and tossed her through the air. A scream tore from her lips as she landed on top of the carriage, the sword slipping from her grip and falling over the side. She closed her eyes against the fire racing up her leg. She was in a lot of trouble. This definitely wasn't on her agenda for the day. "I thought you weren't supposed to kill me." By the look on his face, it was the wrong thing to say. He crept around the carriage until he stood by her feet.

They both knew she would never win in a fight. There was only one way out of this situation that she could think of. Taking several slow, deep breaths, she braced her body and rolled off the carriage. When he stepped around the end of the carriage, she tightened her hand around the hilt of the sword that lay beside her leg. She lifted the weapon and swung at him. He jumped back, screaming as the blade cut through the flesh of his leg. He collapsed onto the ground, clutching the air where his leg used to be. Ignoring his screams,

Lanis grabbed the side of the carriage and stood. It was looking more and more like she wouldn't make it out of this alive. She had to stay strong. Tion was still out there, and so was the last rider.

"You'll pay for this." He beat his head back on the ground.

"Maybe, but not before you." After steadying her balance, she stepped next to him. By the amount of blood on the ground, he wouldn't last much longer. She lifted his sword and plunged it into his arm, pinning it to the ground. Limping to her whip, she bent down and picked it up. Bracing her hands on her knees, she emptied her stomach, cringing at the amount of blood on the ground. If that was any indication, she didn't have much time left either. Her eyes focused on her leg. The cut was deep and ran half the length of her calf. Running would be hard, if not impossible. This was all Anya's fault. If not for her, she wouldn't be in this mess. She tore a piece of the cape off and wrapped it around her leg. She shook her head to clear her thoughts. There wasn't any time for pity. She started walking in the direction Priestess Tion had headed.

The farther she walked, the more the trees around her started to close in, and the darker the night became. She spun around, as the shadows danced around her. Losing her balance, she fell through a pile of foliage and landed on her back. The pain spread like a raging fire from her toes to her head. Her eyes locked on the stars and her thoughts turned to Anya. Her anger toward her vanished with the realization that she may never see her again. It would be easy to stay on the ground and let death take her. When she didn't make it to Malora, someone would eventually come looking for her. She rested her hand on her chest so she could feel each beat of her heart. The slow, steady beat helped put her at ease. She closed her eyes when her fingers brushed the rabbit pendant that hung around her neck. Hundreds of memories flooded her mind at once. She had too much to live for to give up so easily. She was a mercenary, Protector, and a Ramden. Surrender went against everything she believed in and was taught. Her body might be failing her, but her mind was strong. Rolling onto her side, she pushed onto her knees and said a silent prayer. Grasping a small tree, she pulled her body up and stood on shaky legs. Putting one foot in front of the other, she continued toward Tion. After what seemed like an eternity, she spied a small clearing through a grouping of trees and stepped through. The moon illuminated the entire area in front of her and she could clearly see Tion standing near the edge. Why would she stop? She should have kept running, or at the very least, tried to stay hidden.

Lanis limped closer to her. "One of the men rode in here. Did you see him?"

Tion shook her head, hands on her hips. "No. What happened to you?" She eyed her up and down but didn't offer any assistance.

"Not important," she said, waving off Tion's question. "I took care of the other two. Let's hope the third man is the last one, but considering I'm in pretty poor shape, I don't know what I'll be able to do. We should get going." Lanis walked past her, but stopped when Tion didn't follow.

"What do you mean, you took care of them? Did you kill them?"

Lanis stiffened. The coldness of the Priestess's voice sent shivers down her spine. She slowly turned to her, not sure what to expect. "Yes, I killed them. We need to leave before the other rider shows up."

"Too late."

Lanis whirled around and placed herself in front of the Priestess.

"You're hurt." The man snickered. "Not going to be much of a fight."

After making it this far, she couldn't let him win, not now. "We'll see." She advanced and punched him in the face. He grabbed her leg and pulled on it, knocking her off her feet.

"Don't kill her," Tion shouted.

"I have a right to avenge their deaths," he hissed.

"Not with her you don't. If you kill her, I will kill you. Understand?"

Lanis climbed to her feet, not believing what she was hearing. The Priestess was working with these men. Staring into her eyes, she was not looking at the same woman she rode in the carriage with. Magic held a lot of different forms and she was staring at one right now. "Who are you?"

"Priestess Tion."

"No, you're not." She was in trouble. There was no way she could fight them both. It kept getting worse by the minute.

"Are you sure? I look like Priestess Tion and I talk like Priestess Tion. How can you be so sure I'm not Priestess Tion?"

"A Priestess of Nia would never be working with these men." She clutched her whip. "What do you want with me? The way it stands you don't need me alive for it."

Tion wagged her finger. "You, my dear, are my ticket into Malora."

"You're a Priestess; why do you need me?" Maybe

the more she kept them talking the more time she had to figure a way out of this mess.

"I want to go in unnoticed. I need you for that." Tion started pacing.

"I see. You have to realize I won't go with you willingly. Besides." She shrugged. "I'll probably die before I make it that far."

Tion smiled and crossed her arms across her chest. "I figure I have two reasons for you to go along with anything I say."

Lanis furrowed her brow. Two reasons. She could only mean her parents. She had to trust that they were safe and this person was only taunting her. She turned her head when the rider pulled his sword, then stumbled back and grabbed her side as Tion stepped away from her. A small jewel-encrusted dagger was sticking out of her side. A black liquid had already stated to ooze out of the wound. "Why me?" Her words sounded hollow even to her ears.

"Like I said. I need to go in unnoticed. We need each other," Tion said, pointing between them.

"I'll take my chances." Lanis pulled the dagger out and threw it at the Priestess, missing badly. Tion's laughing stopped abruptly, and she staggered back, as Lanis's knife embedded in her stomach. Lanis stepped to the side and flicked her wrist. The crack of the whip vibrated the air around them and in one swift motion, it wrapped around the rider's throat. She pulled and he fell to the ground, clutching at his throat. She lost her balance and fell to her knees, still holding the whip, and crawled to him. The closer she got to him, the tighter she pulled. Pushing his hands away, she grabbed his head and twisted, satisfied when his head fell limp to the ground.

Now all she had to do was gather the energy to get out of the forest. She unwound the whip and stood, securing it around her waist. Turning back to Tion, Lanis took a step back. Tion stood in front of her, waving the knife in the air. The wound was bleeding, but Tion didn't seem affected by it. Lanis wouldn't be able to win against whatever Tion had become. She turned and ran, her chest tightening with each step.

"Lanis," Tion called out. "You won't win."

Lanis started to doubt her decision when she spied the rider's horse ahead of her. Nothing could have prepared her for the searing pain that shot through her body as she climbed on the beast's back and urged her mount faster down the well-worn path. The open road was more like a tunnel rather than an escape route, the darkness closing in around her. She flinched, but kept her eyes ahead when the familiar thump-thump of horse hooves behind her reached her ears. Heart racing, she grabbed tighter to the horse's mane when it suddenly picked up speed. Out of the corner of her eye, she saw Tion approaching on another horse. The Priestess didn't hesitate to pull her sword and lash out at Lanis's horse, slicing its throat.

Lanis lost her balance when the horse reared back and she hit the ground, scrambling out of the way as the horse landed beside her, its shallow breaths quickly fading.

Tion jumped off her horse and wiped her hands on her pants, then turned to Lanis. "Looks like you still have some fight left. Which, considering the dagger I stabbed you with was poisoned, is quite remarkable." She sighed. "It's a shame you're going to die. Why didn't you listen to me?" She knelt and stroked Lanis's cheek. "See what I had to do."

Lanis pushed her hand away and stood, falling back into a tree.

The Priestess laughed and stood. "Lanis, you poor woman." She turned and walked away. "You do understand that your parents live a—" Her words were cut short by the whip wrapping around her neck.

Lanis tugged on the whip and Tion stumbled back, falling into her. Lanis pulled her knife from the Priestess's belt. "I win," she whispered in Tion's ear, bringing the blade across Tion's throat. In truth, nobody won; she was just as dead as the Priestess. Her death would only be slower. She pushed Tion's body to the ground and collapsed next to it. She fell back and closed her eyes, quickly reopening them. Death was imminent, but not here and not like this, she vowed. Gathering her strength, she attempted to stand and fell over the Priestess's body. Gasping for breath, she swiped her hand across her mouth and watched in horror as it came back covered in blood.

She jerked her head up when a familiar sound caught her attention. Tion's horse stood a few feet away, staring at her. She'd completely forgotten about it. It seemed Nia was looking out for her after all. When she stood up, her steps faltered, then stopped. She couldn't leave Tion's body behind. Whatever had taken her over was gone and she deserved a proper burial. Digging a piece of rope from her bag, she tied one end around Tion and the other end around the saddle. The pain, by this point, had all but vanished and after she climbed on the beast, she couldn't feel anything at all. She lay her head on the horse's neck and kicked it into motion.

Dimitri exhaled and leaned over his desk, looking at the map laid atop it. There were five large X's marked on different locations, spread out all over Adearian. Those X's represented where the first five spheres were found. He slammed his hand on the desk and swung his arm, sweeping the map off and he watched it float to the floor. His men were close to finding one of the two remaining spheres, but he had no clue to the location of the last one.

It had taken him fifteen years to acquire the first five. No one knew what power they held, but he was positive once they were put in their rightful place inside Damrek's original book, everything would be explained. His men were still looking for Damrek's cave, but they weren't having any luck finding it. It would have been much easier if Damrek had left instructions, but no matter how many times he read the book, he couldn't find any mention of such a cave. At times, it all seemed such a waste, but he held such anticipation of what the original Book of Damrek contained that he would never stop looking for it. He believed with his very soul that the cave and the original book existed; he just had to find them.

He already allied with two of the most unlikely of sources. One alerted him to the possible location of one of the remaining spheres, and the second allowed him an opportunity he couldn't pass up, and for that, he needed the help of the one type of person not easily found. A colleague had recommended this particular Jester. Dimitri was both afraid and exhilarated to finally meet one of the most infamous of all sorcerers. He employed Rogues, but this would be the first time meeting a Jester.

All Adearian children were tested at an early age for any type of magic abilities, but a few children either fell through the cracks or were hidden away. If a child was found to have any sort of ability, they were tattooed with a yellow band on their left wrist. As they grew in their abilities, different colored bands were added in each phase of their learning, ending with a white band when the individual learned and excelled in every area of their specialty. The three kingdoms of Laramore, Hadmore, and Candor didn't agree on much, but they all were in agreement that every child should be tested. The stakes were too high to allow magic to have free rein. Four schools within the three kingdoms were specific to the different abilities given. Each child was placed according to their abilities, learned discipline, and given a chance to enhance their gift. Those that went unnoticed either taught themselves or found a mentor to teach them. They were rogue. Rogues weren't seen as a member of any society. Over the years, a small number banded together and gave themselves the name Jester. To this day, some even dressed like a court jester.

If Jesters or Rogues were ever caught, they would be killed on the spot, but no one wanted to get close enough and white-band sorcerers were always too busy or didn't want to get involved. There were probably as many Jesters as there were white-band sorcerers. Compared to white-band sorcerers, Jesters were among the most powerful of the magically inclined, for the simple fact nothing they did was monitored. That made them very dangerous and very desirable for jobs no one else would do. It also made them expensive. Dimitri ran his hand through his hair and jumped at the knock on the door.

"Sir," the guard said after opening the door. "Your guest is here."

Dimitri picked up the map, folded it, and put it in a chest that sat against the wall. He sat, straightened his clothes, and addressed the guard. "Send him in." He hoped he could take care of his problem soon. He looked up when the door opened. The man that walked in actually looked like a court jester. His clothes were colorful and he had an innocent and young look about him. Dimitri hadn't expected that. It was quite disconcerting to know he was staring at a cold-blooded killer. Granted, he killed looking for the spheres, but that was different. "Please have a seat." He gestured to the seat in the front of his desk.

"Thank you." The Jester sat and looked around the room. "This place is a dump." He cocked his head toward Dimitri.

"I don't see how that has any relevance. I asked you here to discuss a matter of great importance."

The Jester stood up and waved off his words. "Aren't they all of great importance? You are no different from anyone else I've dealt with. You have a problem and you need me to fix it." He removed a deck of cards from a pocket in his jacket and walked back to the desk, holding his hand out. "Pick one."

Dimitri hesitated, but did as asked. The queen of hearts. "What now?"

The Jester shrugged. "I just wanted to see if you would."

Dimitri threw the card to the floor and stood, slapping his hands on the desk. "This is not a game. Do you know who you're talking to?"

"I do. Do you know who you're talking to? The best thing you can do is sit back down or I will leave.

You need me. I do not need you."

"I have guards stationed everywhere. You won't make it out of here alive."

The Jester held out his hand. A green orb bounced in his palm. Dimitri backed away. "Do not threaten me. You, nor your guards, can stop me. You say you realize who I am, but I don't think you really do."

Dimitri straightened his shirt and sat back down. He couldn't let his temper get away from him, as he needed this man. "Please have a seat." When he sat, Dimitri went on. "My apologizes. I'm—" They both jumped up when a man landed on the floor, appearing out of thin air. The man struggled to stand. "Henry?"

The Jester gripped the orb in his hand. "Who is he?" he said through gritted teeth.

"Please put the orb away. This is one of my associates. He was on a job for me."

"It doesn't look like he was successful," the Jester said, sitting back down, the orb resting in his hand.

Dimitri gestured to the guard. "Help him to a seat." When the guard helped him into the chair next to the Jester, the Jester moved his chair away. "Henry, is it done?"

Henry shook his head and looked away. "I am sorry," he said. "But no, she got away."

Dimitri bit his lip and pushed back in his seat, crossing his legs. "She is still alive?" He spoke slowly, but clearly.

"There is more to her then we thought. I didn't expect. I...she killed all three guards, sir. She was badly injured and when she ran, I followed her. She killed the Priestess. After that, I returned here."

"She was hurt?"

"Yes."

"I see. I thought we agreed that in order to use her for our purpose she was to be alive, but if things went south, you were to kill her. Was she close to death?"

"I believe so, but she was headed to Malora. I couldn't stick around long after she killed the Priestess. My powers were weakening."

"Very well," Dimitri said. The man should have known never to return. He called the same guard over. "Please take care of Henry for me. He looks like he needs some help." Dimitri watched until the door shut then returned his attention back to the Jester.

The Jester waved his hand and the orb disappeared. He started chuckling. "He has no clue that he's about to die. Won't you get in trouble for killing a white-band sorcerer?"

"I have ways to deal with that. Besides, it needed to be done. Now back to what we were discussing. It seems I now have two things I need from you."

"Go on."

"Since Henry didn't succeed in anything I asked of him, I need you to find out everything you can about Lanis Welsh of Trit. I know she is on an oath mission from Nia. She is currently on her way to Malora then she will be headed to Manight. After you find out what you can, I want you to kill her."

The Jester nodded. "The second matter."

"I have a man on the inside of Malora. He informs me that High Priestess Anya hasn't officially made the notice, but that she will take the Prophecy to Manight herself. I need you to intercept her carriage and bring her and her Protector back here. I want them both alive."

"You want me to kidnap the High Priestess of the most beloved Goddess in all of Adearian and you want me to bring you her Protector." He cocked his head. "What makes you think I can get close enough to her to even try something?"

"You come highly recommended. Besides, I don't believe everything they say about Protectors. Surely they have a weakness; find it."

"It will cost you."

"I'll pay whatever you want."

The Jester clasped his hands. "Whatever I want," he sang.

It took Dimitri a second to realize what he said. "No," he said, shaking his head. "Money-wise, I will pay any amount."

The Jester stood, hopping from foot to foot, swinging his hands in the air. "Dimitri," he said, standing on one foot with his arms crossed. "You must always state what you mean. It could be taken the wrong way." He stepped behind his seat and smiled. "I'll get back to you." He snapped his fingers and vanished.

Dimitri laid his head back and rubbed his eyes. He didn't know how much this would cost him, but any amount would be worth it. Now if only he could fully trust his man in Malora, and his ally in Manight, things would be looking up. He couldn't wait until all the pieces in play started to fit together.

⚜ ⚜ ⚜ ⚜

Anya left the afternoon session with nothing new accomplished. She didn't know why she let them get to her. It seemed that eighty percent of the time, she left angry and frustrated. Her advisers never agreed on anything and all the bickering and fighting only distanced her from them. In the last few years, the disdain each of them felt for one another had grown two-fold, another clear sign of the unrest in Adearian. When one thing fell into place, three others ripped apart. She disliked the politics, but understood their place; however, politics should have no place in the temple.

She quickened her steps down the long hallway, stopped mid-step, and looked at the pictures lining the walls, each depicting a time in Malora's history. Some held happiness, while others spoke of destruction and tragedy. She reached up and touched the picture of High Priest Wiltor. The artist captured the moment he left the temple some five hundred years ago, after Damrek's episode. His actions on that fateful day changed the course of history for Malora. She smiled, knowing it wasn't by accident she stopped beside it. She knew he did what he felt needed to be done and she would do what she needed to, no matter the consequences.

She knew evil existed. She saw it in some form every day, even from her own people. The trick was making sure that it stayed only a small part of the majority, and taking care of the more extreme cases swiftly. Acknowledging that she didn't know what Lanis would face only added to her despair. She knew better than to dwell on the unknowns. They only ate at your soul, leaving you a shell of your former self. She would cast her cares on Nia, where they belonged.

Anya continued down the hall, stopping when she reached her destination. Lanis would need help on her journey, and that help waited for her behind the closed door. She stilled her features and turned the doorknob, entering the room, her Protector behind her. Elson Bri stood when she entered and continued standing until she advised him he could sit. She knew from his file he was twenty-four years old and a Ranger in Malora's army. Tall and trim, he wore his long brown hair tied up and kept his beard well maintained. From the cotton pants and simple blue shirt he wore, she deduced today was his off day. He was also a Soliret, a small group of elite fighters that were entrusted with the task of hunting down and killing members of the Holders of the Spheres. This would be the first time he was called to fulfill such a mission. Some Soliret were sent all over Adearian, while the majority stayed in Malora. To her knowledge, the armies of Malora were the only known group to allocate warriors to this specific task. All the other kingdoms dealt with the Holders; she just didn't know their process. The Holders kept themselves well hidden from outsiders. The problem was that the majority were members of very important parties, as was the case with Councilman Ramus. When it came to light, and a member was confirmed, the Soliret were called on to act. High Priest Wiltor sanctioned the group after the Damrek catastrophe. After all these years, countless numbers of members had fallen, but for every one they took down, two more took his place. The last couple of years they focused more on taking out the higher-placed members. Getting the tip about Ramus would go a long way in accomplishing that.

Sending one warrior on two oath missions was a bit unusual, but she didn't have a choice. The Oracle's words were very specific about the fact that Elson would be sent on both. She held back a laugh when he started to squirm under her gaze. She would be entrusting Lanis's life to this man. She closed his file and pushed back in her seat. "Your commanding officer speaks very highly of you, as do your fellow Rangers. That's quite a compliment for one so young." She ran her finger over his file. It told her all she needed to know about his military career, but she needed more. "Elson." She leaned forward. "Tell me something about yourself?"

He looked startled and unsure before he smiled. "I like to eat."

She laughed, putting them both at ease. Placing both hands on the desktop, she went on. "I asked you here for a very specific reason. Well two, in fact." He leaned forward as to catch every word. "You have been chosen by Nia for two oath missions. First, let me say you have an exemplary record and the loyalty you show Nia is seen in all your actions. You wouldn't be here if they didn't. You are a true man of faith." She scooted her chair back when he stood and kneeled, bowing his head.

"I live to serve Nia, and you, High Priestess. Whatever you need from me I will do to the best of my ability."

"Elson, please sit." His actions told her all she needed to know. "I have sent for Lanis Welsh of Trit. She is on an oath mission from Nia. Your first oath will be to keep her alive. She must make it to Manight; nothing must happen to her. It is of the utmost importance."

"I understand."

"I will go into greater detail about that mission when she gets here." She opened the desk drawer and pulled out a small book. From within its pages, she pulled a small piece of folded paper and slid it in his direction. "Are you willing to sign an oath to Nia to fulfill the duties I ask of you?"

"I am." He signed the paper where she indicated.

"No hesitation?"

"There wasn't anything to hesitate about."

She slid the book back in the drawer and stood. "I have another task for you. Stand and follow me." They only walked a short distance before they entered another door that led to another hallway.

"It feels like we're going down," Elson said.

She smiled. "That's because we are." His observation would go a long way in earning Lanis's trust. When they reached the end of the hall, she stopped and looked at him. He was tense and scared, but hiding it well. "You have nothing to fear, Elson. Once we pass through this door, we will enter a small room. Inside the room will be three additional doors. One of them leads to Nia's temple." His eyes widened, but he didn't say anything. "You must never speak of this room to anyone."

He clamped his right arm to his chest. "I would never disrespect Nia in such a manner."

Anya nodded and led the way into the room. Inside, three chairs sat against one wall and a small table was positioned in the corner. She had them brought down so Lanis would be comfortable waiting for her. She smiled and opened the door on the far wall and walked in. She walked to a small table tucked into one corner and pulled a chair out to sit down, indicating Elson should do the same. She pulled a leather-bound book from an alcove in the wall, and took care turning to the desired page. So many names were written on the pages from countless years of service. Some made it home, but the majority didn't. "You will take an oath with Lanis when she arrives, but this is for your second oath. Place your hands on the table." She rested her hands on top of his and looked into his eyes. "I call on you, Elson Bri of Malora, to exact revenge that you have sworn with the Soliret." He blinked at her, but didn't acknowledge her words. "It has recently came to my attention that Councilman Ramus of the Queen's court in Manight is a member of the Holders of the Spheres. He is a high-ranking member and he has been rumored to have five spheres. When you arrive in Manight, your oath with Lanis will be finished and you will need to take as much time as you need to deal with this matter." She patted his hands and turned the book toward him. "I know this is the first time you have been called on, but I am confident you are the right soldier for this mission. Once you sign your name next to Councilman Ramus's, it is a binding contract. You are giving an oath to Nia and it cannot be undone until your oath is fulfilled. Your first priority is to keep Lanis alive until she reaches Manight. If you don't think you can handle both, tell me. There is no shame in knowing your limits. I need you at your best." She watched all the different emotions play across his face and thanked Nia when a look of determination crossed his features.

He nodded. "I am confident," he said, leaning forward and signing his name. "I can do both and neither one will suffer." He softly closed the book and slid it back to her.

"Sign this next." He signed it and handed it back to her. She placed the book back in the wall and stood, piece of paper in hand. "Follow me." They walked a few feet to the altar set in the middle of the room. It stood waist high and pillows surrounded the base. According to Nia's way of living, the altar was simple in structure. "Kneel and place both of your hands on top of the altar." When he did, she placed a small stone between his hands. "Close your eyes." She threw the piece of paper into the fire atop the altar. When the room grew hazy, she walked behind him and placed both her hands on his shoulders. "Nia, I pray that you will continue to bless your solider and keep him safe and his will strong. Pave his way, my Goddess." She opened her eyes and removed the stone. "Open your eyes and stand." He flinched when she touched his wrist. "This is your oath to Nia and to the Soliret. Once your oath is completed, it will disappear." A simple brown and black leather bracelet was molded to his wrist.

"Thank you," he said, looking at his wrist.

"Do you have any questions?" she asked.

He looked around the room, then turned back to her and smiled. "No. I...I have faith that when the time comes I will have my answers. My training has prepared me for many things and I am confident Nia will guide me. I will not fail her, nor you."

"You have my full support." He was so earnest she couldn't help but believe him. Lanis was in good hands. "I have a room prepared and dinner will be brought to you."

"Don't want me wandering about." He chuckled.

"Actually, no, I don't." She smiled and led the way out of the temple, closing the door behind her. She knocked on the door to the left of the temple and a guard answered immediately. "Show Elson to his room."

"Of course, High Priestess," the guard answered, and held the door open for Elson.

"Elson," she said. He turned back to look at her. "Get a good night's rest. I'll see you tomorrow."

"Of course, High Priestess."

She waited until the door closed, then continued down the hall to the door that would lead to her room.

Stopping midway down the hall, she leaned against the wall, everything hitting her at once. The traitor, the oaths, Lanis. She tipped her head back and closed her eyes. For any normal person, it would all be too much, but she knew who she was, High Priestess to Nia, and Nia would sustain her. She swiped at her eyes and stood up straight. Lanis. Maybe she would see her tomorrow and that would ease the turmoil that surrounded her. She sighed. One could only hope.

❧ ❧ ❧ ❧

Anya tossed and turned, finally flinging the covers off, and sat up in bed. Standing, she lifted the robe off the bedpost and slipped it on. Something was wrong. Without even realizing it, her steps took her to the window. The waters of the Tynuck Sea were calm and the city below was quiet. The moon dancing on the water was pure magic. She wished others could see the world the way she did. Lanis hated being this high up. Anya had told her on countless occasions that sooner or later she would have to put her fear of heights away. She missed her. Pushing away from the window, she walked to a small table set against the wall. Picking up the ladle that rested in a stone bowl, she scooped some water up and shivered as it slid down her throat. Her eyes landed on her Protector as she set the ladle down. That was part of the problem. This wasn't her Protector. Lanis was out there, somewhere. Letting Lanis go on her oath mission would be the hardest thing she would ever have to do.

She turned from her Protector and walked to the foot of the bed, kneeling on the prayer pad that always lay there. She needed Nia's comfort now more than ever. Taking deep breaths, she cleared her mind and let peace surround her. After only a moment, she jerked her eyes up and looked toward the main door. Her heart pounded when the person on the other side knocked again. Louder this time. A knock this time of night could only mean one thing: trouble. She stood when her Protector went to the door and spoke to the person on the other side. A moment later, her Protector opened it and allowed a steward of the Council to enter. The steward wouldn't have disturbed her this time of night if something wasn't wrong.

He wrung his hands and bowed his head. "High Priestess, we have a situation." His eyes darted around the room.

No. This couldn't be happening. "Tell me."

"I was informed that the guards just arrived with a rider. The woman was dragging a body behind her horse. The body was of a Priestess, ma'am." He shook his head. "I don't know who."

Oh Goddess, no. She closed her eyes. "What about the other woman, the rider?"

"I don't know. They were both taken to the infirmary. I do know that the Priestess was dead and the other woman was in bad shape."

"Leave. I'll be down shortly."

"Of course, High Priestess."

Anya bent over, gasping for breath when the click of the door echoed inside the room. Not Lanis, not like this. The Oracle never said something like this would happen. What had she done? Poor Tion didn't deserve this fate. She planted her hands on her knees and closed her eyes. Falling apart wasn't an option, not now. As much as she wanted to be there for Lanis, she couldn't be her lover; she had to be her High Priestess. She threw her robe off and quickly dressed, pulling on loosely fitted tan pants and a long cream-colored tunic, her fingers fumbling with the buttons on her shirt. What would she do without Lanis? The thought of living without her had never crossed her mind before. She stood and took several deep breaths, gathering control of her emotions. How could a routine trip go so horribly wrong? Nodding at her Protector, she grabbed her blue and white cape off the hook by the door and slipped it on. As the door shut behind her, she pulled the hood up.

The walk to the infirmary felt like the longest walk of her life. With each step, she kept repeating a prayer of healing. After what seemed like an eternity, they reached the infirmary room doors. She did a double take when she noticed Merek standing off to the side of the doors. He shouldn't have been notified.

"High Priestess," Merek said, walking up her. "They shouldn't have wakened you. I could have handled this, but they wouldn't let me in the room." He rocked back on his heels and fidgeted with the hem of his shirt.

She narrowed her eyes at him. He wasn't acting like himself. He didn't look like a man who had been awakened from sleep. Had he even gone to bed? "You know protocol, or considering events of late, maybe you don't. I don't know why you're here."

He shuffled his feet before clasping his hands behind his back. "I was up and heard the commotion. My apologies. If you wish, I would be glad to accompany you in the room."

That was the last thing she wanted. "That won't be necessary." She turned her back to him but halted her footsteps. She hated to admit it, but he might be useful. Without turning around, she addressed him. "Merek, stick around. I might need you later on." Without waiting for a reply, she walked to the infirmary doors. She didn't need to turn to sense the smirk on his face. Stopping at the doors, she came face to face with Elson's commanding officer.

He bowed his head in her direction. "High Priestess Anya."

"Commander Ketlin, if you would please, accompany me in."

"My pleasure." He opened the door, allowing her and her Protector to enter before him.

She hesitated at the door before walking in. There should be more people, more chaos, but all was quiet. Kaylynn, the white-band healer in Malora, was the only one in the room, and she stood by Lanis's body. Scanning the room, Anya's eyes fell on a sheet-draped body at the far end on the room. Ignoring Kaylynn and Lanis, Anya walked to Tion's body. "What happened?" she asked when the commander stopped beside her.

He placed his hand across his chest as a sign of respect for Priestess Tion. "The guards on the upper towers spotted a rider and as the rider got closer they noticed a body was being dragged behind the horse. When the rider and body came closer to the city, I sent five of our cavalry out to stop them."

"Why didn't the rider stop on her own?"

"She was unconscious, draped across the beast. I don't know how she didn't fall off. I don't know how she survived."

"Go on." She didn't take her eyes off of the sheet covering Tion.

"They slowed the horse and it was only then we

noticed the body being dragged was of a Priestess." She looked up when he grew quiet. His eyes were locked on Tion and his jaw was clenched. "The only reason," he said, pointing behind him, "the other woman was brought here and not a cell is because of the shape she was in. I don't know who the Priestess is. I know there were a few out on missions."

She grasped the sheet at the top of the table. "I know who she is." She curled her fingers around the sheet and pulled it down, gasping when Tion's face was revealed. She dropped the sheet near Tion's feet. The only thing she recognized was the small tattoo on the inside of her wrist, indicating that she was a Priestess to Nia. She knew she didn't have a choice, but she had to know. If she found what she thought she might, things were far worse then she could have ever imagined and it would considerably change the way things played out. "Commander, could you turn her so I can see her back?" A frown marred his features before he grasped Tion's side and turned her so Anya could see her.

A diminutive square tattoo adorned the small of her back. The mark of Damrek. As far as she knew, it hadn't been seen for over a hundred years. If one carried the mark, it allowed the brander, a very powerful sorcerer, to take complete control of the wearer's body, allowing them to use the body in any way they saw fit. How long had Tion had the tattoo? It didn't make sense. This was Tion's first task in months. If Tion was branded on her last mission, what meetings had she been a part of? No telling what type of information the brander had been informed of. "You can lay her back down." The mark also meant something else. A small group claimed they could raise the dead. She had never seen, nor encountered it, but there were stories in Nia's temple that told of others who had. The one thing all risen people had in common was the mark on their back. The only way to stop someone from rising was to burn the body. Her only comfort now was that Priestess Tion was with the Goddess she served. She took hold of the sheet and covered Tion's body before turning around. "Commander, you can wait outside." Anya turned back toward Kaylynn and watched as she lifted Lanis's shirt and pressed on her stomach.

"High Priestess."

"Kaylynn," Anya said, standing beside her. Small cuts and bruises littered Lanis's face, but nothing like what she was expecting. "How is she?"

Kaylynn sighed and pulled Lanis's shirt up to expose her side. Blood and a black substance oozed from a small wound. Even the familiar red streaks that laced Lanis's torso didn't bring Anya any comfort. "The dagger or knife that pierced her was laced with poison. I've given her something to combat the poison, but time will tell what kind of damage occurred. I've healed some of the deeper cuts and bruises, but honestly," she said, pulling the shirt down, "I don't know how she's still alive." She bit her lip. "She's lost a lot of blood."

All Anya wanted was to reach over touch Lanis. Instead, she stuffed her hands in her pockets. "How much time for her to heal?"

"A lot. She has a few knots on the back of her head that have me concerned and a long gash on her leg. I stitched it, but it is deep. I don't even know how she got on the horse to come here. She had several broken ribs, which I repaired, and her back is a complete mess. There are also numerous other cuts and bruises. I feel confident she will heal, but it could take weeks, even months. That's as long as infection doesn't set in. I will keep a close eye on her."

Months, they didn't have months. Lanis had to leave within the next day or two. She could only see one possibility and she knew she didn't have any right to ask. Kaylynn was a white-band healer and as such had special privileges. White-band healers were given the ability to heal someone completely, but it didn't come without consequences. Some of their healing abilities could be compromised in the right circumstances. They held the ability to heal someone on the verge of death, but it came with a high cost. The healer would be stripped of all abilities, only to be left with the knowledge they learned in their teaching. It also had a somewhat unusual consequence. The healer and the patient would be bonded for life, their souls intertwined, their lives intertwined. They would always have to be in close proximity to each other and if one died, so would the other. Fortunately, that's not what Anya needed, as Lanis wasn't near death. "Kaylynn, may I talk to you privately?" She nodded and they walked past Tion's body into Kaylynn's office.

After sitting, Kaylynn ran her hands through her hair. "What can I do for you, High Priestess?"

She looked tired. From the first moment she met Kaylynn, Anya liked her. She came off a bit standoffish, but she was the best healer she had ever had the privilege of knowing. Kaylynn could refuse her request, but she was hoping she wouldn't. "I need you to heal her."

"I am," she said, throwing her hands up. "But it's going to take time. Her injuries are extensive. I'm doing all I can."

"You can do more. I need you to *heal* her. You can, and I need you to. I know I don't have any right to ask." Anya stopped when Kaylynn closed her eyes and sighed. "I'm not asking you to bond with her, but I am asking you to heal her. Nia called Lanis. She is bound to her oath and she needs to leave within the next day or two. I would never ask under normal circumstances, but this isn't normal circumstances."

"Do you know what you're asking me?" she said softly. She shook her head and stood. "Of course you do." She started pacing. After a few minutes, she sat back down. "I'll do it."

"You will never know the full extent of my gratitude."

"That's not necessary." She waved her praise off. "I will need to be alone for a long while. I'm not sure how long this will take. I cannot be disturbed. If I am, I don't know what will happen."

"No one will bother you. I will also take care of Priestess Tion's body." Anya stood to leave when Kaylynn spoke.

Kaylynn cocked her head and regarded Anya thoughtfully. "Her name is Lanis."

"Yes."

Kaylynn stood and walked around the desk, leaning against it. "She killed Priestess Tion."

"How do you know that?" She figured she had, but she also knew Lanis would have a good reason and she couldn't wait to hear it.

"She told me before she passed out. Said she was sorry and she had no choice."

"Do not speak of this again."

"I didn't intend to, High Priestess."

"Good." Anya walked out, feeling drained. How could so much go wrong so fast? She stepped up to Lanis, biting back the tears that threatened to fall. She reached out and touched her hand, caressing it for a moment before walking out. There was so much to take care of. Lanis would wake soon enough. Merek walked up to her when she closed the door. She didn't wait for him to speak. "I need you to take Priestess Tion's body and burn it."

His shock was only evident for a split second. "Of course."

"I need it done now. I'll wait while you take the body. Take a couple of the guards with you." She waited while they gathered the body and walked down a long hallway that would lead them toward the back entrance of the temple. "Commander Ketlin, no one is allowed in that room. No one, including me, is to disturb Kaylynn. Anyone trying to get in is to be apprehended and either brought to me, or put in a holding cell. Anyone. Kaylynn will inform you when she is done."

"I understand," he said, taking up position outside the doors.

Anya walked down the long hallway, stopping when her foot touched the first tread of the staircase. She could only imagine what was going on inside that room. She started back up the stairs, knowing she wouldn't be getting any more sleep for a long time.

❧ ❧ ❧ ❧

Lanis opened her eyes and quickly placed her hand over them. It felt like tiny pins were poking her in the eyes. She lay still, grateful not to feel pain with every breath. She jumped when a hand touched hers.

"Lanis, my name is Kaylynn, and I'm the healer in Malora. You're safe. Keep your eyes closed. I'll cover some of the windows. I didn't expect you to be awake so soon."

"Okay," Lanis croaked. "Water?"

"Let me close the windows first, then I'll get you a drink." Kaylynn patted Lanis's hand and walked away.

Lanis instantly relaxed. Kaylynn was the best healer in Malora. No wonder she didn't feel any pain. She could hear her talking to someone, but couldn't make out what they were saying. After she climbed on the horse, she didn't think she would wake up again. She couldn't wait to see Anya. Goddess, what she must have felt when she found out. If the roles were reversed, she would have gone crazy.

"Lanis, I've sent for High Priestess Anya. She wanted to be informed the moment you awoke. Before she gets here, I want to examine you again. I will help you get dressed after that. Move your arm and slowly open your eyes."

Lanis lowered her hand, opened one eye, then the other. She squinted, but after a few seconds, her eyes adjusted to the light. Kaylynn stood in front of her, her curly black hair pulled back on her neck. She wore the standard clothes of a temple healer. They were required to wear tan pants or a tan skirt and a long white tunic with intricate stitching on the torso indicating their rank. It was a comfort to see a familiar face.

"Now, lie still while I examine you then I'll get you that drink of water." Lanis lay as still as she could as Kaylynn poked and prodded, wincing when she touched the spot on her side. "Sorry, even though I healed your side and got rid of the poison, it will still be tender for a while because of the type of wound it was. I did all I could." Lanis kept quiet. Only a very powerful poison could have prolonged tenderness after being healed. She knew of only a couple types that would cause that kind of damage and neither one was easy to come by. Whoever attacked them went to great pains to do it. It was not a comforting thought.

"Now," Kaylynn said. "I'm going to help you sit up, because I need to check your back."

Lanis struggled, but with Kaylynn's help, she managed to sit up, pulling the sheet tight against her chest when it slipped. She wasn't modest, but at the moment was a bit vulnerable. She breathed when told to, the light touches on her back sending shivers down her spine. She couldn't imagine the scars she would have. Healers could only do so much. She didn't want to think about what Kaylynn must have done to heal her. "Thank you. I can never thank you enough. I can only give you—"

"Stop," Kaylynn said. "You don't have to thank me. We all have a job to do and when the time comes, when you're called on, you do it. You'll be tired for a few days, but you'll slowly start to gain your strength back. That's mostly from the poison that entered your bloodstream. Even though the poison is gone, the effects will linger for a few days. You were very lucky to get here when you did. Another day and I wouldn't have been able to save you. Let me get your water."

Lanis needed to find out what Kaylynn had given up in order to save her life. To give such a gift, one had to sacrifice something. It seemed cruel and wrong on many levels, but it was the way things were done. Lanis looked at Kaylynn's wrist but she still had all her bands and there wasn't a black mark on it indicating that she had been stripped of her abilities. Lanis smiled when she came back carrying a small bundle and a glass of water.

She handed Lanis a small cup. "Take small sips and here are some clothes. I'm sorry but yours couldn't be saved. I'll help you get dressed then we'll check your balance and let you walk a bit."

Lanis set the cup down and let the sheet fall, a bit embarrassed, but they finished quickly. She watched from the bed while Kaylynn talked with her assistant. The pants were a bit loose, but they fit and the dark brown color was close enough to the black that she normally wore that she didn't feel uncomfortable. The tunic was long, like she liked it, but the dark red color was nothing like she normally wore.

"I had these cleaned," Kaylynn said, kneeling at Lanis's feet and, lifting one foot, then the other, placed a boot on each one before tying the laces. She stood. "They were in rough shape, but they were able to be salvaged. Everything else we put in your bag. You will get it back when you leave."

Lanis choked back her emotions. "Thank you."

"Let me help you up so I can check your balance." Lanis stood on unsteady feet and held onto Kaylynn until she stood comfortably on her own. "Good, now keep hold of my arms and as I walk backward, come to me." They walked around the room until Kaylynn felt comfortable Lanis could walk on her own, ending by a large window. "Good, you can walk back to your bed. I'll send for some food. Relax. High Priestess Anya should arrive anytime."

Lanis kept her steps deliberate and steady, grateful when she reached the bed and sat down. She didn't know what to think, considering everything that happened. She knew her anxiety would ease when she laid eyes on Anya, although she hadn't forgotten what got her into this mess in the first place. Anya should have been honest with her. Maybe all this could have been avoided. She swung her legs onto the bed and lay back. She closed her eyes and tried to relax but snapped them open when a familiar scent drifted her way. She smiled and rose up on her elbows. Anya stood by the door talking with Kaylynn, who didn't look happy. Kaylynn nodded, and she and her assistant walked to her office, shutting the door behind them. Lanis sat up when Anya walked over and stood in front of her. One minute, anger flooded her, and the next relief washed over her. "I'm angry and I don't understand what's going on, but I am so glad to be alive. You're the reason I fought so hard to get back here."

Anya picked Lanis's hand up and ran her thumb across it. "When I saw you after they brought you in…" She exhaled. "It broke my heart. I wish I could do more then hold your hand. I shouldn't even be doing this."

Lanis lifted their clasped hands and kissed Anya's palm. "I understand. I'm sorry about Priestess Tion." It wasn't the grand reunion she had been hoping for.

Anya placed her finger over Lanis's lips. "We'll go over everything later in Council. For now, you need to eat and rest. I have some things I need to take care of." She pulled her hand free. "Later, a guard will escort you to the Council room. I wish I had more time to give, but I don't. You'll meet your traveling companion later as well. Things will move quickly from this point forward. I love you."

"I love you too, always." Lanis watched her leave with a heavy heart. She slammed her hands on the bed and lay back. For now, she would relax, and later she would worry about everything else.

Lanis stood when a guard came to escort her to her meeting with Anya. She nodded at Kaylynn, who smiled before turning and stepping into her office. Lanis licked her lips, contemplating what Kaylynn had given up to heal her. The price must have been great. Nothing was free. To give up so much for a stranger amazed her. She didn't think she could, but would forever be grateful Kaylynn did.

"Ready?" the guard asked, holding the door open.

"I am." She eased off the bed and steadied herself before attempting to walk. By the time she reached the guard, her steps were sure. The hallways were surprisingly empty. Probably Anya's doing. She stopped halfway up the staircase to catch her breath, the stairs more of a challenge than she anticipated. Running her fingers along the rail, she grasped it and continued up. Anya awaited her at the top. Upon reaching the landing, she leaned against the wall, flinching when the guard reached for her.

"Sorry." He stepped back. "You looked unsteady."

"Thanks," she said. He walked to the door, opened it, and stepped into the other room. She eased down in the nearest chair and closed her eyes. She knew it would take time, but at this rate, it could take days, even months, to get back to her old self.

She understood Anya distancing herself, but it still stung. She rubbed her neck and leaned her head back, resting it against the wall. Death had been so close. The idea of dying didn't bother her. The act itself didn't frighten her. Death hung around her like a dark cloud during her missionary years, a cloud she thought she'd left behind. She just wasn't ready, not yet. Life was too precious a gift not to fight for. She opened her eyes and scooted forward when the door opened and the same guard walked out, followed by two men and two women. They each glanced her way as they passed by, but she got the feeling they didn't actually see her, except for Merek—he looked right at her. She didn't trust any of Anya's personal advisers and she knew Anya didn't either, at least not fully. She fidgeted, anxious for the guard to allow her entrance. Her whole body vibrated. Whatever happened beyond that door, she had to remember, would be between oath-taker and High Priestess. To act so unfamiliar, so formal, would be hard.

"She'll see you now."

Lanis braced her hands on her knees and walked through the door. She raised her eyes and locked onto Anya, who sat behind her desk, her Protector behind her. She looked put together as usual. Her beauty never ceased to amaze and take her breath away. She also looked tired. Her long blond hair was pulled up on her neck and from what Lanis could see, she wore a simple pale blue dress. Her ever-present blue and white cloak lay draped over the corner of her chair. When Anya smiled at her, it lit up her entire face. "High Priestess," Lanis said, bowing her head.

"Protector," Anya said, standing. "Wait in the other room."

Lanis cringed. His place was with Anya. He should have never obeyed her order. He was there to protect her, not take orders from her. She would have a talk with him. The anger she built up toward him vanished when Anya stood and stepped around the desk, wrapping her arms around her. Lanis pulled her as close as possible and kissed her neck. She always smelled so good, like lilacs. Being this close, after what happened, felt amazing. Her body cried out when Anya pushed her to arm's length and looked her over.

"I know Kaylynn said you were all right, but I needed to see for myself. For my own peace of mind."

Lanis pulled her back into her arms. "I'm fine. I won't lie, though, I am tired and my side still hurts, but those are things I can't change." Lanis ran her fingers along Anya's cheek and down her neck. "Being with you always makes me feel better." She rested her forehead against Anya's and closed her eyes. Relishing this moment, she held onto every smell, feel, and emotion. She'd always wondered what home felt like. This is what home felt like. Being in the arms of the one you loved. She looked up, startled, when Anya pushed her away and walked around the desk, retaking her seat. She knew their time alone would be brief, but she hadn't expected it to be this brief. That would be all she saw of her Anya. Lanis sat down and looked at her. Good, Anya looked as shaken as she felt. For once, her emotions were written all over her face.

"Do you remember what happened? What happened to Priestess Tion?" She clasped her hands in her lap.

Lanis took a minute to compose herself. "To be honest, I'm not sure what happened. I fell asleep twice. I didn't sleep well the last few days," she said, smiling.

Anya nodded. "It has been a rough few days."

"Yes. When I woke up the second time, everything seemed fine, then I heard them. Hoofbeats, and they were approaching fast. Too fast not to have magic aiding them. There were three riders," she said, rubbing her neck and leaning forward. "Priestess Tion changed in the clearing."

"How?"

"Her whole demeanor was off." She scrunched her nose up and ran her hands through her hair. "In the clearing after I killed two of the men, the way she looked at me when I told her they were dead." She shivered and looked away. "I was not looking at a Priestess of Nia. The woman I saw was pure evil." Lanis turned back to Anya, who didn't look at all surprised by what she said. Lanis held her eyes until Anya turned away. "Really Anya, you knew something like this could happen."

"Look."

Lanis held her hand up. "It would have been nice to know that. Why didn't you say something? Never mind," she said, shaking her head. "It doesn't matter. She's the one who stabbed me. I tried getting away, but when she came after me, I killed her."

Anya took several deep breaths, then spoke. "If I had known what would happen…"

"You would have done the same thing." Lanis smiled to take the bite out of her words. "One of the reasons I love you so much is because of your honesty and dedication to what matters most to you. I know I'll never come first for you, and I'm okay with that."

"You're right, I would have done the same thing, only a little differently. Please understand it had to be done this way. You would have never agreed otherwise."

Lanis scooted her chair closer to the desk and rested her hands on top of it. "I was hurt at first. And you're right, I would have never agreed to it if you'd asked me. I just wish you didn't have to do it this way. I don't know what you know, but I take comfort that you know it."

Anya reached over and squeezed Lanis's hand.

"I needed you to say yes. Nia has chosen you, Lanis, to fulfill an oath to her. The last Prophecy—"

Lanis yanked her hand away. "Wait. What?" She couldn't have heard right. "This is about a prophecy? I almost died for a prophecy?" She ran her hands through her hair. "You have got to be kidding me. How old is this prophecy?" She sat back and crossed her arms, glaring at Anya.

"Do not talk to me like that, Lanis Welsh."

Lanis stiffened at the tone of Anya's voice. She should have never spoken to her that way. She made a mistake by not treating her with anything other than respect. "I'm sorry."

"Do not interrupt me." Anya laid her hands on top of the desk. "I am not your lover right now, nor have I ever been in this room. I am your High Priestess and as such, I expect your respect."

Lanis knew the words were coming, but they still bothered her. She never saw Anya as anything but the woman she loved and fell short in respecting her as High Priestess. She stood and winced as the wound on her side pulled, then knelt in front of the desk and, placing her right fist across her heart, bowed her head. "I am sorry, High Priestess, forgive me and my ignorance. It will not happen again. I live to serve you." When she looked up, they both knew something had shifted in their relationship—an understanding. Lanis stood and sat back down.

Anya continued. "The Prophecy was written five hundred years ago. The last one ever written and sealed before the Oracle was chosen to take over the Prophesiers' position. It is also the last one written before Damrek's catastrophe with magic and it was written by Danath." She bit her lip and sighed. "I know it's hard to believe and it has been ages, but it is time for the Prophecy to be read. We don't rely on prophecies as they did back then. At least one was read every day in Danath's time. Today I rely on the Oracle. Do you know anything of Danath?"

"I know some. He disregarded his vows and told his brother Damrek what the Prophecy said. The story goes Danath was hanged the next day." She wasn't spiritual in the least. She would forever be faithful to Nia, but only because of her love for Anya.

Anya laughed. "It's amazing how stories evolve over the years. What you know is partly true. Danath was the last person ever to write a sealed prophecy. After the incident, High Priest Wiltor did away with Prophesiers and chose one to become Oracle. The Prophecy was sealed and it has been stored all these years in Nia's temple. It is to be read in Manight, at their Festival of the Goddess, in three months' time. The festival is a yearly event they put on to honor Shara. It is of great importance because it is the first time a prophecy has ever been read in Hadmore, and more specifically in Manight."

"Why Manight? It didn't exist then." She might not know her religious texts, but she knew Adearian history. "Is it significant that one has never been read there?" She didn't agree with prophecies and Oracles. She liked to live life, not fear what might happen.

Anya smiled. "It didn't exist then and it is of great significance. Who knows what kind, if any, repercussions will come from the reading. I don't believe in coincidences. In the past, the only place a prophecy was read would have been here in the city. And before you ask, I don't know why, it just was."

Lanis squirmed. All of this because of an

outdated prophecy. What could a five hundred-year-old prophecy possibly contain that could affect their lives so dramatically today? "Where do I come into play? What does this prophecy have to do with me?"

"What I'm about to tell you cannot leave this room. There are things each of us is burdened with that others must never know. I know you've already signed an oath in Trit, but make your promise to Nia that you will not repeat what I am about to tell you."

Anya's voice held such passion Lanis said the only thing she could. "I promise."

Anya stood, walked to the window, and leaned against it. "Danath copied the Prophecy once and let his brother read it and make a second copy. Danath gave his copy to High Priest Wiltor. That copy has been passed down from High Priest to High Priestess over the years as each one of us took our vows," she said, pushing off the wall and walking back to her desk, standing in front of it. "We were instructed to read it and never look at it again or ever discuss the contents with anyone. I remember the day I read it and I remember the words. To this day, I'm still not sure what they mean, but they caused quite a stir five hundred years ago. I'm sure they will cause a stir at the festival."

"I didn't think it was allowed to read a sealed prophecy until the day it was to be read," Lanis said. Anya crossed her arms and Lanis fought the urge to reach out and touch her. She gripped the arms of her chair tighter.

"It's not supposed to be, but High Priest Wiltor thought it to be of great importance. Like I said, I've read it and still don't understand the full meaning. Times were different then, but not like today. Today we have stone walls for borders and we keep ourselves hidden away. So much has changed in a short amount of time. Compared to then, some things in our society are still seen as wrong or going against the natural way of things. I can't tell you what the Prophecy says, but you don't play a direct role in it. Someone mentioned in it must live to fulfill her part. Without you, she will die. Your task, Lanis, is to make sure she lives." She reached forward and grasped Lanis's shoulders. "You have to save her life."

Lanis relished the warmth of Anya's hands. "Who do you want me to save?"

Anya pulled her hands back and sat down. "You have to travel to Manight and arrive before the start of the festival. You will have two people accompanying you. You will meet Elson Bri in a few minutes—he is a Ranger in Malora's army. Once you both reach Klate, you will hire a sorceress to accompany you."

"Who do you want me to save?" She hated asking the same question twice.

"The Prophecy wasn't specific, but from everything that's happened, and from the Oracle and through prayer, the person that you are to save is Princess Jalen, Queen Abigail's first daughter and heir."

That didn't make any sense. "Isn't she a commander in the Queen's Army? I assume she has guards to protect her. What can I do that the people around her can't? Why me?"

"I don't know why the people around her can't protect her. And why you? Because of who...what... you are."

"I see. You need me because of my ability, because I'm Ramden."

"Yes, and I won't apologize for that. We need

someone who can disappear."

"The Veilshield can disappear."

"No, the Veilshield disappear into the shadows. We need someone who can disappear completely. Besides, not much is known of the Veilshield and what they can really do. I know you and what you're capable of."

Deep down, she was glad her mercenary days were behind her. The one hiccup was Klate. She didn't want to go back. Anya didn't know how she received her scar and she never volunteered the information. It seemed everything did come full circle. She just hoped it didn't collapse in on her. At least she wouldn't be alone. "What happens now?"

"Now," Anya said, standing, her gaze never wavering from Lanis. "You will meet Elson, and you both will take your oath in Nia's temple." She gestured to Lanis's feet. "Bring your bag. You won't be coming back here."

Lanis walked behind her and through the door. The Protector stood ready. She would have to deal with him now, as there wouldn't be time later. She had to trust that Anya would be safe in the other room with Elson. Lanis closed the door behind her and walked into the hallway. She waited until Anya walked through the door at the other end of the hall before she reached around the Protector and pulled his mask off, shutting the door before he walked through it. He whirled around, eyes wide. Lifting the mask, Lanis placed it on her face and took a step back. "Ramuk, I am disappointed in you. I need someone who is willing to sacrifice all that they are in order to protect High Priestess Anya. From what I've seen, you aren't capable of that. Are you?"

"I..." He fidgeted, then seemed to make a decision. "Yes, I am."

"I don't really have a choice, now do I?" Lanis wasn't at all sure she made the right decision. "You do understand," she said, circling him, "that High Priestess Anya is never to be out of your sight. No matter what she says." Lanis walked behind him and gripped his shoulders. "It is your job to protect her. Her safety and life is your only concern. When you accept this mask, you forfeit your own life. The only time you are ever to leave her side is when she enters Nia's temple." She smacked him on the side of the head. "Do you understand?"

"Yes," he stuttered.

"You're not very convincing, Ramuk. As Protector, you are given the task to protect her. You have all the tools you need available to you. Use them." She pointed to the door they just walked through. "What just happened in that room must never happen again."

"I don't understand."

"You left her alone. Do not ever do that again."

"But I left her with you."

"So. Who am I? I could be anyone. Do not leave her alone with anyone, even if you think them a friend. No one is really a friend, especially when it comes to High Priestess Anya."

He nodded his head. "I understand and it won't happen again."

"No, it won't. Kneel." She pulled her long sword and rested the blade over his left shoulder. She bowed her head and repeated the words the last Protector had said to her. "Nia is with you always. You have a willing heart and you must accept the mask with your entire being. This is not a job. It is a way of life. Nia grants you the means to protect your charge. Accept who you are and what you must do until the time that the original Protector returns and at such time the mask will revert back to her." This was, after all, only temporary. She sheathed her sword and instructed him to stand. "When I return, I will take over my duties. If I find out you have lacked in your job, I will kill you."

"That...that won't be necessary."

"Your responsibilities are great," she said, taking off the mask. The transformation was so smooth, she shivered. "I want you to memorize my face, because if anything happens to her, I will kill you. Her life is of more significance than yours, or even mine." She reached around him and placed the mask in his hand. "Put it on, open the door, and walk through. I'll be right behind you." He hesitated, then slipped the mask on. He opened the door and walked through, taking up his place beside Anya, who sat in one of the two chairs in the room. Standing across from her was a man. Elson, she assumed. He looked exactly like she expected. Normally she preferred working alone, but they would be traveling a great distance and she would need the support. She knew of the Rangers and what they were capable of. He would be an asset.

Anya smiled, but it didn't reach her eyes. "Let us continue."

※ ※ ※ ※

Anya could only guess at what occurred between her Protector and Lanis. She knew Lanis had other responsibilities besides the oath, and she knew she would find time to settle them. She wished she could give her more time, but time was the one thing she didn't have. She stopped before the door and said a silent prayer before opening it and walking in, Elson and Lanis behind her. She instructed them to one side of the Altar and she took her place on the other.

She looked up when she felt a gaze on her. Lanis didn't look happy, but she seemed resigned. "You both have been chosen by Nia to fulfill her oath, for very different reasons. Elson, you have been chosen to ensure the continued safety of Lanis and to make sure she reaches Manight in order to fulfill her oath. Do you accept this request?"

"I do." Anya poured a clear liquid into a small glass, handed it to him, and he drank. When he handed it back, she turned to Lanis.

"Lanis, you have been chosen to save the princess's life. You must allow the help of others in your task. Do you accept this request even with all the unknowns?"

"Yes." Lanis accepted the cup and drank, then handed it back. Anya held back a laugh, but smiled when Lanis grimaced at the taste.

"You must not let outside troubles and outside forces interfere with your journey. Nia is only a prayer away; she will be with you always. It will be a long trip, and," she said, looking at Lanis, "your attack was only the starting point. I do not know who attacked you, but I do know you both will need to be vigilant. I cannot stress enough that you need to make it to Manight before the start of the festival. Time is of the utmost importance. You both must also accept the help of the sorcerer or sorceress you will hire in Klate. They are not your friend, but someone fulfilling their duties to their council. Do you both affirm that you can fulfill this oath in the time allowed?"

"Yes," they both said.

"Close your eyes." With purposeful strides, Anya walked to a cabinet set back from the Altar and lifted a vial from the shelves. "Place your left hand on top of the Altar." She opened the vial and poured a small drop onto each of their wrists. After setting the vial down, she placed both her hands on top of theirs. "Nia, I pray and ask that you watch over them both. They are your faithful servants. Walk with them and keep your eyes and hands upon them. You have asked and they have accepted your oath. Their lives are not their own, but they are yours. Accept your humble servants' gratitude that they were chosen to fulfill your bidding." She opened her eyes and removed her hands. On their wrists were leather bracelets that wrapped completely around their wrists and melded to the skin. "Open your eyes and stand."

Elson stood and placed his hand out to help Lanis up, keeping his eyes averted. Anya knew what it must have meant for Lanis to accept his help, but she did. "Please, have a seat at the table in the corner." She gathered a small book and joined them.

"I have a few things to discuss with you, then I'll let you get some rest." She pulled two pieces of paper from within the book and slid them across the table for them to sign. When they finished, she carried them to the Altar and threw them in the fire, then retook her seat.

"My bracelet just got tighter," Lanis said, tugging on it. "Is that supposed to happen?" She looked to Anya, then Elson.

"Mine did too," he said, running his hand over and around it.

"Yes. Lanis, you can tug all you want, but it won't

come off. If you both hadn't been telling the truth about your ability to accept the oath, the bracelets would have fallen off. It means you both were sincere in your actions." She laid a map on the table, smoothing out the corners. "I don't mean to be so abrupt, but we do need to get down to business. You cannot get into Manight from the main waterway, which would be the normal route, and to make matters worse, you will need to be as discreet as possible. Don't draw unwanted attention to yourself."

"What about the sorcerer we hire? Can we tell them anything?" Lanis asked.

"The Guild Master will know once he reads the letter. Once the papers are signed, they are in your debt. They have a job to do, and they usually don't care what they are needed for as long as it doesn't go against their morals or the code they stand by. Since you will hire them in Klate, they will be an item sorcerer."

"That means they will follow Shara," Elson said.

"It does."

Lanis sat back in her seat and crossed her arms across her chest. "I've traveled a lot. I know a few shortcuts that could get us there faster."

"As have I," Elson added.

"No shortcuts. Since you are on an official oath to Nia, there are oath houses where you will need to check in, and of course places you need to avoid. You will be able to get a good night's sleep at the oath houses, and they will give you provisions to help you reach your next destination. It will also let me know where you are in your journey." They had to stick to the map or she wouldn't be able to help them, and she needed to know they were okay.

Lanis rubbed her neck and leaned forward. "How

many oath houses?"

"For the two of you, there will be three. If you follow the places set for you on the map, you should reach Manight in a little over two months. You should have plenty of time to figure out what must be done in order to save the princess's life."

"Wait a minute," Lanis said, leaning forward and placing her hands on the table. "You don't know what I'll have to do to save her, so you don't know how much time that will take. And the journey shouldn't take us two months. I figure a month at the latest," she said, looking at Elson.

"I agree," he said. "It shouldn't take us anywhere near two months."

Anya hated to be the bearer of bad news and she knew they wouldn't take it well. "Lanis, it wasn't revealed to me what must be done but I know when the time comes Nia will be with you." She stood and clasped her hands behind her back. "It would normally only take a month, but I'm afraid for you two, it won't. For this trip, you will be on foot. You will not be allowed on horseback. There is too much at stake. You don't need the added burden of taking care of horses, nor the added pressure of someone possibly trying to steal them."

"No horses," Elson said. It was the first time she had seen any break in his armor. "It would make things a lot easier."

"This is crazy," Lanis said, standing. "I'm sure you realize, High Priestess, without horses it won't take us two months, more like three." She pointed to the map. "You have us going over a portion of the Anolk Mountains. We won't make it in time."

"No horses for the reasons I stated." She watched

the indecision in Lanis's eyes and was grateful she didn't let her anger or her temper get out of hand. "And you will make it in time. I don't know how, but I know you will. I cannot stress enough not to let anything distract you from your task. You need to get some rest. You have a long day ahead of you." She wouldn't get her private farewell with Lanis. "I know it's not late, but you will leave tomorrow morning, so please rest. Food will be brought up. Follow me." Instead of walking down the hallway, Anya opened a door to the right of Nia's temple. There was a man waiting on the other side. "If you would please follow Trever, he will show you to your rooms. I bid you both a goodnight." From the look in Lanis's eyes, she knew she wanted to say something, but didn't. Anya watched until she rounded a corner and lost sight of her. She softly closed the door and followed her Protector. She knew she hadn't heard the last of their protests. She would deal with them tomorrow over breakfast.

❧ ❧ ❧ ❧

Lanis stood and stretched, her side only pulling slightly. Sleep had eluded her all night; her mind kept reliving every moment from the past few days. With Anya being so distant from their private life, at times it was hard to connect the two. She would give anything to see a glimpse of the woman she fell in love with before she left. It would be a long time before she saw her again. She slipped her pack over her head. It was her constant companion for most of her life. The fact remained that she never intended to pick it up again. On their last mission together, she had received her scar. As hard as her mother tried, she couldn't get all the blood out of the leather. She didn't intend to clean any new stains either. It was good to have a reminder of how things could play out.

She looked to the door when someone knocked. After tightening her whip, she readjusted her knife. Relying solely on her ability would get her killed, but her weapons never disappointed. She opened the door and nodded at the guard. The knots in her stomach grew tighter with each step. The previous evening, Elson had informed her the bracelet would only fall off when she had completed her oath. Lanis traced the leather, resigned to the task ahead. Her steps faltered as they reached the door leading to the dining room. After straightening her shirt, she walked in. Anya sat at the head of the table and Elson sat to her right. She nodded at them both before seating in the chair across from Elson. When Anya smiled at her, she instantly relaxed. Anya would never know what that one smile meant to her. "Sorry I'm late."

"You're not late. I just arrived myself," Anya said. "Let's bow our heads for a prayer before we eat and discuss a few more things before you both leave."

They ate in silence. Lanis enjoyed silence. It brought her a sense of peace and peace was exactly what she needed right now. She kept stealing glances at Anya as they ate. She looked amazing this morning. The white tunic she wore contrasted nicely with her complexion. Compared to Lanis's black pants and brown leather shirt, Anya looked so out of reach. She smiled to herself, thinking about the past few years. They had brought her such joy and happiness…she wouldn't change a single thing. Even to this day, she had to remind herself to breathe every time Anya walked in the room. She didn't ever want to lose that feeling. Her thoughts were broken when Anya stood and retrieved some items one of the guards held for her. Lanis glanced at the Protector standing directly behind Anya's chair. She was almost convinced that after their little chat he would always be by her side.

"Please clear the table," Anya said before sitting back down.

Lanis frowned, grabbed one last piece of bread and slathered it with honey, laid it on her plate, and pulled it close to her chest. When the table was cleared, she released her grip and pushed it away from her, but still within hands' reach. When she looked up from her plate, they were both staring at her. "What?" Elson shook his head and smiled. Anya grinned at her. "It could be a while before I have honey again," she said, taking a bite.

"Now," Anya said. "I have your map." She laid it on the table. "As you can see, and if my estimates are correct, you should make it to Klate in a week's time. After that, you will travel to the first oath house. You will then travel to the second oath house, which I estimate will take you at least a week or two depending on the weather. It can sometimes be unpredictable this time of the year." She stopped and looked up. "In order to reach the third and final oath house you will have to travel through the Anolk Mountains, or at least a portion of them. Keep to the edges. If you wander in too far, you might not make it out. I wouldn't recommend going around them either. It's hard to say, but my best guess is that it will take a couple of weeks to cross through the lowest part of them. After that, another week until the third oath house, and this is the most important one. They will have everything you need in order to make it the rest of the way and it will give me clear direction as to where you are in relation to where you should be. From there, you will travel to a small waterway. Once you reach it, you will pay a fee and they will take you across the Belir River into Biclin. It is a very small community, but it does hold one of the Guild houses. You will have to check in there. Your sorceress or sorcerer will have to be outfitted with a bronze cuff before they are allowed into Manight. From there, you will enter Manight and then you are on your own." She sat back in her seat.

"So," Elson said. "By your estimates, it should take us around a month-and-a-half or two to make it to Manight."

"Yes," Anya answered.

"I can see that if everything is smooth and we don't meet any kind of trouble," Lanis said. "Which would be awesome, but we have to be realistic. I don't know about Elson, but I have never traveled some of these roads or ever walked through the Anolk Mountains." Anya wasn't the one taking this dangerous journey, and it angered her that she was able to sum it all up in a few dots on a map. She didn't know what they were walking into. Someone had already tried to kill her right outside of Malora. Then she would have to deal with Klate and her past. Lanis pushed back her chair and crossed her legs. "There are too many unknowns," she said, pointing to the map. "You might have a timeline, but I can't stick to any specific one. All I can promise is I will do my best."

Anya nodded. "Now there are a few places you need to steer clear of. Stay away from Laramore and its border towns. If you find yourself near there, you have strayed way off course. Their political attitude is vastly different from Hadmore's. They don't take oath missions seriously because they do not worship Nia. I am sure you both are well aware that in certain parts of Adearian, Nia is looked upon poorly. They also think our way of governing Malora is a joke. Again, we know it to be a different story." She placed her hands on the table. "Laramore is off limits also because it is rumored that a large population of Holders call it home."

Lanis understood the urgency in her voice. She didn't want to deal with any more than she already was. "Stay away from Laramore, check."

"Do not cross into Vashta. The Berrocka are hostile in the best of times and they do not take kindly to anyone invading their lands. They are always unpredictable. And whatever you do, do not go anywhere near the Goddess Falls. Too many unexplained things have happened there. The Falls are one distraction you do not need. Besides the fact that the Berrocka live close to the falls, many warriors have fallen to their deaths, out of their own foolishness to prove themselves."

Lanis didn't understand how Anya could be so calm. There were so many unknowns to begin with and now to add all the do-not's to the list, everything seemed almost impossible. "What else have you got?" she said, pointing to the items sitting beside the map.

Anya folded the map and set it aside. "Here are your notes for each of the oath houses, the money for the Guild house in Klate, and the note for the Guild house in Biclin. The note explains everything the Guild Masters will need to know. This bag," she said, handing a small pouch to Lanis, "contains the coins for the provisions you will need to buy in between the oath houses. Spend it wisely, but if you are ever in need of more, simply give this note to an Oath Master." Anya pushed back from the table and stood. "I don't want to take any more of your time, but there is one other thing we need to discuss. As you both know, Manight is holding their annual Festival of the Goddess. It also happens to be the two hundreth anniversary of the festival, and on top of that, the Prophecy will be read. You will have to contend with many things, and to add one more to the mix, you will run into a lot of people on your way. The festival is a big deal every year, but especially this year."

"How many people are we talking about?" Elson asked.

"Possibly thousands."

"Thousands. Okay," he said, running his hands through his beard.

"I know what I ask of you is great and I cannot guarantee the Goddess will bless you in this lifetime. Just remember what you do now matters."

"I'm already blessed," Lanis said, waving her words off. "Nia doesn't owe me anything. I do what I do out of honor, not for reward." Elson was looking at her with what she could only describe as respect.

"I feel the same way. I have been blessed beyond compare. My life isn't my own, but Nia's," Elson said.

"I am pleased you both feel this way. You are very brave to take on this oath. I will pray daily for your safe return." Anya leaned down, picked two small bags off the floor, and set them on the table. "I took the liberty of putting together these bags for the both of you. It's not much, but items I felt might make your journey a little easier," she said, handing one to Elson and the other to Lanis, letting their hands briefly touch.

The bag wasn't heavy and would easily fit in her own bag. Lanis opened the flap of it and slipped the smaller one in. There were tons of questions, but she would only ask one. "I have a question, High Priestess," she said, standing.

"Of course."

"I know it may be a lot to ask, but I would like you to locate my parents and bring them here. When I was attacked, they were threatened. I don't think the threat held any merit, but it would put my mind at ease. It would take a lot off me if I knew you were looking out for them."

"Of course I will. Elson, is there anyone you would like me to look after until you get back?"

"It's just me, High Priestess. My grandmother died last winter."

Anya clasped her hands behind her back. "Very well. I have a meeting that I can't avoid. Stop in the kitchen on your way out and stock up with what you'll need. I bid you both a safe journey and a safe return."

Lanis watched her walk away with a feeling of deep regret. So that was that. She stood and straightened her shirt, her eyes focused on the door Anya had left through. Would she ever see her again?

"Lanis, we need to go."

"Yes, we do."

⚘ ⚘ ⚘ ⚘

Anya rounded the corner and slumped against the wall, burying her head in her hands, quickly straightening when she realized where she was. This wasn't the time nor place for her to lose her composure. Later, she would have a private moment to reflect on the events that had transpired so far. Being so distant with Lanis tore her apart, but she didn't have a choice.

She would like nothing more than to shout from the balconies what Lanis meant to her. It just wasn't the right time and she didn't know if it ever would be. She had faith in Nia, but at times, like now, it was hard to let the ones she loved go, not knowing if or when she would see them again. She would leave them both in Nia's hands. She had her own troubles to deal with. At the top of her list was the traitor. She knew they would all be motivated to turn on their vows; she just couldn't see any of them actually doing it. She also had to make the decision of who would go with her to Manight and whom she would leave in charge.

She picked up her pace as she neared the stairs, then carefully took them one at a time. Her first meeting this morning was with Merek. When she reached the top of the landing, all four of her advisers were waiting for her. "We will start shortly, but I have a matter I must discuss with Merek first." She opened the door, then took her seat at the head of the table, directing Merek to her right.

"High Priestess, what can I do for you?"

He always looked so smug and she knew he felt entitled because of his position. "I take it you took care of Priestess Tion for me."

"I did. We carried her to the edge of the water and burnt her body. I left her ashes in a small container in the public temple."

"Good. I have also taken care of Councilman Ramus. It will be handled." His smile sent chills down her spine.

"Excellent; we must not allow those without faith to run about, High Priestess."

"No, we must not. Call the others in." Lately, every time Merek or any of her other advisers were around, she got a weird vibe from them. Not scary, just different. As the Prophecy reading drew near, their attitudes grew more desperate. When they sat down, by the looks on their faces, she knew this meeting wouldn't start well. Before she could say anything, Miriam spoke.

"We deserve an explanation about what happened the other day. You haven't mentioned anything or addressed the situation. I have people asking me and I can't tell them anything because I don't know anything," she said, wringing her hands. "A Priestess died and another woman was brought in. I went to the infirmary that day and the commander at the door turned me away."

"I agree," Kerrison said. "As your advisers, we have a right to know what goes on in this temple and why a commander was stationed at the infirmary to begin with."

"I see," Anya said. "Does everyone feel this way?" Everyone nodded in agreement. "It seems, in the last few weeks, I have had to explain to everyone countless times exactly who I am."

"Now wait," Hensley said.

They were getting good at interrupting her. Anya stood and slammed her hands on the table, causing everyone to jump in their seats. She held up one of her hands. "Do not interrupt me again. You will all learn your place. I am not another member of this council. I. Am. Your. High Priestess. As such, you will treat me in the appropriate manner. How quickly you forget you were voted in. I was chosen. I don't answer to you, but you to me. Do you see how that works? Nia speaks to me and I listen. I do not take orders from you. No matter how far you think you can push me, the fact remains you can all be replaced. What happened isn't any of your business. If it concerned you, I would have told you. In our positions, you don't always get all the answers. That's what faith is for and if any of you have lost your faith, you don't deserve your position anymore." They were holding their tempers, but the looks on their faces spoke volumes. She sat down and held each of their gazes. "I respect each of you and I value your insight," she said calmly, "but I do not answer to you."

"It is not every day a Priestess is killed in such a manner. I think I speak for everyone when I say we were all just concerned, maybe a little frightened," Merek said.

His knack for politics never ceased to amaze her. "I cannot, nor will I, share all the information I receive with you."

"We deserve—" Miriam said.

"I won't say it again. That particular subject is closed." She would have to take drastic measures after she got back. "Now, I understand that the latest shipment of goods has arrived. Am I to presume everything is satisfactory?"

"Yes, everything arrived intact as always. Dantar is one of our most trusted trade partners. We never have any problems with them," Hensley said.

"So no other pressing issues with the other Councils." From the beginning of Malora's existence, there had always been different Councils to handle all of the city's business. The Council of Four was Anya's personal advisers and the only Council to have constant contact with her. The Council of Eight, Sixteen, and Thirty-two designated two members to report to each separate council so everyone had someone to be accountable to. Sometimes she wished she dealt with anyone other than her advisers, but then again, she didn't know if she could handle it if her four advisers were multiplied.

"No, nothing pressing," Miriam said.

Anya sat back and searched their faces. She saw neither friend, nor foe. It wasn't a welcome feeling. "Before we close, I would like to discuss my trip to Manight. I still haven't made my decision on who will fill in while I am away. It isn't a decision I will make lightly. I will be gone for at least a month, so whomever I choose will have to preach the monthly sermon, and I know that at least two of you have never done that. But rest assured that will not play into my decision. I know some don't agree with the monthly sermon, but it is very dear to my heart and whomever I choose will treat it with the dignity that it deserves. I also need someone who will continue to keep the city locked down. Even though I trust you all with city affairs, I am not so naïve to think that you don't have your own agendas. Everyone does. But you all have shown and proven yourself to me time and time again. I do know whom I won't be choosing for my replacement, but I have another job for him to do. Hensley, I will talk to you after this meeting." She held up her hands to ward of everyone's questions. "Everyone, please respect my decision, whatever it may be. Nia has not given me a clear answer of yet, but when I do receive it, I will let you know. Everyone except Hensley is dismissed."

As soon as the door shut, Hensley moved to the seat adjacent to hers and spoke. "What can I do for you, High Priestess?" He didn't seem angry, only curious.

"You have strong loyalties to Nia. I don't always agree with you, but I do respect you. While I am gone, your duties will be to counsel and take care of any problems that arise in the city. You will stand in for me in the weekly temple gatherings. The people need a strong leader and you have always given them good advice with a dash of good nature. They respect you. I know you will be fair and honest with them. I do not want any bickering among all of you while I am gone. Nothing should hinder the lives of the people we are sworn to care for and protect. You have never acted like you are better than the people of the city just because you are an adviser to me. You are a humble servant to Nia and that is why I am asking this of you. I'm sure the others would be quite capable, but I feel that your best would be to give yourself to the people. I want to make it clear that I am not dismissing you from filling in for me, it's just I feel your gifts are best used this way."

"I would be honored to do this. I love the people of this city and I would do anything for them." He hesitated before he went on. "Of the three remaining, someone will be left out. You will choose a temporary leader and you will choose someone to go with you. That will leave only one."

"I have thought of that, but it has to be this way. The one who takes my place will need two to advise him or her. If the one left cannot handle that, I will have to do something about it."

"It has to be you that goes." It was more of a statement then a question.

"Yes. Now if you would excuse me, I have somewhere else I have to be."

"Of course. I will do you proud."

"I know." At least she felt she had made one right decision, but still at a crossroads with the other one. She stood and walked out the door leading to the balcony. The sun shone down on the entire city, painting it in a multitude of colors. The city never failed to leave her in awe. She hoped Lanis and Elson were making good time. She turned back to the room when a woman walked in and sat down at the table. She joined her and watched as she pulled several stones from a pouch around her waist. The woman threw them on the table and pushed them around with her finger.

"I see a great sadness ahead for you," the Oracle said. "The sky and the ground are twisted. Blackness and heat. The days get away from you and one will betray you. Keep those you trust far away and those you fear close. Do not let love rip you apart." She moved the stones and said in hushed tones, "One unlikely source will come to your aid. Trust with an open heart and let those that do you wrong receive their fate justly. Do not stop what must be done."

"Thank you." Anya stared out the window as the Oracle gathered the stones and left. The meetings were always quick and to the point. But the real question was, who were her real enemies and who were her friends? The one person she trusted above all others except Nia was on her own journey and she wasn't at all sure she would ever see her again.

⁕⁕⁕⁕

Lanis stopped walking and cocked her head to listen to the forest. They were making good time since leaving their breakfast meeting with Anya, but being this deep in the Windark Forest, so soon after being attacked, put her on edge. The complete and utter stillness and quiet of the forest wasn't normal. Nature should be alive with sounds: birds singing, squirrels barking, or at the very least, the wind blowing through the trees, but there was nothing. She fought the urge to jump when the rustling of leaves stopped behind her.

"You okay?" Elson asked.

As he was a Ranger, she knew he would have had years of extensive training, but she wouldn't feel comfortable until she saw for herself what he was capable of. It was one thing to train and quite another to actually put that training to use. Though to her knowledge, Rangers didn't normally carry long swords and Elson kept his firmly planted on his back. From his armor, to his weapons, to the way he carried himself, he was a complete mystery and one she wasn't looking forward to solving. The only thing she was almost certain of was that he was on her side and that would have to be enough. At least for now. Quickly scanning the area, she relaxed only when the wind whistled through the trees, breaking the eerie silence that had surrounded them all day. Most people were afraid of the forest at night, but for Lanis, the daytime held the most secrets. At least at night everyone was on an even footing. Satisfied everything was in order, she turned to face him, her breath catching when she realized where they had stopped. Forcing herself to stay calm and her expression emotionless, she eyed the clearing. Elson stood in front of her, arms crossed across his chest, in the exact spot Priestess Tion had been standing right before she stabbed her with the dagger. Lanis's hand instantly went to her side. Kaylynn had stressed it would take time for the pain to subside, but Lanis hoped it lessened sooner rather than later. She rubbed her neck, cringing when Elson started setting up camp. There was still plenty of daylight left, but she wouldn't question his decision making, at least, not yet. She had a feeling she wouldn't win this one anyway. He knew exactly where they were. "I'm fine," she said.

He shrugged his shoulders and smiled. "I figured you were, but just now you went somewhere else." He looked away, seeming to weigh his words. "You sure you're okay?" He pointed to her side. "Are you hurting?"

She took up his stance. Since they would be together awhile, she figured honesty would be the best option. "My side is bothering me and it's weird being back here so soon." She waved her hand in the air. "I haven't had much time to absorb everything."

"Then maybe you shouldn't," he said, gathering sticks off the ground.

She scrunched her nose. "Maybe I shouldn't what?"

"Absorb everything." He dumped the sticks on the ground. "I don't know a lot, but I do know two things. One, you should always face your fear head-on, and two, thinking on something you can't change only leads to trouble and is a complete waste of time."

She sighed. "You're right." Thinking about and fearing what happened would only distract her. Her sole focus had to be the oath. She slipped her pack off and helped him set up the rest of camp. Satisfied everything looked in order, she sat on the ground and hugged her legs to her chest. Feeling his gaze on her, she looked up, but every time she did, he turned his face away from her. How much did he know about her attack? Pushing her legs out in front of her, she accepted the cup he offered, inhaling the sweet smell. She closed her eyes and savored the first sip. The Maldorna flower grew native to the shores of Malora. The leaves were a little sweet and a little bitter, the taste uniquely different from anything she had ever had before. The leaves were prized in other parts of Adearian, but since the flower only bloomed a few days every year, ninety percent of the leaves stayed in Malora. Some refused to drink it because the plant itself was poisonous—or at least that's what Malora wanted the rest of Adearian to think. Anya mentioned to her that the rumor started long ago because the plant held amazing healing abilities and only Nia's chosen healers were allowed to use the plant. They ground it down to make an ointment and very rarely gave it out. When Lanis was younger, her Grandma gave her a small vial that she kept in her bag. In the past, she never needed to use it, but she had a feeling that would soon change. She took another sip of her tea and looked at him. He held the bag Anya gave him in his hand, fingering the tie. "Oh," she said, setting her cup down. She opened her pack and pulled out her bag. "I forgot about this."

"I didn't. I've been thinking about it since we left," he said, laughing. "I just didn't want to seem too eager. It's not every day someone like me gets a gift handed to him personally by the High Priestess of Malora."

She often forgot very few people knew Anya the way she did. Moments like this brought her crashing back to reality. Anya was her reason for living, as Anya was his as well, but for completely different reasons. She rubbed her hands on her pants before opening the bag, hoping she found her Anya within the contents. "Let's see what High Priestess Anya packed for us." As her fingers touched the first item, she let everything that had built up inside her wash away. The doubt, the worry, the fear, all vanished when she pulled the small crock of honey out of the bag. Since the first morning she and Anya spent together, they shared a piece of bread slathered with honey. It became their morning ritual. Anya knew how cranky she got if her routine was disrupted. She set it aside and pulled out the remaining items: a pair of wool socks, a pair of leather gloves, a small wrapped package containing hard candies, and a note. She set the note aside to read later when she was alone. "What did you get?"

"Socks, gloves, hard candy, jerky and a note."

By the way he held himself, one wouldn't think anything different had occurred, but she could hear the excitement in his voice. "I got the same thing but instead of jerky, I got honey," she said, plopping a piece of candy in her mouth. Lemon—her favorite.

"I wasn't expecting this. I believe with my entire being in Nia and what she stands for," he said, stretching his legs out in front of him and taking a sip of his tea. "I've talked to many people who serve other Gods. Everyone has some cracks in their faith, but I have no doubts about whom I serve. I don't doubt the other Gods' existence. I know they exist, but I would never serve them. Everyone talks about their High Priest or High Priestess as untouchable and distant. That High Priestess Anya would take the time to do this for us shows me how much she cares. The last time I had rabbit jerky, my grandmother was alive."

While Elson read his note, she drank the last of her tea. So far, he hadn't mentioned anything about her attack and the way it was looking, he wouldn't bring it up. Elson looked up when she cleared her throat. "I don't know how much you know about what happened to me, but I think I should warn you about our journey."

"Don't," he said, holding his hand out. "I put my

complete faith in Nia and I trust High Priestess Anya completely. It is not for me to question what happened and what will happen. My faith is unshakeable and I would fall on my sword for either one of them, and since I took my oath, I will fall on my sword for you. She knows what she's doing. I can't say I'm not a little uneasy and maybe even a little sacred about what will happen, but I think that's a normal reaction to any new circumstance. This isn't just a bracelet," he said, pointing to his wrist. "This is everything to me. Some wait their whole lives to be called. My commanding officer has never been called to an oath mission. I am honored to be chosen, that she thinks I am worthy of such an honor. I would never do anything to blemish what it or she stands for."

He was a true believer and for Lanis, that was a rare quality to find in someone. She knew he would do whatever was necessary to see them through to the end. She wouldn't say anything about his second oath bracelet or his long sword; everyone had their secrets. "So you didn't see me that night."

He turned his head away. "No."

"The attack came from out of nowhere. I'm not a stranger to fighting." She shook her head. "But I've never seen anything like that before. I just wanted to let you know that what we're up against isn't normal, and I'm not sure that if we face what I came up against the other day that I even know how to fight it. Our fight could come from anywhere."

Several different emotions crossed his face. "Our fight could come from anywhere." He nodded. "But I've been trained well and Nia is on our side." He smiled. "Let's put this stuff away and get some sleep. You take first watch." He repacked his things then lay down on his bedroll. He turned toward her and spoke. "Just so you know, I'm ready for anything." His grin flashed in the flames of the fire before he turned his back and went to sleep.

She repacked her bag, plopping another piece of candy in her mouth. She picked up the note, caressing the paper before unfolding it and reading.

Some things don't need to be spoken. You know how I feel. I will always be here and I will continue to pray for your safe return. Go easy on the honey—you won't have another opportunity for more until you reach Klate. Give Elson a chance.

With all my heart.

Yours always, Anya

After standing, she threw the note in the fire and walked the perimeter. The night was quiet, but not the eerie silence that had enveloped them earlier. She wouldn't let her fear override her obligation. The stillness used to bring her peace but now it only added to her sense of discomfort. She shook her head to clear her thoughts. This wasn't who she was: afraid of the dark. Even though Elson's oath was to keep her safe, she would do everything in her power to make sure he came out of this unscathed as well. Time would only tell whether or not he could be trusted, but for Anya's benefit, she would give him a chance. Time flew and after a few hours, she woke him.

He stood and stretched. "Everything okay?"

She shrugged. "Nothing to worry about."

"Good. Get some sleep; morning will come all too soon. Then a full day of travel. Hopefully by the end of the week we'll be in Klate."

"I can hardly wait," she muttered. Turning away from him, she shifted on her mat and closed her eyes, trying and failing to fall asleep. She took a deep breath and forced herself to relax, only to tense when someone knelt next to her. Her fingers tightened on her knife, the blood pounding in her ears. On the count of three, she shifted only to have a hand clamp over her mouth. She struggled against the body next to hers and forced her eyes open. Elson held a finger to his lips. Later she would inform him there were better ways to get her attention, but by the look on his face, now wasn't the time. He pointed to his ear then to the left and right, holding up two fingers. He grinned and headed to the right.

She picked up her knife and stood, heading in the opposite direction. The farther she walked, the more her eyes adjusted to the dark. His hearing must be amazing. The only sound she could discern was the crunching of leaves underfoot. She stopped walking and listened, swinging her head around when she heard it. The leaves rustled ahead and whoever it was wasn't making a secret of their appearance. She leaned into a tree and waited. Her eyes picked up shadows through the trees and her heart rate tripled as the footsteps were within striking distance.

Snap

She pivoted and threw her knife. She heard a grunt, then someone turned and ran away from her in the opposite direction. Pushing away from the tree, she took up the chase. The farther they ran, the darker the forest became.

Suddenly, the person's outline came into focus.

She leapt and they tumbled to the ground. She slapped his hands away and gripped his arms, wrapping her legs around his body and twisted them. He bucked his hips and pushed her off him, grabbed her legs, and pulled her back to him. He straddled her waist.

He winked. "You're mine now."

Her fingers curled around the rocks on the ground. When he laughed, she threw them in his face, pushing his body off her. Ignoring his screams, she stood and kicked him in the face, his body falling backward. Kneeling, she grabbed his neck and twisted. Satisfied he was dead, she pushed his face into the ground and stood. It was an easy kill.

Too easy.

She searched his body but didn't find anything useful, nor did she find any type of wound. Why would he run if she hadn't wounded him? He obviously wanted her away from camp for some reason.

She scanned the area before heading back. Doubt started to creep in that she was heading in the wrong direction when a glimmer ahead caught her attention. A smile pulled at her lips when she spied her knife sticking out of a tree. She pulled it free and slipped it into her boot. Now, she knew he was leading her on. What could the purpose possibly be? As far as she knew, Anya was the only one who knew that they were on an oath mission. There would be time for speculation later; now she needed to find Elson.

Her stomach tightened with each step closer to the clearing and it dropped when she entered and Elson wasn't there. Heart pounding, she ducked and watched an arrow embed itself into the tree she was standing in front of. Scrambling around the tree, she stood and blended.

"I know you're there," a woman said from the clearing.

Surely this woman hadn't gotten the better of Elson. After all, he was a Ranger in the army. If he failed to subdue her, what did that say about her chances? She ran her hand through her hair. This was not the time to doubt her abilities. She'd survived worse. Shaking her arms out, she uncurled her whip and stepped around the tree.

The woman stood by the fire, her bow pulled taut. From the well-worn brown leather boots to the short messy brown hair, Lanis didn't recognize anything about her. Her smile was as cold as her eyes.

Lanis kept her eyes on the woman even when she caught movement behind her. The woman winked and released her bow at the same time Elson swung his sword and Lanis flicked her wrist. Lanis grabbed the arrow out of the air and fell back, landing against the tree. Dropping the arrow on the ground, she watched Elson clean the blood from the sword blade. The woman's body lay by the fire, but her head rested next to Lanis's mat. She walked over and kicked it away, securing the whip around her waist.

"Well, that just happened," Elson said, sheathing his sword.

Lanis rested her hands on her hips. "Yes, it did." She shook her head. Elson smirked. "I took care of the other one, broke his neck."

"She was quick," he said, pointing to the stranger's body. "Doubled back on me." He crossed his arms across his chest and rocked back on his heels. "Impressive the way you grabbed that arrow out of the air."

Lanis shrugged. "I knew it was coming." Her quick reflexes and the training she received over the years had saved her life many of times.

"Still impressive. I couldn't have done it." He reached down and started gathering his things. "I'm pretty sure we got them all. She was good." He looked up. "Morning's coming."

"Is she familiar to you?

"No, you?"

"No. It was too dark for me to notice anything about him either." They searched her body, but didn't find anything useful.

He sighed. "I think we should go."

"Since I'm not going to be getting any more sleep, I agree with you." Lanis tried to be optimistic, but she knew things would only get worse. She had killed five people in less than a week. She stood and slipped her arm through her pack.

"I take it we can expect more of that?" he asked when they were a good distance away.

"I think that's a real possibility."

"Well then," he said, patting her on the back. "We have something to look forward to."

"It would seem so."

❧❧❧❧

Lanis adjusted her pack and stayed a step behind Elson, who had taken the lead that morning. All had been quiet since the attack the first night. She hadn't realized how vast the forest was, never having traveled this far in before, until now. They had agreed they would stick to the map Anya had given them and the route she had laid out for them. Time would tell if they were able to stick to it for the duration of their trip or not.

She plopped her last piece of candy in her mouth, savoring the delicate honey undertones. The candy would only satisfy her for a short time. Considering they were both trained soldiers, their food should have lasted longer. They rationed, but still ended up eating more than they should have. Earlier Elson had pointed out a dot on the map that may or may not be a village. They would have to be careful, as isolated villages were always unpredictable. She stopped walking when Elson halted in front of her.

"Do you hear that?"

Lanis concentrated. She could faintly hear something. "Barely. Do you think it's the dot on the map?" She took a long drink of water before handing it back to him.

"I suppose. These woods are too thick for it to be anything else," he said, throwing his arms up. "But who knows what we've passed in this forest. I've heard some weird stuff," he said, scratching his cheek. "I didn't want to say anything in case you hadn't heard it too."

She laughed. "I've heard stuff too."

"I'm usually not bothered by this sort of thing, but I will be ready to get out of these woods." He took a couple of steps, then turned back to her. "I think you should go in front. I'll be right behind you."

"Okay." She pulled down the sleeves of her shirt to hide her wrist. "Ready." She pulled her whip tight across her waist.

"It would be nice if I could disguise my sword like that," he said, adjusting his pack.

"I don't know, sometimes a sword would come in handy." She took the lead.

"Why don't you carry a sword?"

"Before the Ramden Council chose me, my Papa trained me with his weapon of choice, the whip. From the moment I held it, it became a part of me. In essence an extension of who I am. If need be, I could probably learn to use a sword, but I would never be comfortable with it." She ran her hand through her hair. "Once I started training with my Ramden mentor, he convinced me I should learn to master another weapon. After all these years, using either my whip or knife has become second nature. I don't know what I would do without either one. Don't be concerned though, I'm pretty resilient."

"I'm not concerned. I've seen you wield them." He shrugged. "Only curious, that's all."

She didn't expect much from the village, only hoped they would be able to buy a few provisions and maybe a hot meal. After a short hike, they broke through a patch of dense foliage onto a dirt path that encircled a small village. Even though the village wasn't much, compared to the cramped dark forest, the change felt refreshing until her eyes landed on the buildings lining the street. Some looked ready to collapse, while others stood proudly with fresh paint and new shingles. The sour smell that drifted her way instantly put her on alert. Her stomach turned and she stepped back when several doors opened and the occupants of the village walked out onto the street, in unison, as if they had been waiting for them.

Elson took up position in front of her and addressed the man closest to them. "We are in need of provisions and a hot meal. We have money to pay. We're only passing through."

Lanis shivered and rubbed her neck, eyeing the people staring at them. No one said anything, or even attempted to make a move in their direction. Her instincts were screaming at her to leave. "Elson," she said, touching his arm. "Let's go."

"I'm right behind you." They made it as far as the

tree line when a voice stopped them.

"My, my, my. What do we have here, boys?" A man laughed from behind them. "These folks thought they could walk into our town like they owned it and leave without paying our fee."

Lanis clenched her jaw and ran her fingers along the handle of her whip.

"Hey!" the man screamed. "I'm talking to you two."

From the sound of his voice, she estimated him to be, ten, maybe fifteen feet behind them.

"Turn around and talk to me. Face-to-face. I don't have a problem killing you from here." He snickered. "But I so enjoy watching the life drain from the eyes of my victims."

Lanis swallowed and caught Elson's eyes, nodding at the look he gave her. Doing nothing wasn't an option. She took a deep breath, gripped her whip, turned, crouched, and threw her wrist out. The crack vibrated the air around them. The whip flew through the air, the tip licking the man's cheek. She stood and drew it back to her side. The man stood still, eyes wide as blood trickled down his face. "We didn't come looking for trouble," she said.

"We will defend ourselves," Elson said from beside her. He held his sword tightly in both hands. "We came only looking for a meal. A meal we were willing to pay for and when we leave, you threaten us." He kicked up the dirt at his feet. "We are going."

The man, she assumed the leader, took a step closer to them. "You come into our village and think you have the right to anything you want. We know what and who you are. We worship no God!" he shouted. He wiped the blood off his cheek with his sleeve and gestured to the two men on either side of him. "Allow me to introduce myself and my men. I'm Jack and these are my boys," he said, arms outstretched. "The man on my left is Micah and the man on my right is Lee, and for the record you are going to die today." He laughed.

"We might do more to the woman," Micah said.

"Yes." Lee nodded. "We'll play with her while her man watches."

By now, townspeople packed the streets. "We came quietly," Lanis said, "and that's how we would like to leave, but that's completely up to you."

"Did you hear that, boys?" Jack laughed and pulled his sword. Compared to Elson's long sword, it didn't look like much, but she had seen men, especially desperate men, do incredible things with less. She could tell by the look in his eyes that he was about to do something stupid. When his hand twitched, she snapped her wrist, allowing her whip to cut through the air, wrapping around his throat. She fell to her knees and threw her knife, striking Micah in the chest.

Lee pulled his sword and Elson advanced, swinging out in a wide arc, slicing through his stomach, nearly cutting him in half. Lanis pulled on her whip, knocking Jack off his feet. She jumped up, ran to Micah, pulled her knife from his chest, and slit his throat.

She accepted the hand Elson offered her and stood. She wiped the blood off her knife and slipped it back in her boot then knelt next to Jack. "I told you all we wanted was to go quietly." She uncurled her whip from around his neck and wound it back around her waist. The townspeople still only watched.

Jack sat up, gasping for breath, turning hate-filled eyes toward them. "I'll kill you for this."

"No, you won't," Elson said, plunging his sword into Jack's heart and twisting. He raised his boot and kicked him in the chest, sending his body falling backward and allowing the sword to slip free. Elson kept his eyes on the townspeople as they walked back to the edge of the village. No one spoke a word, or even attempted to make a move in their direction. "We will be leaving and if anyone tries to stop us, or follow us, you will suffer the same fate." They all continued staring.

After a short hike, they stopped to catch their breath. Elson sheathed his sword. "I see what you mean about the whip. I could never do that."

"Most couldn't. It's taken me years to get to the level I'm at." If he wasn't going to mention what happened, neither would she.

"The whip you use is a bit unusual in design. Where'd you get it?" he asked, digging in his pack.

"It belonged to my Papa. He passed it on to me after he retired from teaching. What are you looking for?" she asked.

"Seeing what I have left. I've got a little jerky and a small piece of cheese," he said, clasping his pack shut.

"Sounds good to me. I have a few biscuits and some honey. Let's get a little farther away. I don't want to take any chances."

He nodded. "By my estimate, we should be in Klate in a day or so."

⁂

"It bothers me a little," Lanis said after they had set up camp.

"What does?" He sat on a stump and placed his

dinner offerings beside him.

"We've only been traveling for three days and we've already killed five people."

"They were all justified." He took the biscuit she offered.

"Oh, I know," she said, waving off his statement. "It's just that before we met, I already killed four. So that brings our combined total to nine. Nine people in a little over a week. If this keeps up can you imagine our total by the time we make it to Manight?"

"Well." He grimaced. "When you put it that way, it does seem like a lot. But look on the bright side." He accepted the honey she handed him.

She could hear the playfulness in his voice and accepted the honey back, along with a piece of cheese. "There's a bright side?"

"We're not dead," he said, taking a bite of his biscuit and pointing between them.

She smiled at his optimism. "I guess it's true what they say."

He picked up his cup of tea and squinted at her. "They who?"

She waved his question off. "There is always a silver lining."

He brightened and held up his cup. "I couldn't agree more."

❧ ❧ ❧ ❧

Anya ran her fingers along the windowsill, watching the cargo ships unloading at the dock. The cool ocean breeze swept over her, bringing a smile to her lips, and settling her nerves. The reason for her nerves, High Priest Lantor, had arrived from

Cambridge that morning. He served Novak, the God of strength and protection. Eight years ago, her heart almost burst when Bryan, at the age of four, was brought to her with magic ability, but it broke a little when he possessed the gift of strength, rather than the gift of healing. To receive Novak's gift was even rarer than receiving Nia's.

Earlier that morning, she had sent one of her guards to fetch Bryan. On one hand, she was losing a vital part of her community, but on the other, she got to send one of the young citizens of Malora off to their destiny. She pushed off the window and settled behind her desk. She remembered fondly the last time someone was brought to her with Nia's gift of healing. Casten grew up in the Anolk mountains and wasn't aware she had Nia's gift until she was in her late teens. She was a quick learner and had risen in the ranks as the fastest chosen of Nia's to receive her white band. Her ability to learn and her acceptance of everything she was taught went above and beyond anything Anya had ever seen before. Two years ago, Casten was stationed in Manight.

She knew Lantor would be getting the same with Bryan as she did in Casten. She stood at the knock on the door and nodded at her guard to open it. Lantor entered first, followed by his Protector. He hadn't aged a bit since the last time she'd seen him, years ago. His black hair was cut short and his green eyes were the same vibrant shade she remembered. The black wool pants and cream-colored long sleeve tunic only added to his ego. His ever-present white and gold cloak was draped over his arm. One wouldn't have to wonder about his wealth; he wore it very well. She held to the belief that one didn't have to flaunt their wealth to show others what they were made of. She practiced Nia's words never to act, in any way, above those that looked up to her.

Lantor nodded. "High Priestess Anya, it's been too long since I've been in your company."

"I agree." He looked the same, but his tone told a different story. "Please have a seat." She sat after he was settled. "Time doesn't stop for anyone. Besides, it doesn't feel like it's been that long." She clasped her hands in her lap, comforted by the fact that her Protector stood behind her. Even if it wasn't Lanis. "And what a splendid reason to see you again. We should all be so pleased."

He crossed one leg over the other. "As you might imagine, I am quite excited to take Bryan back home with me." He hesitated before speaking. "He will be well taken care of."

She cocked her head. "I am sure he will be. It is quite difficult to let him go, but I would be just as excited as you are."

"I do appreciate your hospitality. Malora isn't like a lot of towns around. You have kept the integrity Nia is known for. It is quite refreshing." He grinned.

The look in his eyes and the tone of his voice conveyed quite the opposite. Many outsiders detested Nia's way of living. Until now, she never realized he was one of them. "We do keep to what Nia set forth for us. Her followers are dedicated and faithful, as are yours." The three guards in the corner must have sensed her discomfort because they took two steps forward away from the wall.

"They are." He eyed the room before bringing his focus back on Anya. "I hear you have a big day coming up."

She relaxed back into her chair. "It is odd how something so normal in our past is something extraordinary today, and to coincide with Manight's two hundredth anniversary of the Festival of the Goddess will only shine more light on the reading." She shrugged. "It will be an amazing time to read the Prophecy. I dare say I'm looking forward to it."

"To be honest, I'm glad it's you and not me. I'm not a fan of public speaking." He grinned. "Having all those people stare at you, waiting for some great bit of wisdom. And what happens when what you say doesn't live up to their expectation? It's only a thought."

There was no way he knew what the Prophecy said, yet that's exactly how he was acting. She held up her hand when her guards and her Protector stepped forward. "We'll see what kind of response I get when it's read. Riddles and innuendoes usually pepper prophecies. It could be complete gibberish," she said, praying to Nia that Bryan would show up soon. Lantor was worse than her advisers. This wasn't the same man she remembered from her youth.

"It could be." He laughed. "We shall see."

"Are you going to be there?" It didn't seem likely, considering he would be in the first stages of getting Bryan settled.

"Actually, I will. As you said, it will be a wonderful time and I wouldn't pass up the opportunity to see a once in a lifetime event. Bryan will be accompanying me, of course. It will give him a chance to take in one of the biggest cities in Hadmore and, if I may say so, one of the most over-rated." He slipped his pocket watch out and glanced down at it. "Have you ever been?"

"No, I haven't, but I am looking forward to going." She thanked Nia when a guard opened the door and walked in. He leaned down and whispered in her ear before walking back out. She stood and informed Lantor to do the same. "Bryan has just arrived and he is a bit nervous."

"Nerves are good."

She motioned for one of the guards to open the door. Bryan walked in, carrying a small suitcase clasped firmly in his right hand. He was quite a bit taller than she remembered. His eyes remained glued to hers even when Lantor stepped forward.

"High Priestess Anya," Bryan said, bowing.

"Bryan." She touched his arm. "This is High Priest Lantor."

Bryan bowed in his direction. "High Priest."

"My boy, I am looking forward to teaching you. It will be my great honor to raise you in the knowledge of Novak."

"I am looking forward to learning."

Anya felt out of place, as some sort of bond seemed to grow between them. "Bryan," she said, stepping in front of him and placing her hands on his shoulders. "I am very proud of you. Remember that you will always have a home here." She patted him on the shoulder and stepped to the side. "I will leave you two. You both may stay as long as you wish."

"Thank you, Anya," Lantor said, leading Bryan to the council table and sitting down.

She motioned to her Protector and they both walked out the door. Lantor was hiding something. She would get someone to look into it.

❧ ❧ ❧ ❧

Klate was a lot different than Lanis remembered

and a far cry better than the last village they stopped at. Although, she was only slightly more confident they would receive a warmer welcome here. Structures stood as far as she could see along the town's border. Some stood taller than the buildings in Malora, and merchants' stalls were bunched together across the square from them. Her stomach grumbled when the smell of the sweet dough wafted in their direction.

Elson laughed and pointed to the vendors. "We have time."

She shook her head and pulled her hood up. "No, let's get this over with." She scanned the area for any disturbances. So far, so good. It was unlikely she would see the woman again, but she wasn't taking any chances.

"Ever been here before?"

"Once." She wasn't about to tell him her story now.

He scratched his beard. "Good to know. We're early. I'm sure that won't matter. At least it shouldn't."

"Only one way to find out."

He grinned. "Too true."

The farther into the city they walked, the more the crowds thinned, and by the time they made it past the square, only a few people spared them a glance as they walked by. The hill they had to climb in order to reach the Guild house ran from one end of the town to the other. In the middle of the hill, a staircase was built out of loose rocks. Elson motioned for her to climb up first. At the top, they stood side by side, looking down at Orange Lake. To Lanis's eyes, the lake looked bigger than the actual town. A large building stood in the center of the lake, and on either side, four smaller buildings were placed. From her vantage point, she could see a few buildings behind the ones in front, but couldn't make out how many. A wooden walkway that ran the length of all nine structures connected all the buildings. At first glance, it looked like the buildings were on top of the water, but at closer look they were actually floating above the water, as was the walkway.

"It's beautiful," Elson said.

"Yes, it is." An orange glow seemed to radiate off the surface of the water. Lanis stepped down from the hill and walked up to the bridge. The skillfully carved wood was polished until it shone in the mid-day sun, and it spanned a quarter of the lake. A guard stood in the middle of the bridge and he stepped in front of them when they reached him.

"What can I do for you?" he asked, without even looking in their direction.

"We have business with the Guild Master," she said. The guard looked her up and down, quickly dismissing her. "Look." She shut up when Elson touched her arm.

"We have business with the Guild Master," Elson repeated, pulling his sleeve back to reveal his oath bracelet. The guard nodded once and allowed them to pass.

Lanis stepped past him and took a step down. Water lapped at the bridge, but never came over the sides. "The breeze is nice."

"Very refreshing." He agreed as he walked past her and up to the first door. The door was opened immediately after he knocked. A young woman directed them into a small room, informed them to sit, and walked out. Except for the four chairs situated against one wall, the room was empty. "Not much in here."

She laughed. "You took the words right out of my mouth." She fidgeted in her seat. Waiting was not one of her strong suits.

A short time later, the same woman escorted them into another room. Besides the four chairs, this room also housed a large desk, and another door. The Guild Master entered through the second door that stood directly behind the desk. He seated himself behind the desk and pushed his hood back, revealing a wrinkled face and snow white hair. He leaned forward and placed both hands on top of the desk. "How may I be of assistance to you today?"

Lanis instantly disliked him. She pulled the note and pouch from her bag that Anya had instructed her to give to him and lay them on the desk. His expression never changed while he read the letter. He called the same woman back and whispered in her ear. Lanis couldn't hear what was being said, but the look on the woman's face spoke volumes. When she asked if he was certain, Lanis knew something was up. She and Elson exchanged looks and she knew they were both thinking the same thing. She rubbed her neck. That's all they needed, someone incompetent, or someone who couldn't handle themselves. If that were the case, they would be better off without them.

The Guild Master smiled. "Julie will be back shortly with someone I think will be perfect for your needs."

"For what we need and what High Priestess Anya is paying you, they better be the best," Elson spat.

The Guild Master continued smiling. "I assure you, she is. Once we have all this squared away, I have a room prepared and dinner will be brought to you. You can restock your provisions and tomorrow morning you can be on your way. I hope you realize since you're here you won't be allowed back in the city."

Lanis tore her eyes away from his when the door opened and Julie entered, followed by a young woman. The stranger stood at least a foot shorter than Lanis and Elson and her bright red hair curled around her shoulders. Her tight gray leggings and long-sleeved purple tunic hid a slim build, and her knee-high brown boots looked more like a fashion statement than anything practical.

"She's not what I expected," Elson whispered in Lanis's ear. With her red hair and flashy clothing, it would be hard for them to keep a low profile.

She walked up to the Guild Master and handed him a small black book. "Rose," he said. "Please have a seat." She sat next to Lanis, but didn't look their way. "Rose, Lanis and Elson are on an oath mission from Nia. They request your services. I knew you would be the perfect fit for them because they are headed to Manight." He stamped her book, produced a shimmering green light from his hand, and touched the paper. The light traveled from the paper to Rose, circling around her before disappearing. "You will protect them, but you will abide by the laws of this Guild, and the oaths for which you have taken. Do you understand?"

"I do." Her voice, cool and detached, held a strange accent.

"Gather your things, all of your things, and join them in their room." She was dismissed as quickly as she was summoned. She bowed to the Guild Master, gathered her book, and walked out. He turned his attention back to Elson and Lanis. "Julie will show you to your room. Food will be brought in."

They followed Julie out and down the hall to the third building. Opening yet another door, she led them down another hallway before opening the door to their room. Lanis couldn't help but notice guards stationed on both ends of the hall. The room held three beds and nothing else. Not even windows.

"Is it just me," Elson said, walking around the room. "Or does this feel like a prison?"

"It does. Did you get a good look at Rose?"

"Although she is beautiful, she isn't what we need. We need someone like Julie; at least she looks like she could blend in."

"I know. I hope we're not being saddled with a loser."

Elson laughed. "He didn't even tell us his name."

"He made no secret of not liking us." She took the bed by the door, sat down, and laid her bag beside her.

"He didn't have a problem taking our money, though." Elson chose the bed across from her.

"I thought you were going to jump across the desk at him."

"I'm not stupid, but I don't care for anyone disrespecting Nia, or our High Priestess."

"Hopefully, we can get a good night's sleep tonight without anyone trying to kill us." She leaned back against the wall.

"Let's hope no one tries to kill us." He laid his sword on the bed and sat down. "I am hungry, though. I hope the food is good."

Lanis raised her arm and sniffed. "We both could use a bath."

"When Julie comes back with our food, we can ask her. I didn't want to say anything, but you were beginning to ripen." He ducked the pillow she threw at him.

"Rose didn't seem to like her Guild Master." She caught the pillow he threw back and placed it behind her head.

"Nope, and the look she gave Julie, if it could have killed, Julie would be dead right now."

"She did seem to have spunk. We'll ask Julie about her."

"I'm confident Nia knows what she's doing. Have faith, Lanis." He stood and opened the door when someone knocked and held it open while Julie brought their food in.

Lanis stopped her at the door. "I probably shouldn't ask because you all have already been so generous, but is there any way we can get a bath?"

Julie looked horrified. "Of course. How thoughtless of me. I'm sorry I didn't mention it before. At the end of this hall, turn and directly in front of you will be a small bridge; cross over. Someone is always standing guard outside the bath house, but I'll let them know to expect you both."

"One more thing," Elson said, leaning close to her. "Again, we shouldn't ask, but we're a bit concerned. Is there something we should know about Rose?" He stepped back and put his hands to his chest. "Now, I only ask because we need to make sure she is capable of handling herself."

Julie fidgeted and looked around the room before speaking. "I probably shouldn't."

"No, go on," Lanis whispered. Elson winked at her.

"Well, Rose hasn't exactly excelled in her teaching like one would hope. Don't get me wrong, she made it this far and I'm sure she will be able to do the basics for you, but let's hope you don't get into any real trouble. She also doesn't interact well with others. Did you see her clothes? We all find her a bit odd. She doesn't come from around here, you know."

Lanis nodded. "I caught that."

"On the bright side," she said, walking to the door. "She is a blue-band sorceress so she must be good at something. I'll leave you both to your dinner." She pulled the door open and froze mid-step. Rose stood on the other side with her bag and the coldest smile Lanis had ever seen. Julie stepped aside as Rose entered the room, then quickly left, shutting the door behind her.

Rose didn't look in their direction, but walked to the remaining bed and sat down. Lanis noticed the bow and quiver full of arrows she set beside her bag. From the looks of the bow, she must have been very accomplished and from the size of her bag, she didn't own much. Elson handed them each a plate before sitting down and eating his dinner. Rose put her plate on the floor and laid down, facing away from them.

Lanis motioned for Elson to follow her when they both finished eating. They walked out and down the hall where Julie directed them. "I hope she knows what she's doing."

He slipped his arm around her shoulders and pulled her toward the bath. "I'm sure she will be fine. We may have to keep her from talking so much though." He said it with a straight face, but Lanis started laughing. Elson tried and failed not to join her. They were both bent over, trying to catch their breath, when the guard cleared her throat. "I'm sorry," Lanis said. "It's been a long week."

"A very long week."

The guard rolled her eyes and allowed them to pass. Lanis grabbed Elson's arm, forcing him to stop. "She is the right fit for us, right?"

He squeezed her hand. "Yes, she is."

❧ ❧ ❧ ❧

"By my estimates," Elson said, folding the map, and sliding it back in his pack, "and if the map is correct, we should reach the first oath house by dusk."

Since leaving Klate four days ago, tensions had been high. Mainly because Rose had barely spoken to them. Even when asked a direct question, she tried her best to ignore them. The only conversation she initiated she had informed them her Guild Master only gave her the most basic of items for her to use, the ones he felt she would need. Having only received her blue band, she hadn't come close to mastering the art of enchanting items. She could only channel her magic through items previously enchanted. Lanis couldn't have cared less. She neither liked, nor disliked magic; she only accepted it because it was a part of Adearian that wasn't going away. If they were in trouble and Rose helped, she would be worth what they were paying her, but if not, they would make do with their own talents. She did not intend to put her life in Rose's hands.

Lanis rummaged in her bag, pulled out an apple, and took a bite, savoring the crisp, sour flesh. She settled beside Elson on a fallen tree and watched Rose pacing in front of them, her bow firmly in hand. The bow never left Rose's sight. From the looks of it, it was crafted from several different types of wood. The light and dark tones contrasted nicely with the red leaves carved into the surface. Lanis noticed the quiver had the same leaves stitched into the leather. She respected her need to keep it close; she felt the same way about her whip. Hopefully the bow wasn't just decoration and she could actually use it.

Rose stopped pacing. "Oath house?"

Lanis coughed, gasping for breath at Rose's question. Elson reached over and smacked her on the back, dislodging the piece of apple. After taking a sip of water, she answered Rose since Elson kept quiet. "We have to check in at certain predetermined oath houses. We have three stops. Once there, we will stay the night and restock our provisions before leaving the next day. It also lets the oath master know where we are in our journey, and in turn, he can let High Priestess Anya know where we are."

"Look," Rose said, smoothing her tunic out. "I know why you hired me, but to be honest, I'm not sure how helpful I'm going to be. Not with what little I was given." She placed her hands on her hips. "I don't mean to seem so distant, but in my experience, everywhere I've been stationed my welcome has been anything but warm."

"We thought you just didn't like us," Elson joked, but when Rose crossed her arms and didn't correct him, everyone's mood sobered.

Lanis should have been happy with the tension before, but if she didn't think things could get worse, she was wrong. "You're with us because that's what our High Priestess wanted. Neither one of us," Lanis said, pointing between her and Elson, "are magic inclined."

Rose rolled her eyes. "That's obvious."

"Don't interrupt her," Elson snapped.

"We have our strengths and weaknesses," Lanis

said, ignoring both of their glares. "We are oath bound to Nia and you are bound to us, just under a different contract. Remember, you're bound to the contract you signed. We expect you to fulfill your part if it's needed."

Rose laughed. "I know what I'm bound to; you don't have to remind me. I am faithful to my vows and to my Goddess, Shara."

"As are we," Elson said, standing.

Rose sighed and let her hands fall to her sides. "All I mean is it's been a quiet few days and you both seem capable." She bit her lip. "Honestly, I'm not sure what to expect. Before this, the only contracts I've signed were to traveling merchants. I don't know what I've agreed to. It's a bit unsettling."

"It is," Elson agreed. He looked at Lanis.

Lanis fidgeted and blew out a breath. Rose needed to channel her fear in another way, or she and Elson would end up at war all the time. "To be clear, it has been a quiet few days."

"It has." Elson's mood was less jovial than a few minutes ago.

Rose threw her hands up. "That's what I just said. It's been quiet."

Lanis stood and clasped her hands behind her back. "Since we started a week and a half ago, combined, we've killed nine people."

Elson laughed and shrugged. "It's been quite astonishing actually." He slipped his pack on and sheathed his sword.

Lanis smiled when Rose mumbled, grabbed her bag, and walked past them. Lanis walked beside Elson. "I guess we're ready," she whispered.

"It would seem so." He grinned.

A few hours into their walk, the air changed and

Lanis caught a faint pungent smell and caught Elson's eye. He nodded and pulled his sword.

Death.

The more they walked, the stronger the stench became. Rose stopped ahead of them and bent over with her hands on her knees. Lanis picked up the pace, stopped beside her, and touched her whip, but she didn't hear, or see anything out of place. The smell, however, engulfed her. She would never get used to the sticky, sour smell of rotting flesh.

"How protected is this oath house?" Rose asked.

Elson and Lanis exchanged glances.

"I don't know," Lanis said. "I've never been to one. Have you, Elson?"

"No," he said, through clinched teeth.

Rose shook her head. "I sense nothing good from this place. Don't you feel it?"

Lanis heard the frustration in her voice. "I don't feel anything, but I smell it."

"I don't feel anything either," Elson said.

Rose bit her lip. "I'm not taking about the smell. I can't explain it. Let's continue on."

"Wait," Elson said. "I'm taking lead." It didn't take long to reach the first body, or at least, parts of the first body. It was scattered along the dirt road. Lanis scrunched her nose and side-stepped a body part. The way the parts were scattered, it looked like the man exploded from the inside out.

"Elson, do you recognize anything about him?" Lanis asked.

He rolled his eyes and she laughed. "From the little bits of clothing I see, no, I don't. Let's be careful."

Farther down the road, the stench became stronger. Lanis coughed into her arm, trying not to take deep breaths. Ahead of her, Elson stopped in the middle of the road, completely still. When they caught up with him, she covered her nose and bit back the bile that rose in her throat. Rose retched behind them. The smell was almost unbearable by now. The oath house lay in shambles; only one wall still stood. Bodies and body parts were scattered all over the ground. All the animals were dead, most still in their pens. Why would someone do this and where were the Oath Keepers? By the looks of the dead bodies' clothing, they were not the Keepers, but farmers. "What happened here?"

"Evil," Rose said from beside her.

"I know that. But what happened here?" She waved her arm around.

"Lanis is right," Elson said. "Normally if a place is raided, the animals would have been taken, not killed. By the looks of these men, they have been here awhile, yet the wild animals haven't touched them. I've never seen anything like this."

Rose walked around them. "I was being serious. Evil caused this. Can't you smell it?"

"All I smell is death," Elson said softly.

Rose turned to take in the destruction. "The magic still lingers, but it's faint. Very strong magic caused this. Evil." She shuddered.

Without acknowledging anyone, Elson walked to the rubble of the oath house. What used to be a two-story brick building lay crumbled around on the ground. Lanis sucked in a breath when she realized what she was seeing. The house, just like the first dead body, looked like it exploded from the inside out. "Rose," she said. "Let's go see what Elson found." It wasn't like him to be so quiet. "What's got your attention?" When she caught sight of what he found, she crouched on the ground and threw up. She heaved a few times before accepting the hand Elson offered. She took a small sip of water, washing out her mouth then took a long drink.

Twelve bodies lay on the ground, lined up side-to-side, from tallest to shortest. Their heads were cut off and their feet were tied together, crossed at the ankles. Nine women and three children. By the clothes, the three little bodies were girls. They were all holding hands. It took a sick individual to kill, then pose the bodies. Lanis scanned the area, but didn't see the heads anywhere.

Elson's voice cracked. "We have to bury them." Lanis nodded. Senseless death disgusted her. It was one thing to kill armed men, and quite another to kill women and children.

"No," Rose said, taking a step back from the bodies. "No." She shook her head. "We cannot move them, or they may never rest. If you want, you can throw dirt over them, but they must not be moved," she pleaded.

Lanis touched Elson's hand when he clenched his fist. Normally she would have agreed with him, but the tone of Rose's voice and the passion in her words stopped her. "Okay. We won't move them." Rose turned away from them.

"Lanis," Elson said. "What's going on?" He ran his hands through his beard. "I've never seen anything like this. I've never heard about anything like this. The women and little girls. Come on. Only a coward would have killed them in such a manner. I don't understand."

"Me neither. I know the oath houses communicate with each other, but I don't know how often. From the looks of the bodies and the smell, I would say they've been here for weeks. Surely they get in touch more often than that." She rubbed her neck and averted her eyes from the bodies on the ground. "The only upside I see is that I don't think this has anything to do with our oaths."

He squeezed her shoulder. "I'm pretty sure it doesn't either. There is a lot of rage and hate here. We've just started so I don't think anyone hates us this much," he said. "Rose is acting weird."

"Yes, but when is she not? She's holding something back." She squeezed his hand on her shoulder. "Do you think whoever did this is gone?"

"Yes, I believe they are."

"You do realize that this was our last stop before we travel to the second oath house. We need food and supplies."

"I know. We'll look at the map and see if there's somewhere to stop. So far the map hasn't been all that helpful."

"High Priestess Anya warned us about veering from it. While I'm sure she didn't expect any of this, she made her point about sticking to the map pretty clear." She wasn't at all confident in the path they were to travel, but knew Anya wouldn't purposely send them into danger. "I don't know."

He smiled at her. "You're almost out of honey."

"How did you know?" She laughed, welcoming the subject change. It amazed her how fast they bonded. She liked him, which for her, was almost unheard of.

He cleared his throat. "You're getting more irritable. I noticed that you cut back."

"I've been trying to make it last." He noticed everything.

"Is this a private conversation?" Rose asked.

"No," Elson said.

"Should we stay here tonight?" Lanis asked. Dead bodies didn't bother her. She just didn't want to sleep next to them.

Rose shrugged. "I know whatever caused this is gone. The only thing they left was death. As for the area being safe, I don't know. Isn't that something you two should know?"

Elson sighed. "It's true whoever killed these people and animals is gone, but someone ransacked this place. Everything of value is gone. The people that did that are still out there. We'll set up camp by the wall and then search the perimeter. We'll rotate on watch every two hours."

"Very well," Rose said.

"Agreed," Lanis said, resigned to staying the night. She would suck it up and try not to think about the corpses around her as she slept.

"You sure that's the best place to make camp?" Rose asked. A second later, Lanis pushed her to the ground and grabbed an arrow out of the air. She growled when a second arrow pierced her shoulder, knocking her backward. Elson grabbed her and dragged her behind the wall of the oath house. She sucked in a breath when he eased her to the ground. "I hear quite a few out there."

"Yes," he said, rummaging through his bag.

Lanis grimaced. "Where's Rose?" It sounded like whoever was out there was staying put. Elson took off his belt and told her to bite down on it. As soon as she did, he broke the arrow and pulled the tip out. She screamed into the belt and closed her eyes as fire raced down her arm. The pain was different from anything she was used to. She ripped the belt out of her mouth, her breaths coming in ragged bursts, and opened her eyes. Elson knelt in front of her, searching through his bag. "What are you doing?"

"Fixing you up. More specifically, looking for something to put on the wound."

She clenched her teeth. "My bag."

"What?"

"In my bag I have a small vial. Put some of it on both sides of my wound, then tie it up." It was her only choice; she couldn't afford to be hurt. Not right now.

"Rose is over there." He jerked his thumb behind him. Rose knelt behind what was left of the water well, looking at her hand.

"Found it." He pulled out the vile and opened it, holding still when he realized what he was holding. "Okay, how much will it take?"

"Just enough to cover the wound on either side." The churning in her stomach calmed the instant the cream touched her wound. "Elson, what's Rose doing?" Rose stood and stepped away from the well. Elson helped Lanis stand, when much to their disbelief, all the arrows that were directed at Rose bounced off her. She lifted her hand and threw something on the ground. It erupted into a blue fog, rolling away from them and into the surrounding area. She bent down and picked up whatever she threw on the ground, slipping it in her pocket.

"You both can come out now," Rose said, walking over to them. She frowned when she saw Lanis's shoulder.

"It's nothing," Lanis said. It ached, but the cream was doing its job. The pain was bearable.

"What did you do?" Elson said.

Rose waved off his question. "The fog will only

keep them subdued for a short time. I suggest you go find them. I've done my part." She turned to the rubble of the house and sat down on an overturned stone.

"I liked it better when she didn't say anything."

It didn't take long for Lanis to spot the first one. A man, no, a boy really. A very young boy. She shook her head in disgust. Such a waste. She grabbed his hand and dragged him back to camp. Elson met her and took him from her, and laid him beside the two he had brought back. It took them two more trips to find them all. There were eight in total. Seven men and one woman. "Do you know if we missed any?" Lanis asked Rose.

Rose huffed and crossed her arms. "I'm a sorceress, not a physic. Maybe you should have hired one of those. You hired me to keep you alive and I did. A thank you would be nice."

Lanis blinked. "I agree, a thank you would be nice."

"For what?" Rose asked in disbelief.

"How easily you forget that was me that caught the arrow and pushed you out of the way."

Rose's eyes narrowed. "Point taken," she ground out.

"Rose," Lanis said. "There is no place for that here. If I waited for everyone to thank me for saving their life, I wouldn't get anything done. If they wake up, can you do something about it?"

"I could, but I'm not going to. I've done the hard part; you do the rest." She threw her hands up and walked away.

"She walks away a lot," Elson said.

Lanis rolled her eyes. "Do you think there's any more?"

"No, I think we got them all. Do you recognize anything about them?" He kicked the nearest body.

"No."

Elson fidgeted. "It would be nice if she would tell us what's going on with those other bodies."

Lanis didn't see that happening anytime soon. "We all have our secrets."

"That we do," he said, patting her on the back.

"Whatever you're going to do, I would make it quick. The spell won't last forever." Rose took a bite of her apple. "What? Casting a spell makes me hungry."

Lanis pulled her knife and cut the boy's throat first. Her shoulder only pulled a little with the effort. Elson had just plunged his sword into the next to last body when the woman woke up. She caught them off guard when she jumped up and ran. Lanis uncurled her whip and flicked her wrist. When it connected with the woman's leg, she pulled on it, and the woman fell face first into the ground. She clawed at the ground until Elson plunged his sword into her back. He grabbed her foot and dragged her back to the pile, throwing her body on top the others.

"I told you to hurry," Rose said, dropping the apple core on the ground.

"We got her," Elson said. "It was a team effort." He pointed between him and Lanis. "You are now part of that team so get used to it. If we need help, you will help." Rose just smiled. "It should be fine to stay the night," he said, wiping his blade off. "It's getting dark and I would feel better in here."

"Me too." Lanis picked up her bag. She felt more confident now that they had at least taken care of some of the threat. As she was walking to the oath house, Rose stopped her with a question.

"What are you doing with the bodies?"

Before she could answer, Elson interrupted. "Nothing." He shrugged. "They can rot for all I care. I don't have too much sympathy toward people who try to kill me."

"So that's it." Rose planted her hands on her hips.

"Yes," Lanis said. "You should get used to it."

"What, him walking off?"

"No," Lanis said, pointing to the dead bodies. "You should get used to them. If my calculations are correct, that's seventeen dead so far."

"I can expect more of this?" she said, waving her hand at the dead.

"Yes. We told you we didn't have a good start." Did she even listen to them when they talked?

"I realize that. I just didn't expect this so soon."

"Well, get used to it."

Rose continued staring at the bodies. "If I'd known you were going to kill them."

"We had to."

"If I had known you were going to kill them, I would have used a different spell and saved that one."

"What would the other spell had done?"

"Killed them. Next time I'll know better how to handle things." Rose grabbed her things and walked away.

Lanis shook her head. Rose kept surprising her.

"You okay?" Elson asked.

"I think we're going to be okay."

"I told you to have faith. Let's get some sleep; morning will come fast. Let me check your shoulder and then I'll take first watch."

"Sounds good to me."

Lanis pushed off the wall and surveyed the area. All was quiet, too quiet. No birds, animals, no sound of any kind; nothing. That, coupled with the fact that dead bodies littered the ground around her, put her on edge. She barely slept all night and the lack of sleep was starting to catch up with her. In all her years as a mercenary, she never ran into this much trouble. If things kept going the way they were, she knew they wouldn't make it to Manight in time.

As her eyes adjusted, the sky began to come alive in a multitude of colors. Watching the sunrise always brought her a sense of peace, but the destruction around her never strayed far from her mind. To kill every living thing and leave their flesh to rot didn't make any sense to her. She coughed into her arm when the wind turned. The women and children were an entirely different matter. She didn't know if the others noticed, but their bodies didn't smell and one of the little girls had a yellow band on her wrist, indicating she was magic inclined. She didn't know all the ways of the magic community, but she couldn't see them letting something like this go. She uncurled her whip and turned to the bodies, opening and closing her eyes a few times to make sure they weren't playing tricks on her. Confident she wasn't seeing things, she walked backward toward Elson and kicked him.

"What?" he said, rubbing his eyes, quickly jumping up when he saw the look on her face. "What?" He gripped his sword.

"They're gone," Lanis whispered.

"Who?"

She turned to look at him. "The bodies are gone."

She pointed to where the bodies of the women and children should have been. The ground was clean. There wasn't even an indention on the ground where the bodies had laid and from the condition of them, there should have been some sort of disturbance.

"I told you not to worry about them," Rose said from behind them, making them both jump.

Lanis glanced at Elson. "No," she said, pointing her finger from Rose to where the bodies should have been. "What you told us was not to move them and that we could throw dirt over them. You never told us they would disappear." This was not a good start to her morning. From her experience, dead bodies didn't just get up and walk away.

Elson sheathed his sword. "If this is going to work, you're going to have to fully explain yourself when we don't know or understand something. I'm sure whatever your explanation is we should have known it."

"Look," Rose said. "I'm sure you two are not completely ignorant. Only a very powerful magic-bound individual could have done this. And no one who ever went to the academy would have done this. I know a lot of people don't like magic-bonded individuals, but we do have morals and we do follow a strict code, like I am sure both of you do. And there are consequences to our actions. We are held accountable. Not just in the next life, but this one as well. To be honest, I wasn't sure what would happen if we tried to move the bodies and I didn't want to find out. It isn't my place to divulge others' secrets. Have you ever killed a dead body that's been enchanted?"

Lanis rubbed her neck. She didn't need this, not today. "No, but we do have you. Surely you will be good for something."

"I'm not sure if I should be flattered you think I am capable of that." Rose showed them her band. "I am only a blue-band sorceress and I am very proud of that, but what was done here wasn't done by any type of banded magic. Rogues are not a group you, nor I, want to mess with or meet up with. Too many unknowns when you're confronted with someone who has nothing to lose. I, for one, am not going to take one on. I have a lot to lose, as I am sure both of you do too."

"Aren't they called Jesters?" Elson asked.

"Yes and no," Rose answered. "Some have bonded together and formed the Jesters while other have kept to themselves. The latter are much more frightening. At least Jesters have a code they stand by. Don't get me wrong, I don't want to come face to face with a Jester either, but you should beware if you ever meet a truly rogue sorcerer. They are unpredictable and their allegiance is to no one. The only way to defeat a true Rogue is with a white-band, and I am not one of them. At least not yet."

"That's good to know," Lanis said. Out of all her missions for the Ramden Council, none had ever been like this. She faced danger plenty of times, but the kind she was on an even footing with. "You ever see a Rogue?" she asked Elson.

His jaw tensed, so subtle if she wasn't looking she would have missed it. "No, but I have heard of them. I just never anticipated we would meet one. I knew we would have troubles, but I never expected anything like this." He turned toward Lanis. "I will protect you and you will make it to Manight no matter what I have to do."

"I know you will. We need to get going. By the

map, it should take us roughly a week and a half to make it to the next oath house. Let's hope it's still standing."

"Wait," Rose said. "What about supplies? I know a small village not far from here. They would trade, or sell to us, and it would only take us a day at the most, maybe two."

"We have an oath to keep. The High Priestess told us not to veer from the path and to the best of our ability, we are not going to stray. We hired you to stick with us, but in this group we each provide if need be. Understood?" Elson said.

"It just seems to me your High Priestess would have accounted for this sort of thing. What kind of leader is she, if she doesn't take care—" Her words were cut off when Lanis grabbed her and slammed her against the nearest tree. "You're hurting me," Rose said, clawing at Lanis's arms.

Elson laid his hand on Lanis's shoulder. "Lanis, let her go."

Lanis leaned in close to Rose's face. "If I ever hear anything like that come out of your mouth again, I. Will. Kill. You. You will not disrespect our High Priestess in that manner. When you insult her, you insult Nia. Do I make myself clear?" When Rose nodded, Lanis backed away from her.

"I'm sorry. I'm just tired." Rose shook her hands out and smiled, but it didn't reach her eyes. "My intention wasn't to disrespect them, I just meant. Look, I don't know what I meant." She shut up when Lanis glared at her.

Lanis picked up her bag and took the lead. The trees around them had thinned considerably and Lanis liked the new scenery, even though it didn't exactly keep them concealed. They needed provisions, but they would have to make do with what little they had. Lanis stopped and cocked her head when a familiar sound drew her attention. Horses, at least three, and they were gaining on them fast. "Everyone off the road. To the tree line."

"I heard it too." Elson crouched down beside Lanis, into a small ditch along the roadway.

"I don't think we have anything to be worried about, but I didn't want to take any chances. They're moving fast."

"They are," Rose said from behind them.

Lanis looked up as the horses rounded the bend. The rider in front wore a long dark cape, and the hood obscured the rider's face. The two riders in the back were also hooded and all three were moving at an incredible speed. Although none of the riders glanced their way as they passed by, Lanis happened to notice a small red stone hanging from around the first rider's neck. The entire episode was over in seconds.

"Did you see those horses?" Elson whistled, standing up beside her. "I don't come this way often, but I know enough to know those type of horses are not bred anywhere around here."

"No, they're not," Rose said, stepping in front of them and frowning. "They were bred in Manight. I used to stare in awe for hours as they roamed the countryside and wished I could own one. They are bred for the royals, but I can't think of any reason why they would be in this part of the country."

Lanis stood and readjusted her whip. "Well, it doesn't concern us so we should get on our way, but just as a precaution, I think we should move farther into the forest." There was no reason for a royal to be here. Why would someone be going that way?

"Why did we duck when they came by?" Rose asked. "Should we be avoiding them?"

"I don't know. It just felt like the right thing to do. Let's go," Lanis said. It was going to be a long week. She chuckled and relished the moment the first raindrop hit her face. The rain was a welcome change to the unbearable mid-day heat that beat down on them.

⁂

Dimitri sat down in one of the two chairs in the room, draping one leg over the other. He lifted his glass and took a small sip, savoring the floral undertones of the wine. The flames from the fireplace only added to the peaceful atmosphere. It was almost perfect. The only thing that would make this moment complete was if his family was with him, but his wife and two of his daughters were at home, and his third daughter, Ella, left home years ago. He sighed and leaned back into his chair. Instead, he sat in this abandoned cabin, waiting. If his beliefs weren't such a vital part of his life, he would have given up on the spheres long ago. If the people he chose couldn't get two simple things right, then how could he expect them to handle the bigger issues that arose?

He took another sip of the wine. She was late. Later than usual. He paused with the glass halfway to his lips when the door opened and she walked in. He let the wine sit on his tongue for a moment before swallowing it and turning to her. She always knew how to make an entrance.

"Dimitri, I'm sorry. I got waylaid at the Castle,"

she said, taking the seat beside him, and accepting the glass he offered.

The look on her face gave him pause. It seemed she, too, had failed him. "She's alive?"

She nodded her head even before she answered. "Yes. Unfortunately."

Of course she was alive. He tightened his grip on his glass. "What happened?" He stared into the fire.

She leaned back in her seat. "I don't know. I wasn't there. All I know is that she was attacked. As was her entire troop. George brought her back." She turned toward him and took another small sip. "The Castle is in an uproar. This is the first chance I had to come and I can't stay long, for obvious reasons. Queen Abigail has vowed to stop at nothing to find out who would harm her daughter. Heir to the throne," she spat.

The hate in her voice surprised him the first time he heard it, but now it was the only thing he heard. It almost brought a smile to his lips. So many people would be surprised. "How badly is she hurt?"

After a moment's pause, she answered. "I don't know."

He slumped forward in his chair. How could she not know? He stood, threw his glass into the fire, turned, grabbed her glass, and threw it into the fire too. He leaned close to her with his hands gripping the arms of her chair. "What do you mean you don't know?"

"Don't try that; you do not intimidate me." He sighed and sat back down. "Jessop has forbid anyone from entering her room and Queen Abigail would never go against his orders. Even if she wanted to, as Royal Healer, he has the final say. Jalen's personal guards are stationed outside her door on either side. Not to mention the men and women from her troop that are holed up outside her room, awaiting word of her condition and to make sure no one enters. She will be guarded day and night until Jessop feels she is able to see visitors. You know of court matters. Do not get upset with me when you wouldn't even be allowed in to see her."

She was right, but what good was she to him if she couldn't do this one small thing? "Surely," he said, facing her, "you will be allowed in." He knew her reasons and even if he didn't agree with them, she was helping him in the long run.

She rolled her eyes. "You would think so, but not right now. No one is allowed in except the Queen."

Jalen was supposed to die. He clenched his fist. "Is there any indication of what happened?" Hopefully the entire plan hadn't been blown.

"All anyone knows is that magic was involved. A very powerful magic. George said when they found her, she was close to death. That tells me her injuries were severe." She shrugged. "Whatever, or whoever, helped her had to have done so at the last minute. She was attacked and she did almost die. She still could, but she was helped. That I do know."

He laughed. "Almost being the key word. If our plans are to work, she has to die. She will ruin everything." It seemed his days were filled with almost.

"I know. We were so close. I have no idea who would have helped her. It had to have been an extremely powerful sorcerer."

"We have more of those around than people want to acknowledge. Leave it to me to find out who helped her."

"What do you want me to do next?"

"Nothing. We wait until the right time to enact the next phase."

"Doing nothing will be hard."

"I'm sure you can find something to occupy your time." He snickered. "I hear there's going to be a festival."

She frowned, running her hand along the chair arm. "Look."

"What?" Not another problem.

"We might have another problem."

"We might have?" How much more could go wrong?

"I was seen coming here. Usually the road is clear, but not today. There was a woman on the road. I believe a man was with her, but I noticed the woman. It was the way she was looking at me." She shivered.

"How was she looking at you?"

"Like she was taking in every detail about me."

"Did you notice anything about her?" It couldn't be.

"The only thing I noticed was the scar on her face."

She jumped in her chair when he stood, picked up his chair, and slammed it against the wall. If Henry hadn't messed up so badly, this particular problem would have already been taken care of. He hated loose ends. It was time to find out who Lanis really was. From her injuries, she should be dead right now. If need be, he would deal with her himself. He crossed his arms. "I'll take care of her. All you need to be concerned about is our plans. It will happen, only a little later than we expected. Go home."

"Very well." She pulled her hood up and headed to the door, stopping when he called her name.

"Does anyone suspect?"

"No. No one suspects," she said. "I will do what I have to in order to ensure what needs to happen, happens."

"I'm sure you will." He turned away from her and back to the fire when the door shut behind her. He couldn't believe no one had caught on yet. It would only be a matter of time. By then, he hoped his plans were completed. He walked to the table in the corner of the room, poured another drink, and lifted his glass. "To Princess Jalen's death."

Anya looked up from her papers at the knock on her office door and frowned. Everyone knew not to bother her when she prepared her monthly sermons. The guard opened the door and spoke softly to someone on the other side. After a few moments, he opened it wide, allowing Miriam to walk in. In her hand was a white envelope with the Council of Thirty-Two's yellow seal.

"High Priestess Anya, I am sorry to disturb you, but Brytin said it was urgent."

"Must not be that urgent if Brytin isn't delivering it." It wasn't Miriam's place to deliver such a letter. It should have never left his hands.

"I told him I was on my way up. I insisted," she said, holding her hands up. "It was my decision."

"No matter what you insisted, it wasn't your place to bring it, and why were you on your way up here? You know what today is and, yet you were going to bother me anyway." Her council, it seemed, believed they could behave anyway they wanted. "I'll deal with both of you later," she said, reaching for the letter. Miriam placed the letter in her hand, but didn't leave. Anya pushed back in her chair and stood. The guard by the door and her Protector stepped forward. "Is there something else?"

"I...I was wondering if you have made your decision yet?"

"I see." Anya leaned forward. "You interrupted my preparations for the monthly sermon for that? It is unacceptable. I told you I would let you know."

Miriam bit her lip. "You will be leaving next month and if you chose me I would need time to prepare."

Anya waited until Miriam met her eyes. "It won't be you." She watched all the different emotions cross Miriam's face and waited for the outburst to come. It didn't take long.

"I knew it." She clenched her fists. "It's Merek. He doesn't deserve it."

"You will watch your tone with me. Of late, I have had to remind everyone exactly whom you're speaking to. This is my decision."

Miriam nodded. "Not me or Hensley, that leaves Merek and Kerrison. I can't see you picking her, not after she fought so hard against you becoming High Priestess."

"Nia guides me in all decisions. I don't make them on who I like or dislike. That being said, I will let you know, when I know. Guard," she shouted. She took her seat when the door shut. Her heart thumped as she tore the seal and read the words written on the letter.

Princess Jalen attacked outside the Brown Pass. Alive, but condition still unknown. More news to follow.

The letter was unsigned. She laid it down and rested her head in her hands. Deep down she knew this didn't have anything to do with Lanis's oath, but she didn't believe in coincidences. The fact that someone already tried to kill Jalen only escalated matters. Especially for Lanis. If they tried once, they would try again. She normally wouldn't speculate, but Jalen had been stationed at the Brown Pass for the past ten years. She was eighteen when she left home. If someone in the Queen's army wanted her dead, she would have been dead long before now. It would have to be someone who didn't want to see her return home. Who would gain the most by her not returning? Ten years was a long time for hate to fester. Someone who hated that much would stop at nothing to see their plan come to fruition. Things were far worse than she realized and she had sent Lanis into the center of the storm.

❧❧❧❧

The past ten days of traveling had flown by. Lanis shifted her bag on her hip and eyed the road in front of them. A change of scenery would have been nice. The same thing, day after day. Trees and more trees. She lifted the collar of her shirt and fanned her face. The temperature had been steadily rising all morning. She hastened her steps to catch up with the others and closed her eyes, opening them when she walked into the back of Rose. Her hands grasped Rose's shoulders to keep them both from falling over. She opened her mouth to apologize, quickly shutting it when she noticed why they both had stopped. In front of them, in the middle of the road, stood a Jester. Out of instinct, her hand touched her whip. Even though she knew it wouldn't be any kind of defense, it comforted her nonetheless.

His shoes and clothes were colorful and elaborate and he was juggling what looked to be three colored balls. As he walked closer to them, she noticed they were actually three different colored balls of light, roughly the size of an apple, one blue, one red, and one green. For every step he took forward, Elson took one back until he stood beside Rose. The Jester stopped fifteen feet in front of them. He smiled, threw the balls in the air, knelt on one knee, and threw his arms out to his sides. Standing, he jumped in the air and clicked his heels together before landing back on his feet. He reached both hands out and caught all three balls in one hand. They were stacked one on top of the other. Lanis couldn't take her eyes off them as they grew darker in color and radiated light in his palm. He smiled at her, threw the balls back into the air, and started juggling again. Every time a ball left his hand, sparks flew off of it. It amused her, but the look in his eyes put her on edge.

"Will you let us pass?" Elson asked.

"Let us pass. Let us pass," the Jester mocked. Standing tall, he threw the balls back into the air and put his hands in his pockets. As each ball fell, it vanished before hitting the ground. He started to pace. Lanis noticed he didn't take his eyes off of her. "Do you know how many times I've heard that? Countless times." He stopped and pulled a deck of cards out of his pocket.

"Will you let us pass?" Lanis asked, finally finding her voice. He smiled again, but instead of answering, he sat on the ground, spreading the cards out in front of him. She didn't know what he was capable of, but she knew she wouldn't be a match for him. He looked up and she flinched, stepping back. He kept his eyes on her as he lifted one card and, with the flick of his wrist, turned them all over. All the cards were the same, except for one. He jumped up and waved his hand in the air. The cards floated up in front of him until he blew on them and they disappeared. She had never seen magic this freely given. All magic came with a price; she wondered what his was. He snapped his fingers and the three balls appeared again. He started juggling again. Her heart rate increased with each toss of the balls.

"One of these things is not like the others," he sang. "What is a poor Jester to do?" He stopped juggling and all three balls landed in the palm of his hand. He winked at her and the three balls started bouncing, one on top of each other.

Lanis took a step back. "Will you let us pass?"

"Should I?" He grinned. "What to do? What to do?" He sighed and shook his head. He held her gaze, picked the green ball of the top, and Lanis knew his answer. If his smile hadn't given him away, his eyes would have. She stiffened when he threw it at her. It connected, hitting her square in the chest, and knocking her off her feet. She jumped up and doubled over in pain, placing her hands on her knees. With every breath, her chest tightened. She closed her eyes and pushed the pain back. After a few deep breaths, she opened her eyes, and stood up. Rose and the Jester were in a standoff. His hand twitched and the red ball flew at Rose, stopping a few inches from her stomach. Rose's hands cupped the ball, but never touched it. Lanis sucked in a breath when he turned toward her and bowed. He straightened, danced around, kicked his legs out to the sides, and disappeared. She didn't see Elson anywhere. She ran to Rose, whose hands were still cupped around the ball. Rose murmured a few words and the ball disappeared.

"We need to leave, now," Rose choked out.

Lanis gripped her shoulders. "Where is Elson?"

Rose laid her hands atop Lanis's. "He went flying that way." She pointed behind them.

Lanis took off in that direction, picking up her pace when she spotted his boots. He had flown a good twenty feet from where they were. She knelt next to him and breathed a sigh of relief when he took a breath. "Elson," she said, shaking him. "Elson, wake up." She shook him harder. She sat back on her heels when he blinked.

"Where is he?" he asked, looking around.

Lanis helped him stand. "He's gone."

"What happened?" He groaned, rubbing his head. "I tried to get to you," he said, looking at Lanis. "I don't remember anything after he threw that blue ball at me."

"I'm not sure what happened. I know I don't want to be hit with one of those green balls again," Lanis said, but the look on Rose's face stopped her from saying anything else.

"We need to go. Gather your things," Rose said, with an urgency in her voice Lanis had never heard before. They didn't question her as they found their belongings. The whole episode unsettled her on an entirely new level. She would never underestimate someone, or let how someone behaved, or what they wore, color her judgment. Elson caught her looking and assured her he was fine. He took the lead. Lanis stayed back with Rose.

"Is there a reason I wasn't knocked out?" she

asked Rose.

Rose shrugged. She kept her gaze on Elson. "The different colored balls tend to be for different reasons."

Lanis rubbed her neck. Rose didn't sound all that convincing. "You must know what the different colored balls are for." Rose ignored her. "Rose, what are the different colors for?" Surely, she would have learned that in the academy.

"Look, the colors can always mean different things, but they generally tend not to. Blue is meant to knock out. The red is as powerful as the other two, but it makes the body put on a show before the person loses consciousness." She shivered. "It's unsettling to watch. Which is the point."

Lanis was afraid to ask. "What is the green one meant for?"

Rose stopped and turned so she had Lanis's attention. "Death," she whispered. "The green one is meant to kill."

"Come on," Lanis said. "I'm not dead. It has to mean other things." Lanis laughed. "Right?"

"I know you're not dead," Rose said quietly. "I don't know why you're not dead. You should be."

Lanis swallowed hard. "It does mean other things, though, right?"

"Not normally. Green is taken as death in magic."

"You two okay?" Elson hollered. Lanis indicated for him to stay where he was. No need to worry him now.

"How am I still alive then?" Lanis said, reaching for her.

Rose stepped away from her hand. "I don't know," she said through clenched teeth. "I'm just as freaked as you are. I have only heard of one other person surviving a green orb."

"Who?"

"I can't tell you. Not many people know her name. The Jester is right, though," Rose said, pointing at Lanis. "One of these things is not like the others." Before Lanis could say anything, Rose jogged up to Elson. Lanis picked up her pace to join them. She should be dead right now. What could have possibly stopped an attack like that? She wasn't sure what she wished for anymore. She used to want a quiet life with Anya, but now all she wished for was to fulfill her oath. She stepped in front of Elson and didn't look back.

⁂

Dimitri slammed his fist on the desk. He still didn't know who disrupted his plans with Jalen. All he knew was whoever saved her was very powerful in the art of magic. Manight's shields that protected their borders weren't easily disrupted. There could only be two outcomes. Either the person could shield themselves within Hadmore's borders or Jalen's savior was outside Hadmore's borders. The second option was the most unsettling. To save her from outside Hadmore would have taken an extraordinary amount of magic. He pushed back from his chair and stood. For someone to have penetrated the shields, and the Royal Mages not detect them, was unheard of. While his people looked into that matter, he had another one to attend to. The Ramden was causing far more trouble than he expected. His spies didn't tell him anything he didn't already know. They did confirm her companion was a Ranger in Malora's army. He expected the Jester any time with his own news.

It's often said Jester's magical abilities exceed some of the greatest sorcerers of all time. Those that refused to take them seriously found out the hard way who they really were. He didn't intend to make that mistake. Dimitri had just sat down when there was a knock at the door. He waited while the guard answered and spoke softly to the person on the other side.

"Sir, the Jester is back."

"Bring him in." He needed him to have good news. The guard led him in and directed the Jester to a vacant seat in front of the desk.

"I don't know why you insist on blindfolding me," the Jester said, pushing the hair out of his eyes. "We both know I only allow it because I can. If I really wanted to find this place, I could."

"And we both know you don't really care to know where you are," Dimitri shot back.

"You're right. It's a dump."

"I know your opinion of the structure. I didn't bring you hear to discuss the décor. I want to know what you found out. That's what's important."

"I guess it could be seen as important," he said, standing and going into a handstand. He walked around the room. When he righted himself, he went on. "How important is this information to you?"

"Very," Dimitri said through gritted teeth. He hated games. "What do you want?"

The Jester sat back down and crossed one leg over the other. He leaned forward and started juggling. "Did you know that half of all Jesters today don't even know how to juggle? Such a shame." He sighed. "I mean, what do they do, if not juggling?" He stopped suddenly and smiled. He threw the three balls out, each one flying toward one of the three guards in the room, stopping inches from their bodies.

Dimitri stiffened, but kept quiet.

"What do I want? What do I want? We can start with doubling...no, tripling my payment."

He expected that. "Done."

"There is one other thing I want."

"What?"

"I want one of your guard's daggers."

"Why?" Dimitri knew he shouldn't have questioned him, but he knew what it would mean for one of his guards to give up his dagger. Each person who pledged their life to the Seven Holders and Damrek went through a series of trials. If they survived, they were given a dagger. Each dagger was hand crafted and made to fit the receiver. No two were ever alike. None of his guards would give it up without a fight and he knew that would end badly for them. But the information the Jester had was more important to their cause than one of his guard's lives. He rubbed his hands on his pants.

"Why not." The Jester shrugged.

"Agreed." Dimitri noticed that all three guards stiffened and exchanged glances.

"I didn't expect much from this mission, but I have to say I was pleasantly surprised. Lanis was not at all what I expected. And you were wrong; she doesn't have one, but two companions traveling with her. She and her male companion were traveling with another woman."

"Who was the other woman?" This information could work to his benefit.

"No. No. No. That's not how this works. I told you to be specific. You said you wanted to know about Lanis. That's what I'm here to report on. All other information I gathered will be for my own personal use. I do so hope you understand?"

"Of course. How much do you want for that information?"

"It's not for sale," he said, waving him off. "Now, she is a Ramden. I have to say though, there is more to her than you would first expect. I saw strength, determination, courage, fear, and..." he trailed off.

"What?" Dimitri said, leaning forward in his chair.

"I sensed something that shouldn't be there. An unforeseen power around her. It was faint. I'm not even sure she realizes it is there. On her body somewhere, she holds an ancient spell bound in some form to her. At first glance, I didn't see anything that stood out. She wears a necklace around her neck and a cuff on her right wrist. My suspicions were confirmed when, like your guards, I threw three power orbs into Lanis and her companions. The blue one I threw at her male companion," he said, throwing out his hand and setting the blue orb into motion. It slammed into the guard and knocked him back several feet. "The second orb, the red one," he said, flicking his wrist. "I sent to the woman." The orb went flying into another guard. His body dropped to the floor and flopped around before becoming still. "It's not created to kill, but merely to put on a show. The red and blue orbs are meant to merely knock out. Now the green one is a bit different. Did you know that not all Jesters like to play with their prey? Sometimes," he said, drawing the green orb back to his hand. "Sometimes death should be quick." He threw it at the final guard and it slammed into him with such force it left an apple size hole through his chest. Death was instant. "You'll need someone to clean that up."

"Did you have a point?" That was one of his finest guards.

"Yes." He stood and walked over to the dead guard and slipped his dagger out of its sheath. "You see," he said, holding the dagger between his hands and admiring the design etched into it. A two-bladed sword wrapped around the handle. "Lanis was the intended for the green orb. I figured I should at least try and take her out. Do you know what happened?"

"Since I wasn't there, no, I don't." He was getting more irritated by the second.

"Nothing, nothing happened," he said, throwing his hands up. "Well, it did knock her back some. Worrisome and quite remarkable at the same time. She is only the second person I know of to come into contact with a green orb and live." He seemed genuinely astonished.

"How is that possible?" It seemed too unbelievable. What was so special about her? "Who was the other person?"

The Jester stood. "I think that's enough information for now. I've told you all that I will."

Dimitri also stood. "You are under contract."

"You should read the fine print." His hands were glowing a deep blue and sparks flew from his fingertips. "The contract stated that I would gather all the information about her, but it never stated that I had to tell you everything. You should be more careful in the future. We Jesters are only out for one person, ourselves. I do believe you owe me payment."

Dimitri unclenched his hands and walked to the door, keeping his anger in check. He could do nothing. Even the sorcerers he employed couldn't compete with the Jester. He knocked four times and a guard walked in, carrying a small pouch. Dimitri nodded and he handed it to the Jester.

"I do hope this doesn't hamper the rest of our working relationship. I will take care of the other thing you asked me to when the time comes."

"It hasn't." Dimitri needed him and the Jester knew it. "I still want you to bring the High Priestess here when the time comes."

"When the time comes, you'll have to tell me where this place is." He winked, twirled his hand in the air, and disappeared into a thick fog.

Dimitri would never underestimate him, but his playfulness was unsettling. He looked down at the dead guard. Such a shame. The fact that the Jester would kill for a souvenir spoke volumes about his character. "Get his body out of here." He sat at his desk, running his hands through his hair. His frustration continued to grow every day. Somehow, he needed to find out what the Jester knew. For him to keep quiet about the other woman, the Jester's news must be important. He'd never heard of someone surviving a green orb before. He needed to find out who it was. Maybe that would give him insight into Lanis. He knew whatever surrounded her only protected her from magic; otherwise, she wouldn't have almost died in the Windark Forest. He needed to find out who the woman traveling with them was. If he played his cards right, maybe she would be the key to unlocking this entire mess. Everyone had a price.

First things first, though. He leaned back in his chair, lifted his legs onto the corner of the desk, and rested his hands behind his head. He wanted to find out who Lanis was before he got rid of her, but it wouldn't hurt to let them know they were still being followed. Plenty of people would hunt anyone down for a bounty. If he could hold them off, very shortly he would have the one thing that could help him reach his end goal, the Protector's mask, and as an added bonus, High Priestess Anya. As badly as everything was going, things were starting to look up.

ꙮ ꙮ ꙮ ꙮ

Anya swept her hair back from her face and smoothed the bodice of her cream and violet colored dress. She loved preaching the monthly sermon to the followers of Nia. One of the guards who came to escort her informed her there was a record crowd gathered. Before the sermon, though, she first had to address her council. Through prayer and meditation, she finally made her mind up about who would take her place. She walked behind the guard until they reached the council door, thankful she wouldn't have to spend much time with them this morning. Everyone was waiting for her when she entered. She knew not everyone would agree with her decision, especially Miriam, who would be left out of everything and she hoped she wouldn't completely alienate her.

"I just wanted to go over a few things before my sermon. As you know, I will be leaving in nine days for my trip to Manight. I have made my decision and I know it might anger and confuse some of you. I know I don't have to explain myself, but it is not my intention to leave anyone feeling less important than they are. I have already talked to Hensley and I am leaving him in charge of overseeing the people of this city. He will take care of their needs and deal with any issue that arises with them. Whomever I leave in my place will have no say in how he handles things. They will only have a say in the city itself and everything that goes along with it. Understood?"

"Of course."

"Yes."

Miriam didn't comment, but Anya already knew how she felt. "I've thought long and hard, prayed and meditated about this. Truthfully, I am still troubled." She turned to Kerrison and smiled. "Kerrison, you'll be coming with me to Manight. I need someone with me that has traveled before. You have." Merek looked pained.

"I would be honored," Kerrison said, clearly surprised.

"Merek, I am leaving you here in my place. I trust that you will be fair in mind. I expect you to care for this city as I would. Is this something you can do?"

"Yes, High Priestess." He sounded equally happy and upset about her decision.

She held up her hands to ward off any questions. "I won't be answering any questions right now." She clasped her hands behind her back. "I hear I have quite the crowd. I will meet with each of you after the sermon individually. Dismissed." She walked out and down a long hall, stopping before a set of double doors. The guards on either side of the doors opened them when she nodded. The noise that greeted her was deafening. She knew the applause wasn't for her, but for what she represented, and she would never take their acceptance as anything else. She stepped up to the balcony and took in the scene below. The crowd spanned the entire courtyard and beyond.

She treasured these days and wouldn't trade them

for anything. This is why she accepted the position of High Priestess, for the people. They came to hear the word and she would gladly share it with them. She would deal with everything and everyone else later. The people gathered below deserved her full attention and that's exactly what they would get it. "Let us bow our heads in a moment of silent prayer to Nia." She prayed this wasn't the last time she would say those words.

⁂

Two days after their interaction with the Jester, Lanis, Elson, and Rose reached the second oath house. Even though the oath master listened to their description of the destruction of the first oath house, he didn't act bothered by it. He assured them he would send someone to investigate, and would send word to High Priestess Anya. They were dismissed, given a room for the night, and dinner. The next morning they stocked up on provisions and were sent on their way. Normally, the oath master's attitude would have bothered Lanis, but after he gave her a small crock of honey and Elson a small bag of rabbit jerky, her bad mood vanished. Knowing Anya had arranged for them to be given these small tokens only solidified her love for her more. Considering everything they'd been through, she and Elson had discussed their options, but decided to stick to the route Anya had mapped out. He would occasionally stop and check it, but as the day wore on, he would check it more frequently, like now. "Elson, something wrong?" Lanis asked.

He frowned at the map. "I don't know." He shook his head and folded it up, slipping it back in his pack. "By the map, we're following the correct route." He scratched his beard. "But the terrain on the map is different than what I'm seeing."

"How old is that map?" Rose said, searching through her bag. She pulled out an apple and took a bite.

"Not that old," he said.

"So we push on and hope we reach the mountains in the next few days," Lanis said. From where they stood, she could see the tips of the snow-capped mountaintops. Several different tribes called them home and she hoped they didn't encounter any of them, but considering their luck, they probably would.

Elson nodded. "We press on. Let's hope we're going in the right direction." After a few hours, they crested a large hilltop. "Well," he said, looking around. "I wasn't expecting this." He pulled the map out and looked it over.

That was an understatement. Lanis rubbed her neck. A massive desert spread out in front of them. Sand as far as the eye could see. The mountains where barely visible now, where only a few minutes ago they were within reach. She took a sip of water. Another obstacle.

"Oh Goddess," Rose said, taking a step back.

"What?" Lanis and Elson said at the same time.

"You both do realize what we're looking at, don't you?"

The fear in her voice put Lanis on edge. "A desert."

"You both have heard of the Desert of Ram-tar and what lies in its depths? Haven't you?" Rose asked, rubbing her forehead.

"Come on." Elson laughed. "The desert and the beasts are myths. My Grandmother told me the stories to scare me."

To Lanis's ears, he didn't sound all that convincing. She knew the stories. Her father had told them to her when she was a child. She always figured, like Elson, that they were stories made up to scare her. She didn't believe one way or the other. A lot of things existed she'd never seen before. The tales she'd heard said a powerful sorceress created the beasts. The sorceress never intended for the beasts to be viewed as evil or vile, but that's exactly how many people saw her experiment. As those around her turned on her, she turned on them and created a desert for her beasts to roam. The story went that the beasts rose up out of the sand, stalked, and killed those that tried to cross the desert, pulling their captives down into the sand with them. The desert was rumored never to visit the same place twice; it traveled all over, her spell enchanting the lands that surrounded it. No one knew what happened to the sorceress and her name was erased from the history books.

"I've heard the stories." Lanis turned to Rose. "Have you heard of any way to defeat the beasts?"

"It is said there is no way to defeat them. Most people that are faced with them never make it home, and those that do never talk about what happened."

"So," Elson said. "I know we were supposed to stick to the map, but in this one instance I think we should turn around and find another way." He turned back the way they'd come and grew quiet.

"What?" Lanis said, turning to see what he was staring at. The path they just traveled had disappeared and in its wake was the same desert that lay behind them. She placed her hand on her whip and turned back around.

"How?" Elson said.

Rose frowned at him. "For you to be a man of faith and open-mindedness, you sure don't follow what others find as their truth. Magic can do many things. Some good and some bad. This is one of those things. We don't have a choice now. The desert has made the choice for us. I have never been up against something like this before. I have an item that might aid us, but it won't help for very long. I can only do so much with what I've been given, and in this instance, I don't believe my bow will come in handy either."

"It's all right," Lanis said. "Only use it if you have to. We may need it again later on." She sighed. "How does the desert determine where it goes? I mean, why are we faced with it? Is it just by luck we ran into it?"

"Honestly, I don't know," Rose said. "All I know is that it seems to pop up in the most unwanted circumstances."

"So, should we have a plan before we trek across?" she said. Rose shrugged. Elson drew his sword and nodded a couple of times.

"I'm ready," he said.

Obviously, he settled whatever was bothering him. "Let's go." Lanis pulled her whip and Rose took a small blue stone out of her pocket, and took up position between her and Elson. He took the lead. The stories said the beasts could tear a person apart, piece by piece. She wasn't looking forward to meeting them. They made their way down the small hill and stopped at the bottom. Off in the distance, Lanis could make out trees, but it was a *long* distance in between. The sweltering heat only made things worse and she knew that once they stepped farther onto the sand, it wouldn't get any better; more than likely, it would get worse. She pulled her cloak out of her bag and slipped it on, pulling the hood up. Elson smiled at her.

He took a tentative step forward onto the sand. When nothing happened, he continued on, with another step, then another. The desert was a wide open space spread out in front of them. Sand and cracked land as far as the eye could see. The only sign of hope were the trees lining the edge of the desert in front of them. Trees that seemed to get farther away the longer they walked. Lanis grabbed her hood, as the wind caught it, and slipped it back on, noticing for the first time how red her arms were. They'd only walked a quarter of the way across and her clothes were already soaked through with sweat. She stopped walking and shielded her eyes as the sand kicked up around them. "Stop," she called out to the others. After what felt like an eternity, the wind settled and she opened her eyes and squinted through the haze. Sand covered Rose and Elson, as was she. Elson gagged and spit then accepted the water she offered.

"I know it feels real," Rose said. "But it's all an illusion. The sand will not harm you. Your skin isn't really burning."

Lanis eyed her in disbelief, swiping the sweat from her brow. "You're kidding, right? Everything is real. You can't tell me the sweat dripping off your nose isn't real."

"It's getting harder to breathe," Elson said, "at least for me it is."

"Me too," Lanis said.

"As well as me," Rose added. "I know it feels real, but it's not. We need to keep going. The longer we stand here, the sooner death will come."

"Let's go," Lanis said. Nothing made sense. How

could they die if it wasn't real? The sorceress who created the desert must have been extraordinary in the magic arts to create such an illusion. She sucked in a breath and stopped as the sand shifted around them. In a matter of seconds, the beasts surrounded them. The stories of the beasts didn't do them justice. Their four legs supported a body that stood four feet high and three feet wide. A large round head was encompassed in tiny spikes that ran down a wide forehead to the tip of their slightly upturned noses. Small dark eyes stared back at them, blank and empty. Lanis gulped and followed the others' lead when they started walking again. Her steps faltered as she scanned the landscape. With the creatures' appearance, the desert had changed. Rock formations littered the landscape around them and cacti stood proud, scattered in between the rocks. She picked up the pace, stopping suddenly at the crunching under foot. She gulped and was afraid to look down, but did so anyway. Sun-bleached bones covered the ground around them.

"Rose," Elson said, "are the bones an illusion too?"

She shook her head sadly. "No. I don't believe they are."

He nodded several times before pointing around them. "We need to keep going." His eyes widened as a low whistle echoed around them.

The Breeken whistled again. "Rose," Lanis said. "Are they real?" Her heart pounded in her chest.

"Yes."

"Okay." The whistle was meant to warn the birds' prey that death was near. "How can they be part of an illusion?"

"I don't think they are." Rose stood completely

still.

The only time Lanis had ever seen one of the birds was when she was eleven. She and her father were walking home from the far cut of their farm when they heard the whistle. They watched in horror as a man ran in their direction, only for the bird to pick him up and carry him off. From where they stood, the bird was enormous. Lanis dared not look up now, for fear that the birds would attack them. She was curious, but her curiosity would have to be just that right now. She caught Elson's eye and they started walking again, this time at a faster pace. For every step they took forward, the beasts took two. Her heart rate tripled as the beasts closed in on them. Her gaze locked onto a large beast that broke through the others, its eyes locked on Rose. The beast stomped its feet and reared onto its back legs, nostrils flaring, then made a run at Rose. Lanis threw her arms around her, hugging her tightly. The breast screeched to a halt inches from them, its drool dripping onto Lanis's arm, burning the skin. All of a sudden, a mixture of dirt and seawater assaulted her senses.

The beast backed away from them, as did the rest of the herd. Lanis's heart fell as they started to emit some sort of fog from their necks. If the beasts closed in on them, they wouldn't stand a chance against them. They had to get across; now. "Elson, run!" The faster they ran the farther the trees got. Elson lost his balance and fell backward onto the sand when a Breeken landed in front of him. It stood at least ten feet tall and its wingspan had to be fifteen feet wide. A bald head sat atop a narrow body that was covered in black scales. Lanis and Rose grabbed Elson and backed away from the bird when it started flapping its wings. It was beautiful and terrifying at the same time.

"Wow, that just happened," Elson said, standing and dusting his clothes off.

"What do we do now?" Rose asked.

"I don't know," Lanis muttered. In the shape they were in, they couldn't defeat them. What choice did they have? She glimpsed the beasts out of the corner of her eye. They were lined up behind them some twenty yards away. Just standing, staring at them. By this point, three other Breeken had landed and were sitting atop three different rock formations that surrounded them. After saying a silent prayer, she turned back to the beasts. Something felt off. Why didn't the beasts attack them? She'd missed something. Why did they back away when she grabbed Rose? She groaned when it hit her why the beasts didn't attack them. She raised her hand to show the others.

"What?" Elson said, one eye on the birds.

Lanis started walking back to the beasts.

"Lanis, what are you doing?" He grabbed her arm, but she threw him off and continued walking. By the time she made it back, they were stomping their feet and shuffling back and forth.

"It seems to me that besides the Breeken, you're the only thing that is real." She held up her arm and the beasts took a step backward. "Help us out of this. Whatever this is. You had your chance to attack us and you didn't." She pointed behind them to the birds. "Help us."

"Lanis," Rose said, standing to her right. "They don't understand."

Elson touched her hand. "Lanis."

Lanis stood her ground when the largest beast stepped away from the others. After a few tense moments, it nodded and ran at the Breeken, quickly followed by the others.

"Run!" As the beasts kept the birds occupied, they ran as fast as they could toward the trees in the distance. Her heart pounded as the trees grew closer to them and her jog quickly turned into a run. She collapsed on the ground as her feet touched the grass.

"You know," Elson said, a smile in his voice. "I didn't realize all the fun we would have on this trip. It's so refreshing to take a nice stroll through a magic desert and almost get attacked by Breeken."

Lanis stood. The desert was gone, along with the birds, and in its place, the forest had returned. "What magic desert?"

Elson wrapped an arm around her waist. "I know we didn't imagine it, but it's hard to believe it was even there."

"Only the most skilled in magic could have done that. That type of skill is what we all strive for. Remarkable," Rose said, turning to Lanis. "How did you know what to do? How did you know they would help us?"

Elson squeezed her waist. "Yes, how did you know?"

Lanis shrugged. "I didn't know, not really. Didn't it seem strange that they were still there? If they weren't going to kill us, why were they still there? There was something strange about the largest one. It stopped when it ran to attack Rose, and I wondered why." She snapped her fingers. "Then it dawned on me."

"What?" Elson said. "Lanis."

She rubbed her wrist and bit her lip. "When I held Rose, the only thing that was visible to the beast was my oath bracelet. It's all I had to go on. I just figured if they were going to allow us to live then surely they would help us escape the Breeken."

A big grin crossed Elson's face. "Do you remember me telling you Nia was looking out for us? Well, I think we have our proof. Although, I should have been the one to protect her. Lanis, you can't take those risks."

"I couldn't let her die."

He nodded. "What a group we make." He accepted the biscuit Rose handed him.

"Thank you, Lanis, for saving my life," Rose said, handing her a biscuit also.

"You're welcome." Once they stepped away from the desert, her skin had returned to normal, but a small scar remained where the beast had drooled on it. She couldn't deny that someone was watching over them, but as much as Nia, or whoever was looking out for them, it looked like someone else wanted to tear them apart.

❧❧❧❧

They had been walking for eight days and everyone agreed it would be best to bypass the Anolk Mountains altogether. She and Elson both believed it would be in their best interest to veer from the map this one time. Lanis sucked in a breath as the ice-cold water rolled down her neck and down her back. She was crouched at a small stream that ran through a meadow. Vibrant wild flowers, some she had never seen before, surrounded lush foliage. The bright blues and orange of the petals weren't like anything in Malora. Anya would have loved it here. The sweet smell of the flowers brought a smile to her lips. It was times like this she tried to forget what they were doing, but considering why they'd stopped, that wasn't possible. They were being followed. She dipped her hand in the water, splashed it on her face again, and paused when she was covered in shadow.

"They're close, I can hear them," Elson said, kneeling next to her and dipping his head in the water. He flung his head back, smoothed his hair out, and tied it up.

"I hear them too. It shouldn't take them long to reach us." She sighed. "How many?"

He shook his head. "Three, maybe." He never took his eyes off the tree line.

"That's what I was thinking. They're not hiding the fact that they're following us."

"I know. They're confident, but so are we. I don't plan on dying anytime soon. I know my limits, but," he said, slapping her on the back and standing. "I do have you and Rose. We're a team. We'll get through this."

She accepted the hand he offered. "I am just glad I don't have to take them on by myself."

They both turned to Rose as she walked up to them. "Is this a private conversation?"

She carried her ever-present bow clutched in her hand. Lanis pointed to it. "I hope you're good with that bow. I believe we may need it."

Rose grinned. "Oh, I'm good."

"Let's hope so," Elson said.

Lanis stopped laughing when the cool breeze rushing through the air turned stale. "Gather your things. They're coming." Somehow, this fight felt different. She was prepared, but wasn't looking forward to it. "Here they come." Lanis gripped her whip handle and took up position beside Rose. Elson had his hand on his sword hilt, but hadn't drawn it yet. She gulped and took a step back, heart racing, when the four men broke through the tree line. They were huge, bigger than the men she fought in the Windark Forest and twice as big as Elson. Each held a long sword with an odd shaped blade attached. One side of the blade was a smooth line and on the other side, small grooves were cut into the steel.

Rose drew a square stone out of her pocket and mumbled into the air when one of the men stepped toward them. Lanis covered her eyes as the dirt kicked up around them and the air soured even more. Someone grabbed her arm, then her feet left the ground. The whistling of the wind drowned out the pounding in her ears. It felt like they were flying. She moved her hand from her eyes, but kept them tightly closed, not sure she wanted to see what was actually happening. She panicked when the hand left her arm and she flung her arms out, reaching, but never grasping anything. "Open your eyes and brace yourself," someone whispered in her ear. She opened her eyes, but didn't have time to brace herself as she slammed into the ground. Gasping for breath, she rolled onto her stomach and brought her breathing back under control. Easing back onto her knees, she grew completely still as her eyes focused on the scene in front of her. She reached over and smacked Elson in the head.

"What?" he croaked.

"Get up now." Rose had transported them into some type of army camp. The soldiers wore the same clothes as the ones that attacked her in the Windark Forest. This was the worst possible outcome they could have hoped for. She watched in horror and shock as one of the soldiers picked Rose up, who landed a hundred or so feet from them, and threw her over his shoulder. He walked to the largest tent and entered it. All the soldiers stood frozen, waiting. Lanis's eyes were drawn to a man standing in the far corner of the camp who was bouncing a blue orb in is hand. A sorcerer. Circumstances quickly went from bad to worse.

"Run!" she shouted.

They ran toward the opening in the tree line, with four of the nearest soldiers taking chase. After cresting a small hill, Elson turned to the right. Lanis grabbed him and pushed him against the nearest tree, plastered her body against his and covered his mouth with her hand. She mouthed 'keep quiet,' then blended. She felt Elson stiffen and pressed harder into him. It didn't take long for two of the men who took chase to reach them.

"Where did they go?" one man spat.

"I don't know, they just disappeared."

"Treg isn't going to be happy."

"Let's get back. Did you see that pretty little thing they left behind?"

"Do you think they'll come back for her?"

"No, they're gone, but even if they did, they wouldn't get her, not now."

Lanis didn't relax her hold until she couldn't hear the crunching of the leaves anymore. She eased away from Elson and wiped her hand on her pants. Rose had saved their lives from one danger to drag them inadvertently into another one. They walked for over an hour before finding a small outcrop of rocks and crawling inside.

"You do know who they were, don't you?" Elson asked.

"I know they were dressed the same as the men who attacked me in the Windark Forest, but no, I don't specifically know who they are." Lanis cut her eyes at him. "Do you?"

"The Black Brigade."

"What? I know they worship Damrek, but that's about it."

"They are the Gray Division of the Black brigade. They will stop at nothing to kill those they deem a threat to Damrek's ways. They train with a ruthless hand, and some don't even make it through their training. They kill without thought and it doesn't matter if their victims are innocent or not."

"We have to get her back."

"We will. After the magic she performed, she has to be weak. She won't be able to protect herself."

Lanis couldn't believe this was happening. "I guess she was the right pick for us after all." She rubbed her neck. "They had a sorcerer with them. We don't have any way of fighting him. Rose was our defense against magic."

"I know. I saw him." He ran his hands through his hair. "There has to be a reason they employ sorcerers. We'll scope out the perimeter, then come up with a plan. I know we can't leave her, but we also can't take any unwarranted chances. We have to be realistic." He sighed. "If it comes down to us moving on, or risking our lives saving her, we have to leave her. We have an oath to fulfill. We cannot risk our deaths saving her. Our mission is far more important than a single life."

"Is there anything else you know about the Brigade that could help us?" She said, ignoring his last remarks.

He scratched his beard. "I don't know about help, but it is rumored they have the equivalent of a white-band fighter among their ranks. I guess you could compare them to say, a Jester. Let's hope he isn't stationed here. I'm good, but I'm not that good." He grinned.

"How do they compare to Malora's army?"

He sobered. "Well, it all depends on what you're fighting for. I fight for Nia and what she stands for. I will kill if necessary. Unnecessary death is a waste and I would never stoop to that level. The Black Brigade and more importantly for us, the Gray division, only fight for one reason. To kill anyone they deem a threat to Damrek and what he stands for. To be honest, we probably would have stood a better chance against the men in the clearing."

Lanis knew he was right about the oath, but it didn't sit right with her to leave Rose behind. Rose felt like her responsibility, as did Elson, and although her oath didn't inherently involve Elson, she wouldn't leave him in that situation. "We go for her tonight."

He stared at her for a few minutes before answering. "Tonight." He nodded.

"Pull out the map. Let's see where we go from here."

He smoothed the map out on the ground in front of them. After an hour of looking it over, they both agreed on where their current location most likely was. It was a guess, but they didn't have any other choice. "It looks like our best bet would be this." He pointed to a cluster of buildings.

"What is it?"

"The Ancient Ruins of Treko. Are you sure this is where we want to go? Do you know what they are?"

If given the choice she would have stayed far away from them, but they didn't have a choice. Hundreds of years ago, the village was abandoned after everyone inside was killed. The week before the massacre, two hunting parties left and when they returned, they were faced with the dead. The village was a fortress of stone structures built for the worship of all the Gods. Rumor had it that those that worshiped Novak and Shara had the residents inside the village killed because they didn't believe in mixing the worshipers of other faiths together. To this day, no sane person ever entered the ruins of their own free will. They say you could see the ghosts of the dead walk the streets at night. "Yes, I know what they are, and no, I don't see we have any other choice."

⁂

Lanis secured her whip, tightened the laces on her boots, and slipped her knife into its sheath. After laying her bag on top of the pile Elson had created of their belongings, she joined him. She was confident in herself and in Elson, but she would remain cautious until they rescued Rose. The one thought that kept returning to her mind, and the one thought she kept pushing away, was Anya. If she focused on her, she wouldn't get through this. Elson's motivation was to Nia, but she wouldn't lie to herself, her motivation was to Anya and it always would be. The sooner they reached Manight, the sooner she could fulfill her oath, and go home.

"Ready?" Elson asked, gripping her shoulders.

"Let's do this." Walking quickly, but quietly enough not to draw unwanted attention, they made their way back to the Brigade camp. The moon gave off just enough light to help pave their way. The brush was thick and after nearly two hours, they made it to a small hill that overlooked the camp. They lay on the ground and scoped out the area. Where the moon had barely given them any light on their walk back, it seemed to light up the entire camp below.

The camp spanned the entire clearing, at least a half mile long. At least twenty tents ran along the backside of the forest's edge. In front of them stood a massive tent and in front of it, a large fire burned. Twelve soldiers were seated around the fire. Along the opposite side sat at least a hundred smaller tents. As far as she could see, no soldier guarded the perimeter. By her estimate, there had to be hundreds if not thousands of soldiers. When they landed earlier, she only noticed a small number. This wasn't good. She'd been in impossible situations before, but this was at the top of her list.

"Let's take that small ridge." Elson pointed to Lanis's right. "Then go along the backside. You lead."

"Okay." His confidence bolstered her courage. The ridge was steep, but they made it down safely, and followed the tree line to the back of the tents. All was quiet. From their vantage point, she couldn't see any soldiers. Her heart pounded. They were thirty feet from the largest tent, where Rose should be.

"This is a set up," he whispered in her ear.

She nodded. "I'll go. I won't be able to blend with the tents, but I believe I'll stand a better chance than you sneaking between them." She held up her hand to ward off his questions. He clamped his mouth shut and turned away. "Look," she said, touching his arm. "I know what your oath is for, but this," she said, pointing behind her, "Wasn't part of the plan. I can do this. It's what I did for years. Once we get out of this, you can protect me all you like." She squeezed his arm.

He nodded. "Be careful."

She winked. "I'm always careful." With deliberate steps, she stopped behind a large tree and surveyed the area. No soldiers were in sight, but she could hear several men laughing and talking around the fire. This was definitely a trap. She slipped her knife out and squeezed the handle. Trap, or no trap, there was no turning back now. She wasn't leaving without Rose. After one final glance around, she stepped from the tree line, and slid between two smaller tents. Loosening her grip on the knife, she relaxed her fingers, and crouched close to the ground as footsteps drew closer to her. Two men stopped by the tent opposite her and entered without even glancing her way. Lying on her stomach, she crawled to the front of the tent, and eyed the largest one. The flap from the rear door opening was wide open. Hopefully Rose hadn't been moved. Pushing back onto her knees, she climbed to her feet and swiftly moved, stopping next to the opening. Rose lay on a bed set just inside the door. It didn't look like her hands and feet were bound, but she wasn't moving. Lanis focused on her and breathed a sigh of relief when she took a breath. At least she was still alive.

She slid back between the two smaller tents, walked behind them, and came up on the other side of the door. Opposite the bed was a dresser and beyond that was a small table and two chairs. The dresser looked tall enough to blend into. Without hesitating, she walked in and quickly blended with the dresser. The tent was a lot larger on the inside than it looked on the outside. She felt a little more secure being able to blend in an unfamiliar environment. Rose still hadn't moved. Although she didn't see any bindings on her, it didn't mean magic wasn't shackling her. This was way out of her comfort zone. She stiffened when movement at the front of the tent caught her eye. A man stood with his back to her and the hood of his cape down, revealing short, black hair. It could only be one person: the sorcerer. Even if she made it to the bed with Rose, she had no way of fighting magic. Her stomach dropped when he turned to her. His wrist was void of any type of brand. He was Rogue.

"I may not be able to see you, but I know you're there."

His voice, calm and soft spoken, sent chills down her spine. He stood frozen to the spot and his arms hung loosely by his sides. Compared to the Jester, this man was plain. His brown trousers and black tunic wouldn't attract any type of attention. With his black hair and brown eyes, he looked like hundreds of other men. He was forgettable.

His eyes bored into hers as he walked closer to them. "Two things are going to happen. One," he said, lifting one finger. "You are going to unblend, and two, you are going to sit on the bed beside her."

Lanis couldn't say she'd ever been in a worse circumstance before. Her only chance would be to surprise him, and in order to do that, she would have to unblend. Her heart sank as the footsteps of the men outside the tent grew closer to them. If she didn't hurry, Elson would come looking for them. The last thing she wanted was for him to interfere and cause more problems. They needed to get out of here with as little disruption as possible. Making up her mind, she took a step forward as Rose jumped up from the bed and threw something at the sorcerer that sent him flying through the front door of the tent. Lanis grabbed Rose's hand and pulled her through the back door. The coast was clear, so they ran back the way Lanis had come. She pushed Rose up the slope, sliding numerous times, and was grateful when Elson grabbed her hand and pulled her up. All three ran for the outcrop of rocks where Elson had stashed their belongings.

Lanis's footsteps faltered as she caught a glimpse of two men running opposite them. She stopped abruptly and pulled her knife. Both men advanced. Lanis sidestepped, and barely missed the punch thrown at her head. She ducked and threw her leg out, sending the man falling backward. She grabbed his leg, pulled him back, and plunged her knife into his chest.

"Let's go," Elson said, after killing the other man. "More are coming."

In short order, they made it to the outcrop and grabbed their belongings. Elson lead the way. Lanis didn't bother to look back even though she could hear them advancing. "Run faster!" Relief washed over her as she glimpsed the Ruins of Treko in the distance. She hoped they were the only people stupid enough to enter them. She slid to a stop just outside the entrance and Elson ran past her into them. Rose was lagging behind and for the first time, she noticed Rose was limping. Ignoring Elson's screams, she threw her bag inside and ran back for her. She threw her knife as one of the men reached for Rose and it landed with a thud in the man's neck. The other three soldiers stopped beside him. "Rose, go into the ruins," Lanis said, eyeing the men. She didn't know if they stopped because she killed one, or because of the ruins. Elson walked up to her, sword drawn.

"Lanis, walk back slowly." Each step they took backward, the soldiers took one forward.

She was jarred to a stop as her back hit the side

of the stone wall that lined the edge of the ruins. She stepped to the right and was grabbed from behind and pulled inside. Whirling around, she glared at Elson. "I was coming." She turned back toward the men and took a step back. The three soldiers were standing just outside the stone wall. "What are they doing?"

"Waiting," Rose said. "Waiting for us to leave."

"By morning we will be surrounded." Lanis turned away from the men. "Are we sure they won't come in?" There was enough light left that she could see most of the outline of the buildings. The stonework and carvings were exquisite and scary at the same time. She didn't believe in ghosts, but just their luck they would run into some here.

Rose looked appalled. "If I had known where we were headed," she said, throwing her hands in the air. "I would have never come with you. I've heard of this place my whole life. Can't you feel that?" She rubbed her arms, eyeing the structures around them.

Lanis couldn't believe her nerve. "Feel what?" she ground out.

"I feel it too," Elson said from beside her. "The air is disturbed."

"You know what I feel?" Lanis said, picking up her bag and slipping it over her head. "I feel grateful, grateful to be alive. You could show a little more appreciation, Rose; we did risk our lives to save you."

"Grateful, sure. Thanks for saving my life. But it seems to me that I had a hand in my escape. Tell me, Lanis, what was your plan? How did you plan to deal with the Rogue?" Lanis turned away. "That's what I thought. By the way, let's see how grateful you still feel in the morning."

"Oh, come on. If something were going to happen,

it would have already. Grow up, Rose," Lanis said.

"Look," Elson said, standing between them. "Let's get farther into the ruins. Even if I think we're safe here, I would feel better being more protected. If, by the time we make camp, you two still want to bicker, be my guest, but for the time being, both of you can keep your mouth shut."

Lanis looked back toward the men. She would have to figure out how to get her knife back.

☙☙☙☙

Dimitri jumped up, sending his chair falling backward to the floor when a man just appeared in his office. "Treg, what are you doing here?" He hired him to keep one of his Black Brigade camps safe. Treg was one of the most powerful Rogues he'd ever met. He shouldn't be here. He was never to leave his post. Dimitri picked up his seat and sat when Treg bowed.

"I apologize, but something unexpected has happened. As you know, we do not see many strangers on or near the land we decided to make our camp."

"Yes, I know," he said, waving his hand. "Get on with it."

"Earlier this evening three people appeared out of thin air at the edge of camp. Two women and one man." He clasped his hands in his lap.

Dimitri stiffened. It couldn't be. They shouldn't have been anywhere near there. On the other hand, if it was them, this could be the break he had been waiting for. "What did they look like?"

Treg waved his hand and a large light orb appeared. He placed it on Dimitri's desk and pointed at the center of it. An image of Lanis and Elson appeared. He waved his hand and the orb disappeared.

"I knew it," Dimitri said. Now he had to find a way to deal with them. He needed information, but how to go about it. "Where do you have them now?"

"Well," Treg said, scratching his neck. "That's the thing. They got away."

"I'm sorry." He couldn't have heard right. "What do you mean they got away? How is that possible with you, and the army?" Could no one get anything right?

"It's not that simple. All my men were stunned when the three appeared out of thin air, and when the man and woman jumped up and ran, I did have men take chase, but they just disappeared. My men couldn't find them. It wasn't until later I realized the one woman was a Ramden."

"Disappeared." Figured. "You said there was a second woman?"

"Yes. A soldier brought her to my tent. When I realized who she was, I kept the men away from her. A few were insistent, but when I told them who she was, they backed off."

"You know her?"

"As do you. She's your daughter. Your youngest, I believe."

No, not Ella. Dimitri ran his hands through his hair. This could be good, or this could be bad. "How can you be sure?"

"I was in the capital when she graduated. I know what she looks like. I do not believe she recognized me, though."

If it wasn't one thing, it was another. "You said you did have her, or you have her now?"

"The Ramden and the man came to rescue her. When I confronted the Ramden, Ella jumped up from the bed and threw a blinding spell at me. It knocked me out." He laughed. "It took me by surprise. I just woke up a few hours ago. She is very powerful. More powerful than probably even she realizes. The blinding spell was well thought out and executed. She went with the other two. They evaded my men and, looking back on it, they had to have known where they were headed. They ran into the Ancient Ruins of Treko. My men have the ruins surrounded, but they will not enter the ruins themselves."

The last he heard from Ella, she was in Klate. How did she get here? He would have to get her out of this situation. He would never let any harm come to her. The men's reluctance he could understand; he wouldn't have entered the ruins either. Right now, though, Ella was his main priority. "No harm is to come to my daughter. If you can take the other two out without harming her then do it, but if you can't, let them go. She is not to be touched. Understand?"

"Of course. That's why when the men took chase, I informed them not to harm her. What do you want me to do now?"

Dimitri smiled. Ella had always been gifted and for Treg to sing her praises meant a great deal to him. She had talents that neither one of her sisters possessed, but that didn't make her any more important to him than the other two. He could only think of one thing to do and he hoped everything worked out. "Jimle," he said to the guard standing in the corner. "Send for the Jester." Dimitri looked at Treg and leaned back in his chair. "This is what I want you to do."

After setting up camp, Elson asked how she managed to get Rose out of the tent. Lanis shrugged. "We ran after Rose threw her spell. It worked quite well and gave us the chance to escape." By this time, Lanis's temper had cooled.

Rose squirmed in her seat. "I didn't expect it to work as well as it did, and not against a Rogue. I learned the blinding spell when I started school. I've used it before, but it has never performed as well as it did this time." She stood up. "I overheard the Rogue tell one of the guards that I wasn't to be touched."

"Isn't that odd?" Lanis asked Elson.

He nodded. "It is. I've never heard of the Black Brigade going easy on a prisoner."

"I'm glad you came for me," Rose said, quietly.

"We may have our differences, but we would have never left you there," Lanis said. "You both should get some sleep. It's been a long day. We can talk about this tomorrow. I believe it's my turn for first watch."

"You won't get any arguments from me," Elson said, lying down, followed by Rose.

Lanis watched until they feel asleep, then sat down on an overturned stone, and buried her head in her hands. They were so far off their path. She wondered if that is why Anya told them not to stray from the map. It would be a long-shot now if they made it in time. The Prophecy was real and important, even if she didn't believe in it. She had never failed a mission before and she didn't intend for this to be her first. She leaned her head back against a tree and opened her eyes. The stars shimmered, and lit up the entire sky. The same sky Anya loved to look at nightly. It hurt too much to think about her, so she didn't. At least she tried not to, but at night, it was hard to keep thoughts of her away. Nighttime was usually the only time they had to spend together. The only time Lanis could take her mask off and be herself. The day they were reunited couldn't come quickly enough. Some people lived their entire lives searching for, but never finding, their purpose. She found hers four years ago. Although, the way things were looking, they wouldn't even have a future together. She had to be honest with herself; things weren't looking good.

Lanis leaned her head back and her eyes closed of their own accord. Her head fell forward and her eyes shot open. She blinked and scrubbed her hands down her face. She jumped up, shook her hands out, and stretched, her arms freezing in midair. By the line of the moon, she'd only been asleep for a few minutes, but the darkness that enveloped the ruins told a different story. How could that be? Her fingers grazed the handle of her whip as she scanned the surrounding area. Nothing looked out of place, but she couldn't be sure. They should have searched the ruins more closely before turning in.

The perimeter was as silent now as the first time she walked it, but it felt different. She circled the camp and her heart rate tripled, as a light in the distance caught her attention. The Brigade wasn't foolish enough to have such a bright light burning, alerting anyone to their position. There shouldn't be anyone else here. Before she knew what was happening, or could stop herself, she was already walking in the light's direction. Her mind conjured up countless explanations, but she dismissed the idea of ghosts. It was more likely someone trying to escape some form of reality, or at least that's what she would keep telling herself the closer her feet took her to the light.

Her footsteps faltered as a heavy haze encircled her. The farther she walked, the heavier the fog became. Even if she wanted to turn back, she knew deep down she wouldn't be able to. Slowing her pace, she squinted into the distance, her hand instantly going to her whip, as the image of a man started to materialize through the fog. She flattened her body against one of the walls of the buildings lining the path and kept a slower pace until she drew closer to him. For each step she took, the man kept up his position and never once looked her way. She had never heard of anyone guarding the ruins. The pounding of her heart slowed as she drew closer to him and realized what he was.

It was a statue, carved of the finest stone. The lines of his face and uniform were exquisitely detailed by, what she assumed to be, an accomplished stonemason. She reached out to touch his face, but drew her hand back at the last second. She took a step away from him and took a deep breath. Statues were just that, statues. Stealing her resolve to finish this, she turned from the man only to freeze to the spot. The fog rolled away to reveal dozens more statues lined up shoulder to shoulder on either side of the path. She knew they weren't real, but they *looked* real. The details of their faces and the precise lines of their weapons were just as intricate as the first man's and would be enough to give anyone pause. The thought of walking past them didn't sit well with her. It shouldn't scare her, but it did. Her eyes locked onto the light in the distance. It called to her and she couldn't deny the pull it had over her. Jerking her tunic down, she gripped her whip handle and walked past the first one, then the second. By the halfway point, it felt like someone was watching her, following her. The thump, thump of heavy footsteps echoed behind her. Instead of turning around as she passed the last statue, she continued on to the light. It shone down from a circular window set high up in a tall stone tower. It was one of the only buildings that looked as if it hadn't faced any type of destruction, except for a few stones on the exterior, missing here and there. Of course it had to be the tallest window of the tallest tower. She hated heights. Running her hand through her hair, she walked around the tower, looking for a different way in besides the window, and for a split second, she contemplated turning around, but knew that wasn't an option. There was no way she was walking past the statues again, and she wasn't looking forward to finding a new way back to camp.

She groaned and looked up, knowing her only way in would be to climb up to the window. After eyeing the structure for several minutes, she reached up and placed her hand in a slot where a brick once stood and pulled herself up. She didn't know where the courage came from, but she kept putting one hand in front of the other until her fingers brushed the sill of the window. Taking a few deep breaths, she pushed her body up and over the edge. Yelping, she flung her arms to her sides, but couldn't stop her momentum as her body fell to the tower floor, a good ten feet from the window.

Who in their right mind puts a window that far from the floor if it's the only way in? Raising up, she rubbed her head, wincing when her fingers brushed a tender spot where a lump was already starting to form. She stood and leaned against the wall to get her bearings. She swung her head around when she heard movement behind her and froze, her heart in her throat. A young woman stood in the middle of the room, staring at her.

Her chestnut hair swept her shoulders and her hands were clasped in front of a white, floor-length dress. Lanis reached for her whip only to realize it was gone. When the woman smiled at her, Lanis took a cautious step forward, her eyes taking in the entire room. A few lanterns were scattered throughout and the shelves that ran along the walls were filled to overflowing with books. Lanis rubbed her neck. There wasn't any visible way out. She didn't have a choice but to address the woman. "I saw your light."

"Indeed you did." Her voice was smooth and silky.

Her curiosity always did get the best of her. "Who are you?"

"Who we are matters not."

We. Lanis scrunched her nose up and scanned the room again, but they were the only two in there. "We?"

The woman brushed her hand in the air. "What is it you seek, my child?"

Lanis stilled. The voice had come from behind her. She gulped and turned, but the space behind her was empty. She cut her gaze back to the woman in front of her. "How many people are here?" She asked the question, not sure she wanted the answer.

"We are old."

"We are young."

"We are somewhere in between."

Their voices echoed throughout the entire room.

"By numbers we are three."

"Three by three."

"Three."

The voices came from everywhere, but the woman in front of her never moved her lips. "Are you real?" Lanis asked. Maybe she should have listened more closely to what walked these ruins. She knew she didn't hit her head that hard when she fell.

The woman cocked her head and smiled. "As real as we can be."

"What does that mean?" Lanis hated riddles.

"It means what you need it to mean. What do you seek?"

"I know my destination. I don't seek anything and if I do, I'm not sure what it would be." In the future, she would rationalize every situation before jumping in. She didn't know what possessed her to climb up by herself. She ran her hands through her hair, trying and failing to clear her thoughts. How in the world would she explain this to Elson and Rose? On second thought, maybe she would keep all this to herself. Who would believe her anyway? The woman in front of her never even blinked. "I'm not sure I'm even supposed to be here."

She spread her arms wide and smiled. "Yet, here you are. Those that seek us never find us."

"I didn't seek you."

The woman only smiled. "What is it you seek?"

She was persistent; Lanis would give her that. Even though this whole experience was odd, she wasn't scared. All the fight left her. "I honestly don't know what I seek."

"Come here." The woman pointed to a spot in front of her.

Lanis only hesitated a second before making her way across the room. The woman placed her hands on Lanis's shoulders. Without warning, Lanis's knees buckled and the room started spinning. Shadows started dancing around her and Lanis had to close her eyes to ward against the movement.

"Lanis, open your eyes."

Lanis stood on unsteady feet, opened her eyes, and took a step back. Standing in front of her where the young lady once stood, were three very old women. She wouldn't even try to guess their age. She could make out every wrinkle and crease on their gaunt faces. They stood at least two foot shorter than her and their backs were slightly bent. The dresses they wore looked more like rags then actual clothing. Before Lanis could do, or say anything, one of them stepped toward her. Her movements were steady and strong for someone who looked so frail.

"What you seek will be freely given," the first woman said.

The second woman walked to a shelf on the far wall, pulled down a well-worn book, and laid it on a table that was pushed against the wall. The leather cracked when she opened it and dust flew off the pages. "Come here."

As soon as Lanis reached the table, the third woman grabbed her hand and pressed a small square stone into her palm, and told Lanis to make a fist around it. "Are you ready?"

"Yes."

The second woman started reading from the book in a language Lanis didn't recognize. After each word the woman spoke, the stone grew warmer in her palm. When the first woman took over reading, the stone started to glow, light spilling out from between Lanis's fingers. By the time the third woman finished reading, the stone had grown cold.

Lanis uncurled her fingers to reveal a round pink stone. "What's it do?"

The women wore blank faces. "When the time comes, you will know," the first one said.

She didn't know these women and she knew she would never see them again, but she would never forget them. "How will I know?"

"You will know," the second one said. "Now, a little advice from three old women. Always trust your instincts."

"Choose your friends wisely," the first one said.

"Doing the right thing sometimes means making the wrong decisions," the third added.

Lanis glanced down at the stone. "What does that mean?" She looked up, but all three women were gone.

"Open your eyes."

Her eyes were open so she closed them, then opened them again. The young woman from earlier stood in front of her.

"I take it you found what you needed," she said, pointing to Lanis's hand.

Lanis opened her palm. "Yes, I guess I did." She couldn't explain it, but she knew she had gained an important piece to the puzzle. It brought her a bit of comfort to know, at least, one thing was taken care of. Even if she didn't know what that was. She slipped the stone in her pocket.

"Very well." The woman nodded. "You can leave by that opening over there. No need for you to climb up to the window." She winked.

A door stood ajar in the corner of the room. "Thank you," she said, turning back, but the woman was gone. She spun around when someone called her name, but there was no one there.

When she turned back to the door, she heard it again.

"Lanis!"

She whipped her head around and grabbed the door to steady herself.

"Lanis!"

She slumped to the floor as sharp pains sliced through her body.

"Lanis!"

She closed her eyes. It felt like someone was shaking her.

"Lanis, wake up."

She sat up, gasping for breath. Elson and Rose were both on their knees beside her. Elson looked terrified. "What...what happened? How did I get back here?"

"What do you mean get back?" Elson said, looking at Rose. "You never left. We've been trying to wake you all night." He ran his hands through his hair. "We..." He sat back. "I thought you were dead."

Lanis rubbed the back of her head, tensing when she felt a tender spot. If she had never left, how did she get that? "Are you sure? It was so real."

"What was real?" Rose asked. "Where did you go?"

Lanis rubbed her hands on her pants and felt the stone in her pocket. Who were they, and why did they give her the stone? She slumped forward and rested her head in her hands. What a mess. She attempted to stand when Elson grabbed her arm and helped her up.

He steadied her and looked into her eyes. "You okay?"

Lanis pushed him away and leaned against the wall. "I can't believe I fell asleep." She waved off his concern. "I'm sorry."

Rose touched her arm then quickly pulled her

hand away as if she was burned. "I woke first and when I couldn't wake you, I woke Elson. We were really worried you wouldn't wake up." She turned and walked away.

Lanis laughed. "It must be this place." She didn't want to get into what she saw or did.

He leaned against the wall beside her. "Where did you go in your dreams?"

"I woke up here, only it was different." She shook her head. "I can't explain it." It couldn't have all been a dream. She rubbed her neck. She could do nothing about what happened and there was no sense in trying to figure it out. "Anything out here change since I've been asleep?"

He sighed and let her drop the subject. "We're surrounded on all sides. We haven't seen the sorcerer, or anyone else, but then again, we haven't been looking."

The women told her she would know when to use the stone and she knew this wasn't the time. She pushed off the wall and walked to Rose. Elson was right behind her. "Rose, how many arrows do you have?"

"Eight. Why?"

"We need to take out as many as we can. We'll split up, but we should stay within the ruins. The last time I fought men like this, I almost died, so be careful. We will not interact with them outside of these ruins. Agreed?"

"Yes."

"What are you going to do?" Elson asked.

"I'm going to go back to where we came in. Rose, you head toward the east of the wall and Elson, you the west." Lanis kicked out the fire and slipped her bag over her head. She walked to the spot where they entered the day before and the same three men stood just outside the border of the ruins. She uncurled her whip, letting it slide down her pants leg, and started pacing.

"If you think you can take us with that whip, come on out here," one of them taunted.

She stopped pacing and stared at him. "I'll take my chances." She leaned against one of the pillars. "Do you honestly think we'll stay here? We got away once, we'll get away again."

He shook his head. "You can't stay in there forever."

She looked on when the guards straightened and turned away from her. While they were distracted, she threw her whip out, catching one of the guards around his leg and pulled, sending him crashing backward

She winced when his head connected with the ground. Flicking her wrist, the whip flew sideways into another guard when he reached for it. She pulled it back and wrapped it around her waist.

"You'll pay for that," he spat, wiping the blood off his face.

"Maybe I will, maybe I won't." She smiled when she heard footsteps behind her. "Everything okay?"

"Yes," Elson said.

"Good." She nodded. "Rose?"

"I haven't seen her," he said. "Looks like you got one." He pointed to the guard on the ground.

"I was bored." She shrugged, then noticed movement in the distance. "Rose is coming."

They met up with Rose, who continued on to the remaining guards and took them out. Lanis took the opportunity, ran outside the ruins walls, and retrieved her knife. They waited for her to catch up. "Good," she said to Rose.

"Yes." She seemed tense.

"You okay?" Lanis asked.

"I'm fine. I think everything's starting to catch up with me."

"It was bound to happen," Elson said. "There's still plenty out here."

"We have to take our chances. How long until we make it to the falls?" Lanis asked.

"Well." Elson tapped his finger on his chin. "That depends."

"On?" Rose said.

"If a desert appears, a secret brigade, Jesters, Rogues…"

"Stop." Lanis laughed. "I think we both get the picture. How long in normal circumstances?"

"By the map, I figure if we travel all day, we should be there well before nightfall, maybe sooner if we push ourselves. Once we reach the falls, my hope is that we won't have any trouble and will have time to make a safe climb down. From all that I've heard, it will probably be a death sentence to climb down."

"So," Lanis said, turning around and walking backward. "Just another day."

"Exactly," Elson said, turning her back around and continuing on. Lanis looked back and noticed the frown on Rose's face.

"I am a bit troubled by the climb down," Rose said, in answer to Lanis's unspoken question.

"Me too," Lanis added. "There is a reason no one climbs down them. Too many have lost their lives out of their own foolishness."

"Well then," Elson said, putting an arm around each of their shoulders and pulling them into his sides. "Fools we shall be." He led the way to the edge of the ruins and held his hand up for them to stay back. "I can see five of them in the distance." He turned back to them. "Ready?"

"As I will ever be," Lanis said and Rose nodded. Lanis gripped her knife and followed behind him. They kept close to the ruins until they had no choice but to enter the forest. "They see us, but they're not following."

"I know," he said. "I'm just not sure why they're not following us."

Lanis picked up the pace and walked beside him, scanning the forest around them. She touched him on the arm and pointed to the left. He nodded. There were men on both sides of them, but no one made a move toward them. She kept her eyes on the guards when they reached the forest's edge. They stepped onto the road and were a good ways down when she turned around. The Rogue from the Brigade tent stood at the edge of the forest, staring at her. He smiled, nodded, and walked back into the forest.

"What was that about?" Elson said.

"I don't know, but we need to get out of here." Lanis turned toward Rose, whose back was turned to them. "Rose, you okay?"

She turned slowly toward them. "I'm fine. Let's get out of here. Who knows when they will decide to come after us?"

"Agreed." Elson took the lead.

Lanis didn't know about the others, but something didn't add up. Why, after chasing them, would they just let them go? She would keep her ears open and her eyes on Rose, who was acting funny. That's all they needed, someone else to cause them problems.

Anya walked down the familiar hallway and ran her fingers along the stone wall. She hadn't been down here since giving the oath to Lanis and Elson. Nia's temple never failed to humble and give her a deep sense of oneness. Word arrived late the previous night that they had arrived safely at the second oath house. After learning of the circumstances of the first oath house, she dispatched soldiers to investigate. They hadn't reported back yet, but from the way the oath master talked, Lanis, Elson, and Rose were lucky to be alive. She prayed daily that Rose was the asset they needed to get to Manight safely. She had deliberately given them a route not usually taken in order to throw anyone off their path.

Not that long ago, she and Lanis were standing in this very hallway. Lanis had removed her mask and they walked hand and hand toward the temple. Anya closed her eyes and remembered vividly the way Lanis tugged her to a stop and pulled her close. The kiss that followed left her weak, but when their lips parted the look in Lanis's eyes almost brought her to her knees. Her eyes always gave her away; they conveyed what words never could. Lanis had run her hands down Anya's cheek and placed gentle kiss on her lips before putting the mask on. Anya opened her eyes and blinked, slamming back to reality. She was here and Lanis was out there, somewhere. Of late, she found herself thinking about what life would be like away from all this. No advisers, no mask, no High Priestess, just her and Lanis. They could settle down somewhere quiet and live out the rest of their lives peacefully. It sounded like a dream and that is exactly what it was: a dream. Her life wasn't her own. It never had been. She started walking again, making her way to the temple door. She could never leave this. Nia had staked a claim on her long ago and was literally a part of her. She didn't have it in her to turn her back on Nia, or her people. She would give up almost anything for Lanis, including her life, but she would never give up who she was. Lanis understood that; she may not agree with her, but she understood. She was exactly where she belonged.

After waking that morning, she handed her traveling bag to a guard to take to her carriage. For good, or bad, today was the day. She would be lying to herself if she didn't admit to being nervous. After prayers, she and Kerrison would leave for Manight. The journey itself would be short, but the in-between held many unknowns. She didn't expect trouble; she just couldn't shake the feeling of dread that seemed to wash over her that morning. She nodded at her Protector, turned the handle, and walked into Nia's temple. Time didn't slow for anyone and she didn't want to be late. Praying was her primary reason for coming down here, but she also needed to retrieve the Prophecy. As far as she knew, she was the only one who knew it was kept in Nia's temple.

Kneeling at the Altar, she bowed her head, inhaled, and tensed for a moment when a familiar scent drifted her way. After a few minutes, she felt him kneel beside her. He never stopped amazing her with his timing. He always visited when she least expected it. She had a feeling this meeting would be vastly different from the rest, though. The first time he knelt beside her, she was startled, but in a previous meeting with the Oracle, she had told her to expect the unexpected. It was certainly unexpected for anyone to find their way into Nia's temple without permission. From that first time he showed up, they had formed a tentative friendship. They watched each other grow in age and confidence. She didn't judge him and he didn't push her into anything, or try to use his power against her. She kept her head bowed. "It's been a while." She never told Lanis of their meetings.

He didn't waste pleasantries. "You have a traitor."

"Yes." It amazed her what he knew.

"Do you know who?" Anya didn't answer him. "I know you will never ask me," he said, pushing a piece of paper into her hand. "I have grown fond of you over the years. I enjoy our talks and I don't want to see anything senseless happen to you that could have otherwise been avoided. In my line of work, it's best not to form attachments, and I'm not a religious man, but I have formed an attachment to you. You're different. You are genuine and your heart is always in the right place. I have talked to a lot of other priests, leaders, and monarchs, but you are the only one I believe when you speak. I warn you, our paths will cross again, but do not fear me or what I must do. We both have tasks to accomplish, and do not hate me, for I will do things that will make you doubt me."

She grabbed his arm when he attempted to stand. "I forgive you for what you must do, for I have done things that cannot be undone. We all have a fate that we must follow. But always remember," she begged, clinging to his hand. "There is always someone you can turn to. As long as I draw breath, you can always come to me without fear of being persecuted. You are always welcome here."

He slid his hand out of hers and bowed. "And as long as I draw breath, I will do everything in my power to ensure your life continues."

She stood and leaned against the Altar, for what seemed a lifetime, when he disappeared into the shadows. The piece of paper felt like hot coals in her fist. She would have never asked him for the name and he knew that. With shaky fingers, she opened it and read what he wrote. It shouldn't have hurt, but the betrayal felt like a knife to the gut. All those years of commitment so easily thrown away. She threw the paper in the fire.

She left the chamber and informed the guard standing outside to gather her advisers for a meeting. She didn't have a choice. When she entered the chamber, her advisers were already waiting for her. "You don't have to sit, this won't take long. There has been new information brought to my attention and my plans have changed. Merek, you have ten minutes to pack, you will be coming with me. Miriam, you will be in charge." She held up her hand to ward off any questions. "Everyone except Miriam is dismissed."

"Miriam, please have a seat." She chose her words carefully. "I know at times you think I'm playing favorites, but I trust you, and truthfully, I don't like any of you better than the others. You know what is expected as High Priestess. Let Hensley do his job and allow Kerrison to do hers. There are things happening that are beyond my, or anyone's, control. Plans have been set in motion for a long time. I need to know now if you're willing to take over my duties."

Miriam's eyes held a sadness Anya had never seen before. "You're acting like you won't be back. You will be back, won't you?"

Anya honestly couldn't answer, because she didn't know. "I need your assurance that you can handle things."

"Of course I can," she said, leaning forward in her chair. "But you didn't answer my question and that tells me you don't know. I know you probably won't answer, but I'll ask anyway. What's going on? You're starting to scare me."

Anya stood and pushed her chair in. "I'm fine. I trust in Nia and I trust that everything will turn out as it should. I need to go," she said. With her hand on the doorknob, she turned back toward Miriam. "Be ready for anything, and above all else make sure this city is protected. Everything and everyone isn't what it seems." The trip down the stairs was the longest she had ever made. Before she passed through the door leading to the carriage, she turned toward the closest guard and handed him a wrapped bundle. "As quickly as you can, take this to Kaylynn and tell no one what you have done."

He bowed. "Of course, High Priestess."

She pushed through the door and only spared a brief glimpse at Merek before climbing into the carriage. Her Protector sat beside her, Merek opposite her.

"High Priestess."

"Merek." He knew that she knew what he had done. It was only a matter of time. "Let's get on our way," she said.

"Very well." He knocked twice on the door to set the carriage in motion.

There was no turning back now. She knew if anything happened to her, and Lanis found out about Merek's betrayal, she would stop at nothing to hunt him down and kill him. Anya only hoped she was alive to see that smile wiped off his face.

After a few hours of travel, Lanis knew they were being followed, and their pursuers weren't being quiet about it. "We need to speed up," Lanis said, starting to run. She ran as hard as she could, and ignored the tree branches that were slapping her in the face. Heart pounding, she ran through the overgrown brush, and stumbled to a stop.

The Falls were deafening. The sheer size of them was more than she could have ever imagined. It amazed her how the forest had masked the sound of the water. They would never make it down before the men attacked, at least not safely. Lanis walked to the edge, stopped, and turned back to the trees when she heard Elson and Rose break through.

"This wasn't what I was expecting," Elson said. He looked as frightened as she felt. "It will be getting dark soon. We need to take care of these guys then make our way down. I'll try and find us the safest avenue possible." He pulled his sword and took up position beside Rose.

Rose drew her bow. "I don't have the magic to get us out of this."

Lanis cringed and uncurled her whip. She closed her eyes and took a deep breath, calming her nerves. As soon as she opened her eyes, three men and two women broke through the tree line. They weren't wearing the uniforms of the Black Brigade. Two of them pulled swords, while the other three held battle axes. She took a step back, clinching her hand around her whip when the biggest of the five lifted his sword. His clothes were soaked with sweat and he had a wild look in his eyes.

Without warning, his eyes dulled and his entire body jerked before freezing in mid-step. Lanis looked to the other four and they looked the same way. Frozen.

She glanced at Rose, who looked as surprised as she did, even a little frightened. Elson shrugged and took a step forward when his body also froze. Lanis clutched her whip when Rose collapsed to the ground. She scanned the entire area. Her entire body tensed and every inch of her skin chilled when the Jester walked out from between two of the trees. She wouldn't have recognized him if not for his smile. Gone were the flashy clothes and in their place were a pair of pants and a shirt in different shades of brown. He waved his hand in front of him and the men and women disappeared. He took a few steps forward and stopped. For some reason she withstood the green orb, but there were plenty of other ways to kill her. She didn't stand a chance against him. That's one reason magic was so regulated. It gave your opponent an unfair advantage. The longer he stared at her, the louder her heart beat.

"I ask nothing from you in return. You need to leave this place as quickly as possible. You don't have much time." He winked. "This will be our little secret." He snapped his fingers and disappeared. Things kept getting more wild and strange. She needed to find out what he really wanted from her. After a few minutes, Rose and Elson started to come around.

"What happened?" Rose asked, accepting the hand Lanis offered.

"Yes, what did happen?" Elson kept his eyes on the tree line.

"I don't really know. It all happened so fast," Lanis said.

"Where did they go?" Elson squinted at her.

"I don't know. We need to get out of here. There are bound to be more to follow." She caught Rose's eye. "Something wrong, Rose?"

"No, not with me."

Elson looked between them and shook his head. "I'm going to find the best way down."

Lanis turned her back on Rose and took in the scene before her in utter amazement. Even though many considered it a death trap, the falls were spectacular. They dropped at least two hundred feet down into a deadly looking river. Admiring the view and climbing down were two entirely different things. She looked over the edge and wished she hadn't. If one of them slipped, they wouldn't be getting back up. When Elson called her name, she joined him and Rose.

"This is the best way down I could find," he said. "It's not going to be easy, but none of us expected it to be. Honestly, I've never attempted anything this far down before, but I'm confident we'll make it down. Rose, how are you with heights and climbing?"

"I should be fine, but I would prefer not to."

"Lanis," he said, grinning at her.

She glared at him. "You know how I feel."

"Excellent. So we know where everyone stands." He rubbed his hands together. "First, we need to get our belongings to the bottom."

Lanis wasn't about to throw her bag over the edge. "Rose, do you have a spell that can transport us down there?"

Rose cut her eyes at her. "What kind of sorceress do you think I am? No, I don't have a spell to get us down there. I didn't know I would be facing certain death when I signed on for this."

"Certain death." Elson smiled. "What else did

you expect?" Lanis knew he liked to joke, but she also realized it was his way of dealing with less-than-ideal situations. "Ready?" he said. "Trust me."

"I do," Lanis said and she did trust him. What she didn't trust was the rocks.

"Rose," he said, pulling her to him. He pointed to a small outcropping about halfway down the wall. "See those trees." She nodded. "This is what I was thinking. Lanis and I both have rope packed. If we can tie one end of the rope to your arrow, do you think you can hit those trees?"

She looked offended that he would doubt her abilities. "Of course I can."

"We can then slide our things on the rope and down to the outcrop. When we reach it, you can do the same thing so we can get our stuff to the bottom safely."

"I can do that, but I won't need rope and I can get it to the bottom first shot." She looked between them. "I can only do this once."

"Okay," they said, looking at each other.

"Put all of your stuff in a pile by me." Lanis slid her bag off her shoulder and laid it on top of Elson's sword. Rose laid her bow and arrows on top of the pile. She pulled out a small stone and clasped it between her hands. She lifted her hands and chanted. Dropping her hand, she threw the rock on top of the pile. Lanis jumped back when a purple fog engulfed the pile. It circled around the pile and disappeared when Rose waved her hand. Magic would never cease to amaze her.

Rose picked up her bow and circled the pile in a slow motion with an arrow. As Lanis watched, a deep purple rope appeared tied to the arrow and bound around the bags. Rose nocked the arrow onto the bowstring, stepped to the ledge, and released it. One by one, their belongings flew off the ledge, chasing after the arrow. Everything slid down the rope and stopped near the ground, hanging in the air before dropping down beside the arrow. Rose let go of her bow and it flew off the ledge, landing on top of the pile. The fog once again engulfed the entire pile before it disappeared.

"That was incredible," Elson said. "Okay," he said, rubbing his hands together. "Now it's our turn."

"What are we waiting for?" Lanis said, with more enthusiasm than she felt. No point in being afraid. They had to do it. It would be dark soon.

"I'm not going to lie. It won't be easy. I have faith, though. Lanis." He grasped her hand. "We were sent on this oath mission for a reason. I have no reason not to doubt Nia is with us. We can do this." He squeezed her hands.

It was all she needed. "I'm ready."

"Me too," Rose said.

"I won't let anything happen to either one of you," he said. When he sat down on the edge of the cliff and his feet dangled over the side, Lanis's heart started pounding. When he disappeared over the side, she thought her heart would stop, but she pushed it back and sat down. Without thinking, she slid over the edge just as he had. She clung to the side, her fingers digging into a hold until her feet found a secure position. She could do this. She made a mistake when she looked down. She couldn't believe she was doing this. Elson was moving at a pretty good pace.

"Lanis, you have to actually move your body," he called up to her. "I'll wait here until you make it down to me."

She took a deep breath and started slowly making her way down, at times her fingers scrambling for a hold. When she was a few feet from him, she looked up. Rose didn't seem to be having any trouble at all. They were a quarter of the way down when her foot slipped. She searched for a hold, her fingers gripping at the loose rocks. Her panic threatened to overwhelm her when she felt a hand on her back.

"I've got you," Elson said, voice strained.

"Okay." She calmed, hugged the wall, and felt him guide her foot into a hold.

"Ease away from the wall," he said. "The rocks are slippery. About thirty feet down, we'll come to the outcrop where we can take a quick rest. We can't be up here when it gets dark and night is fast approaching. Rose," he called up. "Did you hear what I said?"

"Yes," she said tightly.

"You okay?"

"I'm good."

"Okay," Lanis said. "I'm ready." If it hadn't been for them, she would have already given up. Her hands were raw and her whole body ached. When it seemed like she couldn't go on, she reached the ledge. Elson grabbed a hold of her, and she let him pull her onto it. A few minutes later, he did the same for Rose.

"That was the hardest thing I have ever done. The scariest, too," Lanis said. She was leaning back against the rocks with Elson beside her. Rose sat in front of them.

"I agree," Rose said, accepting the water Elson handed her. Lanis noticed her hands were raw as well.

"It's not going to get any better. As we get closer to the bottom, it gets steeper. We'll have to watch our step," he said.

"Steeper," they both said.

"Ready?" he asked, after only a few minutes of rest.

It was a lot trickier to maneuver the second time. The rocks weren't as wet, but he was right, it was steeper. The rocks seemed to go in on themselves. Lanis shook her head. She had to keep her mind on the climb. She didn't come all this way to die rock climbing. She had only made it a few feet down when her foot slipped, her hands clawing at the rocks until her fingers found a hold. It took all her strength not to let go.

"Lanis, hold on, I'm coming," Elson called to her.

"No," she shouted. "Just give me a minute…" The rock she was holding gave way and she fell backward. She grabbed for her whip, but it slipped through her fingers. Her body bounced off the wall then stopped, suspended in the air. Elson had somehow managed to grab her foot. She was hanging upside down, thirty or so feet from the ground. Elson held tightly to her foot with one hand while his other hand was wrapped around a root sticking out of the rocks. She said a quick prayer to Nia when she noticed his feet were barely planted. How long before his grip slipped, or her boot came off?

"I'm going to slowly lift you up," he said, his breathing labored. "There's a small place by my feet that you should be able to grab a hold of. When you get to my legs, wrap your arms around me. You'll have to turn yourself around. Rose," he called up. "Stay where you are until I get her ready, then you can continue down."

"You don't need me?" Rose asked.

"No."

"What?" Lanis said. "You're barely holding on yourself. How are you going to hold on with me wrapped around you?" Elson didn't answer her, just started lifting. When he stopped, she hugged his legs.

"I'm going to let go and give you a little push sideways. Do not worry about me. I won't let go of this root. Your body will fall fast so be prepared to keep a grip on my legs, but it will be up to you to change your hand and arm position. If you lose your grip, I can't help you."

"Okay. We need to move fast. I'm getting a little lightheaded." He let go and gave her legs a push. Her body fell quickly and as she turned, she loosened her grip on his legs, and let her body fall naturally. At the last second, she grabbed onto his ankles and hung upright. Before she changed her mind, she glanced to her right and, seeing the foothold he told her about, reached over and grabbed it. Thankfully, as she transferred her body weight, she was able to find a place for her feet to rest. Only after she got her breathing under control did she allow herself to look up. Elson was hugging the wall as tightly as she was.

"How about that," Lanis said.

"Yes, how about that," he said. "Are you okay?"

"Shouldn't I be asking you that?"

"I know you hit your back pretty hard. Are you able to continue down on your own? If you can, we need to start down again," he said.

"I'm sore, but I don't think anything's broken. I didn't hit my head. Tomorrow will probably be a different story though." Since she had a moment to rest, the adrenaline was wearing off. Her whole body throbbed. "I'll go first since I'm already down here."

"No, I'll go first," he said. "I'm coming down now.

It's my job to protect you."

"Fair enough." She was too tired to argue with him.

"You sure you're okay?" He said from beside her.

"No, I'm not sure. Let's just get down." When she paused for a breath, she realized Rose was right above them. "Rose, you okay?"

"Better then you, I would imagine."

"True." They made their way down without incident. Lanis was only a few feet from the ground when she felt hands on her back. She would forever be grateful Elson had been chosen to accompany her on this oath. When her feet touched the ground, she placed her hands on her knees, and took a few steadying breaths before standing. She couldn't believe they had all made it down safely.

"Hopefully the climb up won't be as eventful," Rose said.

"Yes, and we do have one thing to look forward to," Lanis said.

"What's that?" Elson asked, sheathing his sword and handed Lanis her bag.

"We also have to cross the river before we can climb up." The way the water rushed by, it seemed unlikely they would make it to the other side. It had to be at least twenty feet across and she wouldn't even guess the depth.

"I wouldn't worry too much about that," Elson said. "We can go down farther. It doesn't look too bad there."

"I can hardly wait," Lanis said. She took the apple Rose handed her.

"It's getting dark and we need to make camp." Elson said, looking around. "I'm sure we'll be safe here."

Lanis walked away from them and stood by the river. She touched her back and winced. Why did it always have to be her back? She wouldn't look until morning. No telling what her body would look like after this was over. She smiled when Elson walked over and stood beside her.

"Are you sure you're okay? That was some fall." He frowned. "For a moment, I thought—"

"Don't." She held her hand up. "I'm sore, and trust me when I say I've had worse, much worse."

※ ※ ※ ※

Anya leaned back in the carriage seat and gazed out the window. The trip so far had been routine and although the scenery was unchanging, she could definitely feel a shift in the air. It had been gradually changing since they left Malora. Merek had been uncharacteristically quiet, but she could see the change in his demeanor also. He was even more confident than before and he was continually pushing his boundaries. When she knelt to pray after awakening that morning, he had knelt beside her, and although it wasn't unusual for him to pray with her, his closeness was far too near for her liking. She knew Nia wouldn't leave her, but the unknown was still frightening.

She braced herself when the carriage turned suddenly and the road became rockier. She could definitely feel the change now. Whatever her fate, Merek and whomever he was working with held it in their hands. She would have never forgiven herself if she had left him in charge of Malora. As the carriage came to an abrupt stop, she knelt on the carriage floor, bowed her head, and prayed. Surely her Protector would step in if someone tried to harm her. She felt Merek shift, the door open, then the carriage swayed as he stepped out. She whipped her head around when the other door opened and her Protector stepped out. She didn't hear any signs of fighting or arguing.

"You let him get away?" Merek said from outside the carriage.

"I didn't let him get away. My orders were for the High Priestess first, then the Protector. It isn't my fault he got away. Didn't you have men at the ready?"

Oh Goddess, she knew that voice. If he was involved, this was far worse than she first thought. She clinched her fist when her door opened and Merek whispered in her ear. "You're not in charge now."

Anya gasped as a cloth was thrown over her head, he dragged her from the carriage, and her body fell to the ground. She cried out when he jerked her up and tied her arms behind her back.

"You will not touch her in that way."

"Now wait a minute," Merek said. "I got her here. You wouldn't have even got close to her if it wasn't for me."

"I would have found a way. I'm in charge of getting her back in one piece and that is exactly what I will do. Whatever issues you have with her, you can deal with in your own time. We're leaving. You'll have to find your own way." He led her away from Merek. "Brace yourself, it may be a bit bumpy," he said, drawing her to him. "I am sorry to touch you this way." She hoped that when Lanis found her, the destruction she left in her wake didn't destroy all of Adearian.

Lanis knelt by the rushing water and splashed some on her face. She had awakened before the others and couldn't go back to sleep. They were still a long way from the falls, but the sound of the falling water still drowned out everything around them. Even if she tried, she wouldn't be able to hear anyone approaching. The power the water held was something that always fascinated her. That's one reason she wasn't looking forward to crossing it. That and the fact that her entire body hurt and was covered in bruises.

"You look deep in thought," Elson said, coming to stand beside her.

She bit back a groan as she stood up. They stood side by side, quietly watching as the sky turned a dark pink over the falls. He wasn't at all what she expected when they started off. He was a good soldier, and a faithful follower of Nia. She was used to working alone, but if it weren't for him, she would be dead right now. "I'm not looking forward to crossing the water, or the climb up."

He crossed his arms and rocked back on his heels. "How bad are your injuries?"

"Not bad." When he didn't look convinced, she went on. "I'm sore and I have bruises where I didn't know I could get bruises, but nothing's broken. I'll do what I have to; I just might be a little slower at it for a while."

Elson sighed, knelt down, and splashed some water on his face. When he stood back up, he had a weird look on his face. "Rose," he hollered. "Can you come here?" He waited for her to join them before going on. "What I'm about to tell you can never be repeated to anyone. As you both know, I'm a member of Malora's army and, as a Ranger, I was taught certain things. I can't tell you how, but I can get us all across the water safely. You both will have to trust me. While you gather your things, I'm going to walk the water's edge and find the right spot to cross."

"Okay," Rose said, walking off.

"I'll get my things." Lanis joined Rose.

"You okay?" Rose asked.

"I'm sore, but I'll live. Thanks for asking." Lanis stood with her bag and watched Elson as he walked along the cliff's edge. He seemed to make up his mind when he turned back and joined them.

"Ready?" He asked, picking up his things.

"Yes," they both said.

"Follow me," he said. "Let me have both of your bags and I'll carry them across first, then I'll take you both across."

"Wait," Lanis said. "Why can't we just follow you?" Maybe she should have asked if he hit his head.

"I learned a lot in my training and I cannot, nor will I, tell you what that was." He shrugged. "It's just one of those things. I'm sure you both have things you don't want to tell me."

Lanis could understand that. "Okay."

"You're okay with this?" Rose said to Lanis. "You trust him that much?"

"I do."

"Good," Elson said. He picked up the bags and confidently stepped onto the water. It looked like he was walking across the top of it. Lanis walked to where he entered and dipped the tip of her boot in. She pulled it back when it broke through the surface. He had a big smile on his face when he came back to them.

"Who's first?" he said.

"Rose will go first," Lanis said. She knew Rose didn't want to go at all, so it would be best if she went first. Elson knelt and Rose climbed onto his back. He slowly stood back up, careful not to drop her.

"Rose, not so tight," he said. She loosened her grip from around his neck.

Lanis watched in amazement as, yet again, he walked across and dropped Rose off, then came back for her.

"Ready?"

"I guess we do all have secrets," she said.

He grinned. "That we do. Climb on," he said, kneeling. As his feet touched the water, she couldn't believe how surreal it felt to be crossing on top of it. When they reached the middle, she tapped him on the shoulder to stop. She knew it would probably be the only time she would ever experience this. The Falls were even more impressive from this view. It was incredible.

"Lanis, we have to go."

"I'm ready."

She felt honored that Elson would share this with them, but at the same time knew he didn't have a choice. She breathed a sigh of relief when her feet touched the ground. "That wasn't so bad," she said.

He laughed. "No, but it is nice on solid ground."

"I second that," Rose said.

"We need to start our climb up," he said, handing them their bags. "This time we will be tied together. I didn't want to use rope before because we don't have that much, but after what happened to Lanis I think we need to tie ourselves together. I will be tied first, then Lanis, then you, Rose. If something were to happen to both of you, I should be able to hold you both. Rose, if you were to slip, Lanis would be able to help you, but if you were first, and me or Lanis slipped, you wouldn't be able to hold us up and we would all go down."

"Makes sense," Rose said.

"Rose," Lanis said. "Is there any way you can get our bags up like you did down?"

"No, I'm afraid not. What stones I have left we need to save. After what's happened so far, we will probably need them."

"I figured that." Lanis bit her lip. "To make things easier, we should distribute our belongings evenly between our bags." After they were done, Elson first tied the rope around his waist, then Lanis's. He then tied the rest of the rope around Rose's waist and through each of her legs.

"It won't be pleasant if someone falls, but it will stop you." There was a few feet slack in-between each of them and he tugged on them to make sure they were secure.

"Wait," Rose said when it was time to climb up. "Neither one of you seem too worried that we're getting ready to enter into Vashta. The Berrocka don't take too kindly to people invading their territory."

Lanis stared at her blankly, then turned to Elson. It hadn't occurred to her where they were headed and it was a costly mistake. This was their only way out and it could get them killed. The Berrocka were known for being unfriendly and unforgiving to anyone that entered their lands without an invitation. She could understand that, because it was the same for the Ramden people. They would have to take their chances. "We don't have a choice. Those men after us aren't going to give up."

"No, we don't, and honestly, I can't believe it

hadn't crossed my mind," Elson said. He turned to Rose. "Lanis is right. We'll have to take our chances. Once we reach the top, I pray that Nia will let us be spared from their wrath and give us a chance to explain. At the top, let's not make any sudden moves." He looked toward Vashta and scratched his chin. "Have either one of you ever meet one?"

"No," they both said.

"Our starting point is over here," he said, leading them to the spot he picked. Lanis watched Elson climb up, dreading her turn. With each reach of her hand, she cringed as her muscles pulled tight. After checking herself that morning, she knew the climb wouldn't be easy. She ignored her body's protests with each movement. At the halfway point, she released some of the anxiety that weighed her down. Her breathing increased when the air around them changed. She jerked her head to the left as an arrow embedded itself in the rocks where her head was seconds before.

"Elson!" she screamed, "Move." They picked up the pace as arrows struck the rocks around them. Her grip slipped and she slammed into the rocks when the rope pulled taut. She scrambled to regain her hold and looked down. Rose lay slumped over into the rocks, an arrow sticking out of her shoulder.

"Rose."

"I can't climb up," she said through clenched teeth.

"Lanis," Elson called out.

"Elson, move down, I have to get to her. We don't have a choice." She made it to Rose, slid down beside her, and pressed her body into the rocks. "Hold on," Lanis said. The arrow had gone clean through her shoulder. "I'm going to break this end off. Brace yourself." She didn't wait for a response, but Rose's screams echoed through the ravine as she pulled the arrow out. "We have to climb, Rose. We have to go now. You'll be between me and Elson. We won't let you fall." Lanis untied the rope from around Rose then from around herself.

"Lanis, what are you doing?" Elson said.

"It's our only choice," she said, tying the rope back around Rose. Out of instinct, she looked back toward the falls and five men stood by the edge. Considering the distance, magic had to be involved. They needed to keep going. She gritted her teeth when an arrow skimmed her shoulder, and looked up in time to see Rose's foot slip. She placed her hand on her back to steady her. She moved her hand against the rocks as Rose regained her footing, screaming as an arrow pierced her hand.

"Lanis!" Elson yelled.

"Keep going." She grimaced with every movement of her hand. She looked up to gauge their distance and her heart sank. Two Berrocka stared down at them. From one danger into another one. With rough movements, they jerked first Elson, then Rose over the side. As her fingers grazed the top of the cliff, hands grabbed her and threw her on top of Rose and Elson. A scream tore from her throat as the arrow was ripped from her hand. Rolling onto her back, she clutched her hand to her chest and closed her eyes. She pushed the pain back as much as she could and opened her eyes, instantly regretting it. A Berrocka stood over her, his spear pointed at her chest.

❧ ❧ ❧ ❧

The constant dripping of water combined with

the musty, dirt encrusted sack covering her head only added to the list of things that were attempting to throw Anya into a downward spiral. Fear was never her first instinct, but the cold floor beneath her and the rough stone she rested back against, along with the other factors, only meant one thing. She was in a cell. Where, she had no clue. She had a sinking feeling she was nowhere near her final destination, though. Merek had more than betrayed her. He had betrayed Nia, along with her followers, and in essence, all the Gods and Goddesses and what they stood for.

On impulse, she attempted to pull her hands in front of her, forgetting for an instant they were tied behind her back. Heart thumping, almost to the point it would beat out of her chest, she swallowed, trying to slow her breathing. She closed her eyes against the blackness of the sack and prayed. A calmness she had never felt before washed over her and brought a smile to her lips. No matter the circumstances, Nia was always with her.

She swung her head around and opened her eyes as voices drifted toward her. After a moment of eerie silence, she heard the all too familiar sound of a door being opened and she squinted into the sack as a soft glow seeped through the fabric. Even with Nia's comfort, she forced her body not to react when footsteps headed in her direction and someone squeezed her shoulder. Not being able to make out any features, or discern any shapes, was more unnerving than anything she could have imagined. A part of her hoped it was Merek, if only for the familiarity.

Without warning, the sack was ripped from her head and she braced herself when she was pushed sideways to the ground. Biting back a groan as her head hit the dirt packed floor, she counted to ten before opening her eyes against the light that suddenly flooded the room. Merek knelt in front of her, grinning. She felt sorry for him. His life was forfeit and he didn't even realize it.

"I am only going to ask once," he said, leaning close to her. "Where is your Protector?"

Anya kept her expression neutral while his eyes bore into hers. Was this about her Protector or was this about her? "I don't know," she said quietly. "I just assumed you had him."

"You mean to tell me that the High Priestess doesn't know how to get in touch with her Protector? Do you take me for a fool?" he spat, and brought his hand down hard across her face. He grabbed her chin and forced her head back around to face him. "There is no one here to stop me, now is there?" he whispered in her ear. "Where is your Protector?"

"I don't know," she said. "My Protector is never to leave my side. So no, I don't know where my Protector is." She jerked away from his grasp and scooted back to the wall. Grasping the stones behind her, she fought her way into a sitting position, ignoring his smug smile. His eyes held a coldness she'd never seen before. Who was the man kneeling in front of her? Was his entire life's dedication to Nia a lie? A week ago, she would have said no, but now she knew better. Out of the corner of her eye, she spied him scooping up a handful of dirt from the floor. She wouldn't give him the satisfaction of her flinching. Instead, she closed her eyes, but when nothing hit her face, she opened them. The dirt hovered in the air in front of her.

"Merek," the Jester said, standing his ground when Merek jumped up. "Childish games aren't necessary." He waved his hand in the air and the dirt disappeared. "Even if she knew where her Protector was, do you think she would tell you? Besides, she is right, her Protector is never to leave her side." He placed himself in front of Anya and pushed Merek back several feet.

"Don't touch me," Merek snapped.

"To tell you the truth," the Jester said, juggling. "I wouldn't put much stock into this Protector. Running at the first sign of trouble. I mean, really," he said mid-throw, "who does that? Especially someone who is rumored to be immortal."

"Let me do this my way." Merek attempted to step around him, but the Jester threw his arm out to stop him.

"Your time with her is up."

"Now listen," Merek said, poking him in the chest.

"My contract isn't with you. I would gladly kill you for my own satisfaction, but I gave my word I wouldn't." He pointed to the door. "Get out."

Merek pivoted on his feet and walked away, stopping at the door. "This isn't over."

After losing sight of him, Anya allowed herself to relax somewhat. She licked her lips, not sure what to expect next.

"Have faith," the Jester mouthed, slipping the sack back over her head.

Her stomach dropped as the door slammed shut. The silence, normally a welcome friend, tortured her with its presence. She bowed her head and prayed.

❧ ❧ ❧ ❧

Lanis tensed, frantically looking for an escape

route, but there wasn't one. Berrocka surrounded them. The soldier's feet stomped in sync with the distant beating of a drum. Lanis paled as the tip of the spear inched closer and closer to her chest. Looking from the tip of the spear, to the necklace hanging around most of their throats, confirmed what only few had ever seen. They were made out of teeth and bone. It was rumored that after the Berrocka killed their first animal they carved the tip of their spears from the animal's hind legs and they made a necklace of the beast's teeth and wore it around their neck. Her eyes darted to their heads where only a few wore a cap made out of their twentieth kill's fur. The man holding the spear on her stepped forward and grinned, pressing the tip into the center of her chest. Lanis closed her eyes, snapping them open when someone shouted for the man to stop. A young boy weaved his way through the crowd and whispered to the woman who was holding a sphere to Elson's chest. Lanis swallowed when the spear was removed and bit back a groan when she was hauled to her feet next to Elson.

"Here," Elson said, ripping a piece of his shirt off and wrapping it around her hand.

"Thanks." She cursed their luck when one of the Berrocka picked Rose up and carried her off.

"We'll get her back," Elson said, leaning close to her, keeping his voice down. "They're bigger than I expected."

Lanis agreed. The men stood at least seven feet tall and most of the women weren't much shorter. Their thick tanned skin only added to their intimidating presence. Along with a spear, the man leading them also wore a bone carved knife on his side. But it wasn't their size or weapons that made them stand apart; it was their eyes. They were a soft cream color. Lanis pulled her gaze away from their escort and concentrated on where they were headed. The farther they walked, the deeper into Vashta they went, and the less likely they were to escape.

It didn't take them long, with the quick pace their guides were setting, to reach an enormous clearing. As they made their way through the center of the village, she could feel dozens of eyes on her. To be completely surrounded brought reality crashing back down. Elson squeezed her hand when they stopped at a large hut set back amongst the trees. Every voice inside the hut halted when they walked in. Berrocka were seated on either side of the aisle and from the sneers on their faces, it wasn't hard to deduce they weren't happy to see them. When their guide stepped out of the way, Lanis got her first look at the King of the Berrocka. He stood taller than the rest and the cap on his head hung down his back. He stood with his arms across his chest and two guards stood on either side and behind him. They each held a spear in their hand. Lanis planted her feet, willing herself not to take a step back as the King took one forward.

"When I was told of who graced our lands I couldn't believe it." The King's deep voice reverberated around the hut. "Oath wearers venturing onto our lands." He spread his arms wide. "Were we supposed to accept you with open arms? Uninvited guests, I might add." His voice rose with each word he spoke. "Not only did these two step foot on our land, but they also disgraced us with the presence of a sorceress." He stomped his foot and spit on the ground. Until this moment, Lanis hadn't realized how much the Berrocka hated magic. The King reached out and accepted the spear one of his guards handed him. "What God do you serve?" He sneered, pounding his spear into the ground.

Before Lanis could speak, Elson took a step forward and answered for them. "We serve Goddess Nia." He brought his right arm across his chest and placed his hand over his heart.

The King halted the pounding of his spear and turned to Lanis. "I want to hear who you serve from your own lips."

"I also serve Goddess Nia." She brought her hand across her chest, leaving a trail of blood down the front of her shirt when she dropped it back to her side.

The King handed the spear back to the guard. "You acknowledge your Goddess without shame and prejudice and with such honor." He shook his head. "Hold up your oath bracelets for everyone to see." They raised their arms high and lowered them when the King nodded in their direction. "We, as a whole, do not believe in, nor do we worship any of the so-called Gods. Out of all the Gods, Nia's followers, compared to the other God's followers, are the only ones to ever show our kind respect. Which in today's society is very hard to come by. You're lucky that someone happened to see your bracelet. We do not take kindly to strangers entering our lands. Most would be killed on the spot. I am sure, however, you would both find our ways distasteful."

Lanis took a step forward. Now was not the time to cower. Nia had gotten them this far; it was up to them to get themselves out of this mess. "I was not born in Malora. My people feel as you do. Trespassers are not looked on kindly and most who enter our lands never make it out. I truly am grateful you've allowed us this long to live."

The King turned away from them, climbed two steps onto his platform, and sat down in a simple wooden chair. "I see," the King said. "Your honesty is refreshing." He accepted a piece of paper from a guard, unfolded it and held it up. "Do you know you have a bounty on your heads? It's a shame, really, they only describe your scar." He crumpled it up and threw it on the ground. "It has always amazed me how all people see is a glimpse of someone and not really see the person at all. Now me, I would have described your strength and beauty. Both which are clearly evident. The scar, at least to me, was an afterthought. Maybe because we all have them. Whether they're visible to the naked eye or not." He turned to Elson. "They only described you as a large man in the Malora army who travels with the woman with the scar. These men are not very imaginative, or thought provoking." He laughed.

At least now she knew why they were getting attacked at every turn. She shrugged when the laughter died down. "People see what they want to." She touched her chest and locked eyes with the King. "Some would see you as a beast, not fit to roam where others would. Me, I see a man who loves his people and would do anything to keep them safe. A leader capable of making the hard decisions, whether they are for the right, or wrong reason. But what is right for one person isn't necessarily right for another. You protect your people and I respect that."

"Would you have respected me if I had allowed you to be killed on the spot?"

"I would have. My people would have done the same thing. It takes the right person to make the wrong decision for the right reasons." She ran her hand through her hair. "May I ask a question?"

"You may."

"Were we spared because of our oath bracelets, or because of the bounty?" He laughed and stepped down from his chair and extended his hands to them. Lanis accepted, as did Elson.

"I am King Strunkot of the Berrocka and it wouldn't have mattered about the bounty. You're wanted dead or alive." He stepped back and planted his hands on his hips. "What are your names?"

"I am Elson, a humble servant of Nia."

"I am Lanis." She noticed a subtle shift in his demeanor at her name. He took a step back and everyone turned to the back of the room when the door slammed open, a woman stepped in, and made her way to Strunkot's side. She whispered in his ear, then stepped to his right.

This couldn't be good. Elson stepped toward her and placed his hand on her back. Whoever the woman was, she had the entire hut in an uproar. She wore a thick cap on her head and a long necklace around her neck that was adorned with dozens of different size teeth. Besides the spear in her hand, she had a bow strapped to her back. She was a warrior.

"I ask that everyone please leave the room," Strunkot said, not leaving any room for any doubt that what the woman had to say was important. When the room was cleared, he turned back to them. "I am sorry, Elson, but I must speak to Lanis alone."

He shook his head and wrapped his arm around her waist. "I don't think so."

"Elson," Lanis said.

"No, don't. We've discussed these matters."

"Elson." She placed her hand on his shoulder. "I am all right. I'll meet you and Rose later." She looked back at the King. "I will meet them both later, won't I?"

"You will."

"If not," she said, turning back to Elson. "You can tear this whole place apart. Please go." He hesitated, but let four of the Berrocka guards lead him away. It wasn't like him to be so possessive. He must have been really on edge. She couldn't blame him - so was she - but she had to know what was going on. She stepped back when both the King and the woman bowed. "I don't understand. What's going on?"

"Please accept my most humble apologies, Protector," the woman said.

Lanis stiffened, but kept her face expressionless. "What are you talking about?"

"You are...please do not think me a fool. You are Protector of the High Priestess of Nia," the woman said.

"You don't have to confirm," Strunkot said. "Which makes me wonder why you're here and who is taking care of High Priestess Anya. Though, it was prophesied that you would come. We as a people do not believe in magic, but to have the gift of a seer is not magic to our people. It is an honor and a gift passed from mother to daughter. It was also prophesied I should help you, so that is what I will do."

This was the last thing she expected. No one, least of all these people, should have known who she was. She knew Elder Helt and Anya would have never told anyone and they were the only ones who knew. It was more than a little unsettling that this woman knew about her. She and Anya would have to have a long talk when she got home. King Strunkot may not have killed them yet, but he was up to something. She didn't believe for one second he wasn't above disregarding a direct vision for his own gain.

"Where are you headed?" the woman asked.

She hesitated at the question, but they could only be headed one place. "Manight."

"I find it my duty," the King said, "to inform you Manight is in a bit of unrest at the moment. You would never know it to walk through the city because they hide it well."

If Anya had known, she would have informed them; it must have been a new development. Something else they had to deal with. "I am sure they have a lot to deal with, preparing for the festival and the reading."

He nodded. "They do, but Princess Jalen was attacked on her way home from the Brown Pass. She almost died from her injuries and Queen Abigail vowed that she wouldn't stop until she found those responsible for the attack on her daughter, who also happens to be her heir. They say magic was involved. I always wondered how long it would take magic to make its way into Manight. It's taken almost five hundred years."

She could have cared less about the magic, but Jalen being attacked was another matter. If she was attacked once, the culprits wouldn't stop if they really wanted her dead. They needed to get to Manight sooner, rather than later. Since they knew who she was, hopefully they would let them go unharmed. "My friends are all right, aren't they?"

"They are."

"Rose was taken from us earlier. I hope to get medical attention."

"Yes, she was taken to one of our healers," he

answered, and held his hand up. "And before you ask. We do employ healers. We may not believe in, or practice magic, but we also aren't stupid. Healers are a necessity."

"They do come in handy. We will need to leave as soon as possible." She would explain everything to the others later.

"Very well. You will stay the night. We have food and shelter for you. In the morning, you and Elson will be escorted to the border, where you will cross the bridge into Hadmore."

Lanis crossed her arms across her chest and held her ground. He may have been a foot taller than her, but she'd never let anyone bigger than her get the best of her and this wouldn't be the first time. "That's all well and good, but we are not leaving without Rose." She wouldn't allow these people to keep her and she wasn't feeling up to another rescue.

"That's not the way things work," he bellowed, and the woman took a step back. "The vision plainly stated three would arrive, but only two would leave. She stays with us."

"No, that's not the way I work. My High Priestess ordained this and she is a part of my group. She will be leaving with us."

"You will not tell me what to do," he said, accepting the spear from the warrior.

"You do what you must and I'll do what I must. If we are not allowed to leave together, I will make it my life's mission to wipe your people out of existence." She let her hand slip to her the handle of her whip when his knuckles turned white on the spear.

"How dare you. I do not take lightly to threats. I should kill you where you stand."

"King, the Prophecy," the woman said and stepped back when he glared at her.

Lanis was thankful for prophesies when he handed the warrior back the spear.

"I don't make threats lightly. It has been a long road for the three of us and we will make it to our final destination as a whole."

After a moment of silence, he spoke. "I will allow the three of you to leave, but be warned that you are going against one of our direct visions. Things will not turn out like you hope. Are you willing to take that chance?"

"Yes."

"All three of you will be escorted in the morning. Lanis, your past will come back to haunt you."

She bowed her head. "When has it not?"

The warrior walked up to her and took her hand. "Let's get you to the healers." Lanis's feet never halted even though she could feel everyone's eyes on her. They walked down a long dirt path and entered a moderate sized hut. Cots lined one side and tables lined the other. Elson sat by the fire and stood when she walked in. The relief on his face was a welcome sight compared to the hostility of the Berrocka. Rose lay on a table next to him. Her shoulder had been wrapped and it looked like she was sleeping. Lanis turned when a healer walked up to her and lifted her hand.

"I don't think the arrow hit anything vital, which is a plus," she said, turning Lanis's hand over, and examining it. She carefully laid it down and looked up. Lanis's stomach dropped at the look in the woman's eyes. She wasn't Berrocka. "I can heal your hand and your friend's shoulder completely, but not without something in return."

Lanis sighed. It never failed. That's how this was going to work. It seemed lately everybody wanted something from her. A favor for a favor. "What do you want?"

The healer leaned forward and lowered her voice. "When you get to Manight, I want you to kill someone for me."

If it was just her and her hand wasn't in such poor shape, she would have ignored the woman, but it wasn't just her. "Elson," Lanis said, without turning away from the woman. "How bad are Rose's injuries?"

"They removed the arrow and stopped the bleeding, but the healer said she would never be able to use her shoulder the same again. She'll live, but not without problems. The healer also said, with her type of injury, she will have to rest before we move on. They offered to keep her here until she is able to get on her way. Like we would ever allow that to happen."

Lanis smiled at his words. Seemed he had grown fond of Rose as well. She would never be able to live with herself if Rose was permanently hurt. What was one more death on her conscious? "Who?"

The healer's cold, calculating smile gave her pause, but she still accepted the piece of paper she handed her. Lanis slid it in her pocket and climbed on the table. She cringed at the cup the woman handed her. A deep crimson liquid stared back at her.

"Lanis," Elson said, coming to stand beside her. "What are you doing? Rose didn't have to drink anything."

Ignoring him, she downed the contents, then handed the cup back to the healer. "Getting another healing." She knew the drink was an oath to the woman, but she didn't have a choice. She winced when the woman spit on her hand and rubbed some sort of powder into the wound. She closed her eyes and relaxed back onto the table.

"Lanis."

She opened her eyes. Elson stood beside her bed. Considering how much the fire had died down, she must have been asleep a while. "Why didn't you wake me?"

"I figured after everything we've been through, sleep was the one thing you needed right now."

"How's Rose?" She accepted his hand and pushed off the table. Her legs wobbled and he placed a hand on her shoulder to steady her.

"She'll be fine. Let's wake her so we can go to our quarters for the night."

"We will rest tonight, then we'll be escorted to the border in the morning."

"Good. I'm ready to leave this place." He pulled her to a stop before they reached Rose. "What did the healer hand you?" He held his hand up. "And don't tell me it was nothing. The healer that took care of Rose told me he had no way of healing her more than he already had. He said there wasn't anything else he could do for her. Now she's completely healed. What did you do?"

"What I had to and that's all I'm saying. We are all burdened with things that we have to deal with. Please, let it go." She pulled away from him, walked up to Rose, and shook her shoulder.

Rose groaned and opened her eyes. "What happened?" Elson helped her sit up. She rounded her shoulder and frowned. "What happened to my shoulder? It doesn't even hurt." She looked from Lanis to Elson. Elson turned his face away from her. "Guys."

Lanis shrugged. "My hand is healed also. Must be Nia looking out for us. As I told Elson, King Strunkot has been gracious enough to allow us to stay the night and provide us dinner. In the morning, we will be led to the border where we will cross into Hadmore."

Elson frowned, but nodded. "If you're ready, Rose, let's go." Rose nodded and he helped her down. Lanis patted her pocket when they exited the medical hut, where a guard waited to lead them to their quarters for the night. She kept back a few feet from the others, unfolded the note, and came to a complete stop when she read the name on the paper. She crumbled the note and threw it into the nearest fire then caught up with the others. She couldn't believe this. It seemed her list of things to do kept getting longer and longer. Stupidly, she hadn't even asked the healer's name. The one name she did know was the name printed on the paper; Lady Sara. She would have to find a way out of this one. There was no way she could, or would kill her. She was Queen Abigail's wife. Things just got a lot more complicated and not in a good way.

❧❧❧❧

"Ready to get out of here?" Elson said, breaking Lanis from her thoughts.

"Yes." Sleep had been elusive, especially since she couldn't take her mind off of Strunkot. She wasn't new to the game. He was up to something. Even the sprinkling of purples and pinks ascending the horizon couldn't shake the anxiety that had taken a hold of her when they were pulled over the edge. She rubbed her neck. They were so close. From the border, it would take at least three days on horseback to reach the royal estate. She drank the last of her tea and slipped the cup back in her pack, turning to Elson. "Things aren't adding up. We've been targeted from the beginning." She ran her hands through her hair. "I guess what's really bothering me is not a lot of people knew about our oath."

"I know," he said. "We know the bounty was put on us before Klate. Rose wasn't on it." He shrugged. "Or they do know about her and only want us. Look," he said, patting her shoulder. "We don't know why someone told and who they told; all we can do is what we we're asked to."

"That doesn't comfort me in the least," she said.

Elson laughed. "We'll be extra cautious in Manight."

"I'm ready," Rose said, tying her bag. She stood when she saw the look on their faces. "Why do you both look so worried? Just another day, right?"

"Well," Elson said. "We're not out of here yet and we," he said, pointing between himself and Lanis, "do have a bounty on our heads."

"True," Rose agreed. "And I won't be able to use magic in Hadmore, but I will have my bow," she said, holding it up.

"Yes, it is a good thing you have something to fall back on." Elson smiled.

"Yes, good thing. Look," Rose said, running her hands through her hair. "What happened to me? I know I was struck with an arrow, but that's all I remember until I woke up in that hut. I was in pretty bad shape."

"You weren't going to die, but your shoulder was in pretty bad shape. See." Lanis held up her hand. "She healed my hand too."

"Usually there's a price to pay for that kind of

healing. Who paid mine?" She looked between them both.

"It was my price to pay," Lanis said. She couldn't make out the look that crossed Rose's face. Shock, relief, sadness.

"You saved my life?"

"Like I said, your life wasn't in danger. I saved your shoulder. Besides, I just opened the door for it to happen." Lanis turned and watched a Berrocka approach them, carrying a platter of food.

"You are to eat and then King Strunkot will escort you to the border. What you don't eat you can take with you." She handed the tray to Lanis, turned, and walked away. They ate and packed what little was left into their bags. It didn't take long for King Strunkot to make an appearance.

"You all look refreshed," King Strunkot said. "I hope you're ready. Follow me."

Lanis kept a discreet distance from the others. Nothing about the King's appearance or continence was different, but something was throwing off alarm bells in her gut. By the way Elson held himself, she could tell he sensed something was off also. The walk to the border took a little over two hours. Lanis blew out a breath and eyed the bridge, or more appropriately, what was left of it. For some reason, she had expected it to look more secure. The wood was rotted and cracked in several areas, making it impossible to determine its age, other than old. The ropes that ran the length were brittle and breaking. The distance across seemed unimaginable. In reality, it was at least a mile long, maybe more. Below the bridge, a massive structure stood some hundred feet down. Considering the trees and vines had taken over the outer walls and roof, the building was ancient. That type of damage didn't happen overnight. Time and the elements had destroyed what once was more than likely an amazing piece of architecture. Time slowed for no man or thing.

Elson pointed to the ravine below. "Some drop."

"What do you make of that?" she said, pointing to the ruins.

He squinted where she pointed. "What do I make of what?" He eyed her, then the ravine. "Do you see something?"

She closed her eyes then opened them and the ruins were gone. She stepped back from the bridge, heart racing. To her knowledge and experience, buildings didn't just disappear. She knew what she saw, but obviously, Elson hadn't seen it. She grasped his arm. "It's nothing. I didn't get much sleep last night."

He narrowed his eyes. "You sure?"

"Yes."

"Okay." He looked from the bridge to Strunkot. "You can't expect us to walk across that."

King Strunkot shrugged. "It is the only way. Either you walk across, or we push you off. Your choice."

"Elson, Rose, let's go. He won't change his mind. I wish we could tie ourselves together, but we don't have any rope left." She would die before letting someone else decide her fate.

"We'll be all right," Rose said. Lanis noticed her patting her pocket. Maybe things weren't as dire as first thought.

"Good luck," the King said, smiling.

"We don't need luck." Lanis held her breath as Elson took his first step onto the bridge.

"It's a bit spongy, so watch your step and keep your hands tightly around the ropes. Whatever is left of the ropes, that is," he murmured. He took a few more steps, and Rose followed behind him. She was having a harder time than he was. Lanis still couldn't believe they were actually walking across it. She stepped onto the bridge after Rose because she wasn't sure how much weight it would hold. She hated heights. She stopped when Elson halted ahead of them. She didn't feel comfortable stopping. The slight sway of the bridge made her stomach queasy.

"There are a few boards missing, and I don't want to risk jumping. That might cause this thing to give way. We'll need to walk on the edges of the ropes until we get past these few missing boards. Make sure your feet are secure. I'm not going to lie; this isn't going to be easy. We don't have a choice." Elson easily stepped onto the ropes along the edges and, in a couple of steps, he was across. Lanis held her breath when Rose tried and failed to spread her feet the width of the bridge. Her legs weren't long enough to span the length comfortably.

"I'll come back over and carry her across," Elson said. "Lanis, stick close behind in case something happens."

"Won't it be too much weight?" Rose said.

"Doesn't matter. We don't have a choice," Elson said. It didn't take long for him to come back across. He made it look so easy. "Climb on." He knelt down.

Their combined weight would be a lot and the bridge's sturdiness was questionable. They were only a quarter of the way across. Elson made it safely across and Lanis braced herself to do the same.

"Come on, Lanis," Elson said. "I'm afraid I can't carry you across. Our combined weight would be too much."

"Are you trying to tell me something?"

"No, not at all. Don't tarry," he said, seriously.

She placed one foot on either side of the bridge. It felt unnatural for her legs to be in this position, so far apart. She slowly moved one foot then the other, when her foot slipped off the rope. She grabbed a board at the same time Elson grabbed her arm and pulled her onto the other side. They both scrambled back from the edge and Elson laughed.

"You sure are making it a habit of me saving you," he said, standing. "Let's carry on. Strunkot doesn't look happy. He's up to something."

"I know. He's been up to something since last night," Lanis said.

"Yes, he is," Rose said from behind them.

Lanis accepted the hand Elson held out to her and stood. He took up the lead with Lanis in the rear. The closer they got to the border, the more secure she felt and the more secure the boards felt under her feet. She felt compelled to look back and her heart dropped. She watched as, in slow motion, Strunkot raised a sword. "Grab a hold of the rope and hold on. Brace yourself!" she screamed.

"Why?" Elson hollered.

"We're about to…" Lanis screamed when the bridge beneath her feet collapsed. Her heart was in her throat as they flew through the air. Her heart rate tripled as the cliff walls came closer and closer. She held on tightly to a plank as they slammed into the rock wall. She didn't have time to think, just react, when Rose slipped and fell into her. One of her hands held tightly to Rose and the other gripped the rope. "Rose, you're going to have to grab onto a plank. I can't hold us both." Her shoulder was on fire. When

Rose reached up and was able to hold on, Lanis swung her body around and placed her hand on the opposite side. Rose was between her and the bridge. "Elson, you okay?" He was holding tightly to a wood plank.

"I…yes…just give me a moment. I…think," he gasped, pulling his right hand out from behind the bridge, "my hand's broken."

"I'm fine, but my shoulder is killing me and Rose slammed pretty hard into the wall." Lanis knew they hit hard, but they should all be dead right now. There was only one explanation for why they weren't. Magic. "Rose, you okay?"

"Not really. My head is killing me, but on the bright side, the spell worked, some."

"That it did. You're going to have to climb up, or I'm going to fall off."

"I'm going to give it my best shot."

Lanis cringed with each step that Rose took up, and was ready if her foot slipped again. She glanced past Rose, gauging they were halfway across when Strunkot cut the rope. He would pay for that; she would make sure of it. She rested her head on the bridge and counted to ten. They were so close. Giving up now wasn't an option. "Elson, we're going to climb up until we reach you. Then we'll figure something out."

"Sounds like a plan." His hand shook on the ropes.

Lanis grabbed a plank, pulled herself up, and was grateful when it held. She climbed one, then another, finally reaching Rose. "Rose, you have to help him. I can't climb above you."

"Oh Goddess," Rose said, looking down then jerking her face back up. She touched her cheek and cringed.

"You're okay, but we need to start climbing up. We don't know what else the King has in store for us. Elson needs our help."

"What am I supposed to do? His hand's broken. How is he going to make it up?"

"I'll do my best," he said. "I sure didn't expect this. I'm telling you, Lanis, I've had more adventure with you than I have ever had before."

He was barely holding on. "We'll do what we have to. Rose, you have to calm down. You don't happen to have something that can help him."

Rose shook her head, then stilled. "I might have, but it will only be temporary and I've never actually used it on a living being before."

"I'll take my chances," Elson said.

"Elson, hold still," Rose said. "I don't know what side effects it will have. I don't know if it will even work. Ready?"

"I don't have a choice so, yes, I'm ready. I don't know how much longer I can hold on."

Rose took a small pink stone out of her pocket and asked Elson to put his broken hand behind him. His hand was twisted, swelling, and turning a deep shade of purple. Several of the bones were sticking out at odd angles.

"I'm sorry." Rose placed the stone in his palm and closed his hand around it. Lanis didn't know what kept him from screaming. Rose bowed her head and spoke a few words before blowing on his hand. A faint pink mist encircled it and quickly turned a brighter pink, almost red. He flexed his hand and tentatively placed it on the plank above his head. He pulled up and stood firm.

"That's amazing," he said. "How long will it last?"

"I don't know, but I don't think you have much time. When the brightness starts to fade, the spell will soon wear off and the pain will be incredible. We will need to be at the top because I don't think you'll be able to hold on once it wears off. We need to move."

The first hundred feet or so were pretty easy and Elson moved at a good pace. The closer they got to the top, the more the damage to the bridge became quite apparent. Elson started slowing down and Lanis struggled to keep up with the others. She might have done more damage to her shoulder then she initially thought, plus the bruising from the day before didn't help matters. The pain rippled down her neck to the tips of her fingers. She halted and looked up when Rose stopped above her. Lanis sucked in a breath when Elson's body shook against the bridge; his arms were wrapped tightly around the plank. They were only a quarter of the way from the top, but he wouldn't be able to make it any farther on his own. The spell, by this time, had almost completely faded. They didn't stand a chance if they didn't keep going, and she wouldn't leave him here. "Elson, you have to keep going."

"I…I'm…trying."

Lanis's eyes widened when she heard, then saw movement above them. Four men peered over the edge, staring down at them. In her experience strange men usually meant trouble. She exhaled when she noticed their uniforms; they were blue and black, Hadmore's military colors.

"Hold on," one of the soldiers yelled down. "You will have to climb a little farther up in order to reach the rope." He stood back to allow another man to drop a rope over the edge. A once unattainable goal now seemed within reach, but the fact remained they were still a good twenty feet from the rope.

"Elson, you can't stop," Lanis said. "We're almost there." He didn't answer her; instead, he reached up, grabbed the next plank, and struggled to pull his body up. As his hand clasped onto the plank above him, the plank ripped off, and Lanis watched in horror as he struggled to hold on with his broken hand. He swung his body back and forth and hugged the bridge. Rose climbed up and steadied his feet. If he could climb up a few more feet, he would be eye level with the rope.

"Elson, you've got this," Lanis called out. When he looked down at her, she allowed some of her worry to wash away at the determination on his face. He nodded, reached for the next plank, and the next. The rope was now within his reach.

"How do we know we can trust them?" Elson said.

"We don't," Rose said.

"She's right," Lanis said. "There is no other way. Besides, you're the biggest of the three of us. If they can pull you up, we know they can handle Rose and me."

He laughed. "Makes sense." In order to reach the rope, he would have to use his good hand. Holding on with his broken hand seemed impossible considering the pink mist had all but vanished. Lanis held her breath when he bowed his head, then reached over, and slipped his hand through the loop at the end of the rope at the same time that he let go of the plank. His body swung in the air, and she let out the breath she was holding when they started pulling him up. It didn't take long until he disappeared over the edge and the rope was thrown back down.

"Rose, your turn."

"Yes." She didn't sound the least bit excited. Lanis could relate; she wasn't either. She didn't trust easy and at every turn of this trip, all she faced involved trust, in one way or another. The people, the places, the experiences.

Rose reached the plank next to the rope. "Guess it's my turn."

"You'll be okay. Do the same thing Elson did. Hold tight with both hands."

"Okay." Rose reached for the rope, but it slipped from her grasp and she plastered herself against the bridge. Lanis scrambled up the planks and placed her hand on one of Rose's legs.

"Stay calm, you're fine. Take a deep breath and try again." Lanis leaned away from her when she grabbed the rope and her feet left the bridge. She should have listened when Anya told her to get her fear of heights under control. Now the choice had been taken out of her hands. She looked to her left as the rope landed next to her. It was her turn.

"Ready?" one of the men asked.

"I am." She didn't have a choice. It was her only way out of this mess. She reached over, slipped her arm through the rope, and held on with both hands as she pushed off the bridge. It was an odd feeling, being suspended in the air. When they started pulling her up, she felt such relief she almost cried. The last few days were starting to get to her. A person could only take so much, no matter how strong they claimed to be. She couldn't wait to get this over with and go home. She opened her eyes when the pulling stopped. A soldier grabbed her and pulled her over the side. Feeling the ground beneath her feet was, at the moment, one of the best things she had ever felt before. She placed her hands on her knees and bowed her head, giving a silent thanks to Nia.

When she stood, the guard who pulled her over spoke. "Elson told us a little about what happened with the Berrocka. You're lucky," he said. "They usually don't let those that wander into their lands live."

"A few weeks ago I would have said we were lucky, but now, now I know someone is watching over us and for that I will forever be grateful. For her and for you. Thank you." She searched the area for the others. Elson was propped up against a tree and he held his bandaged hand close to his chest. Rose stood beside him. "How do you both feel?" she said, walking over to them.

"I've had worse." He winked at her.

Rose shrugged and touched her face. "I'll be okay, but I wouldn't say no to a healer right now."

"I hear you," Lanis said.

They all turned when the same guard that helped them approached. "I didn't get a chance to introduce myself to you," he said to Lanis. "I'm Captain Ricks of the Queen's Army. You have just entered Hadmore." He rocked back on his heels. "I couldn't help but notice the bands on your wrists. Is your business in Hadmore?"

"Manight," Lanis answered. He looked typical of a solider.

He shook his head. "I understand. You are currently in Lardon. We will escort you to our Army Guild house, where one of our healers will see you, and you will be given something to eat. I'm sorry." He frowned. "I can only imagine what you've been through, but it is at least an hour's walk away." He didn't wait for them to answer; he just turned and walked off, expecting them to follow. Lanis did find it a little strange they didn't question them. Maybe that would come later. They fell in line behind him and after a mile or so, he spoke again. "These next couple of miles are downhill and the rocks are slippery, so watch your step."

Lanis was starting to think she had done major damage to her shoulder when she slipped a third time and fell backward, landing on it. She didn't say anything, just let Captain Ricks help her up. She was grateful when the landscape evened out and they finally reached the Guild house. The Captain took them directly inside to see the Commander, who greeted them and instructed them to sit.

The Commander leaned forward and folded her hands. "I've been in this position long enough to know when to not ask questions. I assume you," she said, pointing to Rose, "Are a sorceress?"

"I am," Rose said. They were all in pretty poor shape. Couldn't these questions wait until later? They needed to see a healer.

"Once you reach Belir, you will have to check in at your Guild house. You will receive your cuff bracelet."

"Yes, ma'am, I know," Rose said through clenched teeth.

"Good," the Commander said and stood. "You will see our healers and get something to eat. If you want to leave after that, I will have three horses ready for you. Once you reach the Guild house you will have to surrender the horses, but you will receive new ones for your journey into Manight."

They walked out of the office and entered a large room. "The healers will be with you shortly," the Commander said and left.

They each sat on a bed and Lanis laid back on hers. "What a trip."

"You're not kidding," Elson said. "This is the most action I have ever seen."

"I agree," Rose said. "The people back in Klate would never believe what I've been through and actually survived. If it wasn't for both of you, I would be dead now."

"As would we. We might not have started out on the right foot, but you have been a great asset to us, Rose, and our trip isn't done yet. I estimate once we reach Manight, we will have to travel at least three days before we reach the Estate," Lanis said.

Everyone grew quiet when the healers walked in. When the healer assigned to Lanis grabbed her shoulder, she growled.

"Oh hush," the woman said. "You warrior types are all the same. Now hold still."

Lanis instantly liked her. She reminded her of her mother. Stern, but gentle. She missed her parents. She only hoped Anya got to them before anyone else did.

"Take your shirt off," the healer said, reaching up and pulling a curtain around them. Lanis hadn't even noticed the curtain. She reached down to lift her shirt when the woman gasped and stepped back.

Lanis sighed. She didn't have time for this. "I am Ramden, is that going to be a problem?"

"Well…I."

Lanis pulled her shirt back down. "Maybe you should get your Commander."

"Good idea." The healer practically ran out of the room.

"What did you do?" Elson asked.

"I guess she didn't find my streaks all that appealing."

"I don't know," he said, "I find them quite fetching."

"Funny guy." She laid back and waited. She struggled, but sat up when the curtain opened and the healer and Commander stepped in.

"What seems to be the problem?" The Commander said, looking between them both.

"You didn't tell her?"

"I thought you should be the one to," she said, looking away.

Good grief. Lanis lifted her shirt as far as she could. Her streaks were a deep, dark maroon. The healer stepped back.

"They weren't that bright when I first saw them," the healer said.

"If I'm correct, the reason the streaks are brighter is either because she's upset, or she's in pain."

Lanis instantly relaxed and the streaks begin to lighten. The Commander knew what she was and didn't seem bothered in the least. "I've had a long day."

"Yes, you have," the Commander said, turning to the healer. "Is it going to be a problem for you to heal her?"

"No. I just have never seen anything like that. I've heard about the Ramden, but never actually seen one before. It just surprised me."

"Really?" The Commander said, and crossed her arms across her chest. "In the future, when I send someone to you to be healed, I expect you to heal them, no questions asked. I have never, nor would I ever, put you or any of the other healers in danger. Did you even notice the oath bracelet on her hand?"

The healer's eyes widened and she gulped. "No."

"I see. You were too busy judging her."

"Yes." She hung her head.

"If I may, Commander," Lanis said. "I can understand her reluctance. I am a bit different from her so I can understand the shock she must have felt. Let's move on from this. If she's still willing to look at my shoulder, that would be great, seeing as it feels like it's going to fall off my body."

"Oh my. Of course. Of course. Commander, please leave us," the healer said, pushing the Commander back through the curtain.

"Good luck." The Commander nodded and left.

"I'm going to need it." Lanis stood and allowed the healer to help her take her shirt off. She gasped when the healer hit a particularly tender spot.

"I think you have a few broken bones. There is extensive muscle and tissue damage. Good grief. What happened to your back? You do realize you are not indestructible. This is going to take longer than I expected. Goodness, you're covered in bruises. Close your eyes and lie still."

Lanis didn't remember falling asleep, but when she opened her eyes, she was alone. After slipping her shirt on, she slid off the bed, and rounded her shoulder. The pain was completely gone. Not seeing anyone in the hall, she continued past the Commander's office and into the main room. She stopped short when the woman standing at the window turned around. Kaylynn, the white-band healer of Malora, was staring at her. "What are you doing here?"

"Lanis," she said. "I didn't expect to run into you here. I saw Elson and your companion outside."

"I didn't expect to see you here either. I thought you always stayed in Malora." Lanis had to keep in mind that Kaylynn only knew her as the woman she saved. She didn't know her as Protector.

"I actually came early for the festival. So much has been happening that I thought some time away would be good and High Priestess Anya was gracious enough to grant me the time off."

"Time away is good for the soul," Lanis agreed.

Kaylynn swallowed. "Yes, it is."

"Kaylynn, I have what you were looking for." The Commander stopped just inside the door. "It's good to see you up, Lanis. Your friends are outside. They were waiting for you to wake before they got something to eat."

"Thank you, Commander." Lanis turned back to Kaylynn. "High Priestess Anya was very kind to me. I hope she was well when you left?"

If the question surprised Kaylynn, she didn't show it. "High Priestess Anya left a few days before I did. She took the Prophecy to Manight. She should have already arrived."

"I see." Anya hadn't told her that she would be leaving. She should have been with her instead of on this journey. The only good thing about reaching Manight is that she would get to see Anya when she got there. "That's good." Lanis felt drawn to her and didn't know why. She couldn't turn away from her pull. Not a sexual pull, but more of a spiritual one.

The Commander cleared her throat and looked between them both. "I take it you two know each other."

She had to get out of here. It felt like the room was closing in on her. "She saved my life. Literally brought me back from the edge." She looked in Kaylynn's eyes. "I will forever be truly grateful, although, her hard work was almost for naught after what we've been through."

Kaylynn straightened and frowned. "There has

been trouble?"

"I don't think trouble is a big enough word," Lanis said.

"Are you kidding me? Trouble doesn't even cover it," Elson said, laughing and walking in the room. "You look good. Shoulder okay?"

Rose waked in behind him. "We were waiting for you so we could eat."

Lanis nodded. "All seems well, but really, at this point, who would know?"

"I hear that," Elson said, turning to Kaylynn. "You look familiar." He squinted at her.

"She's the healer in the central temple in Malora," Lanis said.

Elson snapped his fingers and frowned. "You're a long way from home."

"As are you," Kaylynn said.

"Too true." He smiled and turned back to Lanis. "Ready?"

"I am. Commander, thank you for everything. Kaylynn, it was good to see you again. Let's go, I'm starving." Lanis felt a sense of loss when they walked outside. She turned back to the building and Kaylynn stood at the window, staring at her.

"Lanis, come on." Elson patted her arm.

"I'm coming." She didn't know what was going on. There wasn't any reason for Kaylynn to be here. She hoped it didn't involve Anya, but if it did, she could do nothing about it.

⁂

After an enjoyable meal of beans, potatoes, flatbread, and a thick sauce Lanis couldn't identify, they were escorted to Lardon's border. Their guide instructed them if they kept to the main road, they would reach Belir within a couple of hours. Time flew and Lanis felt a deep sense of relief when the Belir sign came into view. By all standards, the town wasn't large, but it was well organized, and with the clear instructions their guide had given them, they were soon standing before the Guild House.

Compared to the basic, simple design of the town, the Guild House looked out of place. Intricate stone detailing and carved wood pillars adorned the outer walls. A stone statue of Shara, dressed in a long flowing dress, stood in front of the building, welcoming visitors. In her outstretched hand, an orb sat at the ready to defend her people. Lanis and Elson stood quietly by as Rose knelt in front of Shara and prayed. Rose touched Shara's hand and rejoined the others. "Ready?" she asked.

They both nodded and Lanis lead the way. As soon as her foot touched the first step, the guards on either side of the doors took notice. Stepping in front of them, she pulled back her sleeve, revealing her oath bracelet. The guard to her right nodded and opened the door for them to enter. A man stood by the window and turned toward them when they walked in. "What can I do for you today?" he asked.

"We're here to see the Guild Master," Elson said, from behind her.

"Also," Lanis added, "The Guild House in Lardon instructed us to turn our horses they lent us over to you."

The man nodded. "I will have someone take care of them. Do you have something for the Guild Master?"

"Sorry." Lanis handed him a folded note bound

with High Priestess Anya's seal. He accepted it and left the room.

He returned a short time later and pointed toward the hallway. "He will see you now. First open door." He sat at his desk without another glance their way.

Lanis shrugged and walked down the hall. She hesitated briefly, then walked through the only open door. The man behind the desk stood when they entered. He wasn't at all what she expected. He looked too young to hold such a position. He kept his long hair down, tucked neatly behind his ears, and like Elson, he kept his beard neat and short.

"Please have a seat," he said, pointing to the three chairs in front of his desk. "When you are ready to leave, there will be three horses ready for you. I took the liberty to send word to The Green Dragon Inn and booked three rooms for you tonight. It is located just as you enter Manight, a good hour from when you leave here. For the rest of your stay in Manight, you will have to find your own accommodations, but since you are early for the festival that shouldn't be a problem." He then turned his full attention on Rose. "Rose, please come here. I have received word from your Guild House and they have instructed me to expect you. Please hand over the items you have left. You will get them back when you leave the city." Rose hesitated, but laid two round stones and one square one on the table. When he looked up sharply, she took a step back.

"That's all I have left," she said. "With respect, Guild Master, we have had a rather unexpected journey so far. Things haven't exactly gone like I expected."

When he still didn't look convinced, Lanis chimed

in. "I'm not sure what the problem is, but we hired her to help in any way she could. I assure you, sir, what she used was necessary. If it hadn't been for her, we would all be dead."

"Oh no, I'm sure we would all be dead," Elson added happily.

"I see. What other items did you have in your possession?" When she told him, he got a weird look on his face. "That's all he gave you?"

She fidgeted. "I am not sure my Guild Master is confident in my abilities."

"Is that so? Give me your hand." He clasped her hand between his. "Close your eyes." The room quickly filled with a gray fog that vanished when he let go of her hand. "You certainly have had quite the adventure and your former Guild Master truly underestimated your abilities."

"Yes, sir."

He reached inside his desk and took out a deep colored bronze cuff. It looked much too large for her wrist. "Have you ever worn one of these?"

"No," Rose said.

"At first you will feel a bit of numbness in your wrist, but that will soon give way to a feeling of warmth. It will dull your sense of magic, but you will still have the ability, however, not the means to use it within the city. When you come back through this way, it will be taken off. Give me your wrist." He slipped the cuff on and it molded itself to Rose's wrist, like it was a part of her. "Does it hurt?"

"No. Just feels weird, different."

"That's expected. Okay." He stood up. "Follow me and we'll get you on your way."

"That's it?" Lanis asked.

"Of course. Your note and her memories were all I needed." They walked past several closed doors before coming to a stop at the end of the hall. He opened the door and a man on the other side held it open. "Rose, once you pass this doorway you will be in Manight. You might feel a bit of a surge in the cuff. That is to be expected. The shields they have in place are ten times stronger than the ones they have in other parts of Hadmore. They are quite impressive." He motioned for them to walk through.

Rose swayed. "That is quite a feeling."

"It is. Now this is as far as I can go. Jamason will get you all settled. Good luck," he said, closing the door behind him.

"Why does everyone keep wishing us good luck?" Lanis said. Elson shrugged and Rose smiled.

It took them less than an hour to reach The Green Dragon Inn. They stabled their horses and everyone settled into their rooms for the night. Lanis took off her boots and lay down on the bed. After the events of the past few weeks, she couldn't believe they were finally here. There were a lot of people, but not the thousands Anya had told them to expect. Anya. She should have told her that she would be traveling to Manight and that she would be the one to read the Prophecy. She should have been the one to escort her here, not some imposter. And what did Kaylynn have to do to with anything? It was unheard of for a white-band healer to leave their assigned post, especially to travel such a long distance. Anya held a lot of things back, but then, they all did. There was something weird going on with Rose too. Ever since they left the Ruins, she was acting funny, more aloof. She would tell Elson about her suspicions tomorrow. She pulled the blanket up and settled down, comforted by the fact that she would talk with Anya soon. If she had taken the direct route, she should already be here. Her reunion with Anya would have to wait though. She wasn't at all sure what she would have to do to ensure the princess's safety, but Nia had been with them so far. Surely she wouldn't abandon them now.

❧❧❧❧

Dimitri gazed through the small opening in the door at the woman sitting on the bed. She looked so small and pitiful. He chuckled to himself. How easy those of power fall. She didn't look like a High Priestess now. He covered his nose when a foul odor reached it. She didn't smell like a person of power either. Kidnapping her was just a means to an end and it kept Merek off his back. In truth, all he wanted was the Protector's mask, but the Protector had run at the first sign of trouble. They were, in all ways, known as immortal. It didn't make sense. If all Protectors were so easily scared off, that information would come in handy later.

She had been there three days and they weren't any closer to finding the Protector than they were at the beginning. He instructed the guard to take her some water and a bite of food. If it was up to him he would let her starve, but the Jester insisted. He shook his head and walked toward his office where his two guests were waiting. He knew what he wanted to do, but he wasn't sure it was in his best interest. He knew what Merek would say, but he knew the Jester, being a wild card, could throw his entire plan out of order. In the end, the decisions concerning her fate would be his and his alone. Merek seriously couldn't believe that her being out of the picture would guarantee him her position. And no one really knew what the Jester wanted, but he would do his best to find out. His ace might turn out to be Ella. He needed to get in touch with her.

He stopped before he reached his office and opened a door on his right, entered it, and closed the door behind him. A square, black table sat in one corner of the room and a plain, brown chest sat on the center of it. The chest itself would never catch anyone's eye, but what lay nestled within its depths would. He removed a black stone from his pocket, waved it over the latch of the box, and smiled when it made a popping noise and opened. Five small, silver spheres laid nestled within its depths. He ran his finger over each one. What power did they hold? Besides his daughter's births, his greatest joy was receiving the first sphere. The other four weren't as easy to come by and many men had lost their lives helping to acquire them, but the price was well worth it. As for the last two spheres, he knew deep in his gut Jalen possessed one. The last sphere, though, continued to elude him. He waited fifteen years for the first five; he would wait as long as it took for the final two.

Merek approaching him gave him the perfect opportunity to accomplish a lot without having to do much of anything. Some plans fell apart while others continued to grow. Hate could lead a person to do the unthinkable. He hoped Ella carried out her part. He held out little hope that she could, or would even help him. She held her oaths to a high regard, and her loyalty to the sanctity of magic could very well out do her love for him. If, when the time came, she couldn't do as he asked, he would have to find another way. He would never want her to sacrifice her integrity for his cause.

With one final glance, he shut the lid, and walked out of the room. He continued down the hall, opening the last door on his left. He nodded at the guard, straightened his shirt, and walked in. His two guests were already seated. As usual, the Jester looked relaxed and Merek tense. "Gentlemen."

"I don't like to be kept waiting," the Jester said.

Dimitri sighed and took his seat. "My apologies."

"You're scared of him," Merek spat. "He's a joke."

"As you should be too," the Jester said. A white orb appeared in his hand and he floated it in front of Merek. "Alas, now is not the time for games. I do believe we have business to discuss."

"Yes." Dimitri nodded. "I asked you both here to discuss the fate of my prisoner. Since it is looking more and more like she doesn't know anything." He looked at the Jester. "She won't be of any use to me. Why should I keep her alive?" He watched the different emotions play out on both their faces. He leaned forward when the Jester blinked. That little crack in his demeanor spoke volumes.

"I agree," Merek said, standing. "I don't see any reason to keep her alive. In fact, I would be honored if you would let me kill her."

"I know what you want." He directed his next question to the Jester. "What do you think I should do?"

The Jester stood and started to pace. He jumped up, crossed his legs, and floated in the air. "I can see the benefits to keeping her alive and the benefits to killing her. I feel that she would be of better use to you alive."

"What?" Merek shouted, pushed his chair back,

and clenched his fists.

The Jester cocked his head and smiled. "How often do you get a prisoner like her? She is a High Priestess and the followers of Nia love her. Imagine the leverage you could have with her. It far outweighs the enjoyment you, Merek, would get from killing her." He uncurled his legs and stood.

Dimitri stood, walked to the door, and spoke to the guard. A few minutes later, the guard returned, dragging Anya's body behind him. He threw her on the floor and walked out.

Merek covered his nose. "Good grief, the stench is awful."

"What did you expect would happen, throwing her into that kind of environment?" The Jester said, looking down at her.

Dimitri addressed the Jester. "You have one shot to find out what you can from her. I want to know where her Protector is, and for an added bonus, I want to know where the written Prophecy is."

The Jester knelt beside her. He touched her arm, but when she recoiled from his touch, he sighed and closed his eyes. After a few minutes, her body started convulsing. White foam seeped out of the sack that covered her head then her body went limp. The Jester stood and addressed Dimitri. "She has a strong mind and an even stronger spirit. She doesn't have the Prophecy." He smiled. "She's not stupid. She sent it to Manight already." He held his hand up. "I don't know how she sent it, or who she sent it with. It was locked away in a part of her mind I couldn't access."

"You must not be that much of a Rogue if you couldn't access every part of her mind," Merek spat.

"I am a Jester, and you seem to be forgetting she

is a High Priestess. Her faith in Nia is great and her mind is very strong. She will not give up her secrets easily and, to be honest, it's hard to break that kind of faith."

"Is that right? You didn't find out anything about her Protector?" Dimitri asked.

"I have already told you she wouldn't know where her Protector is. She doesn't have a mind connection with her Protector," the Jester said.

Dimitri picked her up and held her in front of him. "What a waste you are. Not much without your Protector, are you? Maybe if I were to kill you, your Protector would try to save you. You disgust me." He grunted and threw her into the wall, only to have her body stop a few inches from it, hanging in the air. Dimitri swung his gaze to the Jester. "What are you doing?" He now knew what the Jester would do if faced with her death. Now he just needed to find out why the Jester wanted her kept alive. What was he playing at?

The Jester held his hand up. "Like I said. She's worth more to you alive."

He nodded and called another guard over to take her back.

"A new cell," the Jester said.

"What?" Merek said.

"Take her to a new cell, and give her proper food and water, and a place to wash up. If she's going to be here for a while, she'll need those things."

"No," Dimitri directed to his guard.

"You can't honestly believe that's the right thing to do," the Jester said.

"Of course it is." Merek laughed.

"Both of you, shut up. Merek, everyone knows what you want, but for the moment, she's worth more to me alive than dead. Forewarning, Jester. That may not always be the case." He needed to find out who held the Prophecy and how to stop them, no matter the cost. "Merek, you can leave." When he heard the click of the door, he sat behind his desk and addressed the Jester. "I have a job for you."

❧❧❧❧

The three-day ride into the heart of Manight didn't bring any unwanted surprises, and to everyone's delight, turned out fairly easy. From their vantage point on the main road, Lanis could see the top of Livingston, the formal name for the Royal estate. The sight was a welcome one. One of the townspeople informed them that the road they were on would lead to the heart of the marketplace. So far, the people they met seemed friendly and didn't seem the least put out by their presence. Elson turned a corner in front of her, and Lanis couldn't have prepared herself for the scene in front of them. There were people as far as the eye could see. Vendor's stalls lined both sides of the street, and the smells were intoxicating. Her stomach growled.

Elson gave her a look. "As much as I would love to explore, let's figure out what road to take, then we'll get something to eat."

"I second that," Rose said.

Lanis eyed the three separate roads that spread out in front of them. "Excuse me," she said to the closest vender.

"How may I help you, my lady?"

Elson coughed and Rose snickered. Lanis ignored them both. "If you could direct us to the inn closest to the Estate and which road we should take?"

"Of course." He smiled. "Take the far right road and at the end of the lane, turn left. Directly at the end of the road are a few inns for you to choose from. Now, if you're looking for something to eat, you will want to take one of the other roads."

"We appreciate it, thank you," Elson said. They trotted to the end of the road and turned left.

"Being so close to the Castle will increase the cost of the room," Rose said

Lanis nodded in agreement. "So everyone needs to be prepared to share a room."

Elson smoothed his hair back. "Share a room with two beautiful women. You won't hear me complain."

"I just bet you won't." Lanis smiled. Rose had been quiet for the last few days. The look on her face spoke volumes. Lanis caught Elson's eye and pointed at Rose. He rode in between them.

"Rose, you okay?" he asked.

Rose scratched her nose. "I'm fine. It's just been a while since I've been back. I'm getting the feel for everything." She rubbed her fingers on her cuff. "Being this close to the Estate has dulled my powers even more. It's throbbing more than usual."

He patted her on the back. "You know what cures all, don't you?"

"No, what?"

"Apple pie," he answered with a straight face, and everyone laughed. Elson led them down a side road, stopped, and dismounted. He nodded at a woman standing by a fabric vendor.

"Ma'am, I was wondering if you could recommend one of the three inns." He shrugged. "Maybe prefer one over the other."

"Your best bet would be the brick building on

the end."

"Thank you," Elson said. When they rounded the corner, it was hard to miss the sign hanging above the building, The Green Dragon Inn Two.

"Well, the first one we stayed at was nice enough. Elson, why don't you go in and get us a room while Rose and I wait out here," Lanis said.

"Sure thing."

Lanis stood against the building, watching the bustling of the marketplace. Her eyes kept wandering with every new sight to adsorb. Being in a city this size was new to her. It was both scary and fascinating at the same time. She didn't like it. She did a double take when she saw a woman standing off to the side of a vendor's stall. She looked familiar, but from the distance between them, she couldn't make her features out. Lanis turned away, swinging her gaze back when it dawned on her who the woman was, but the woman was gone. She would have to keep an eye out for her. "Is that all that's bothering you?"

It took Rose a few minutes to answer. "I grew up here, and I haven't seen my family for a few years. Not since I left the Academy. Everything is different."

"So this is all normal for you," Lanis said, pointing to the marketplace.

"Actually, it's probably twice the size it normally is because of the festival, but yes, I'm used to this and I know exactly which vendor sells Elson's apple turnovers."

"Excellent," Elson said, walking up to them. "Our room is around the corner and it only has two beds, but I don't mind sleeping on the floor. I also had enough money to stable our horses. I paid for the room for a week."

"Let's hope our business is finished before that. It would be nice to enjoy some of this. I can't see myself ever coming back here. Not once I get back home," Lanis said.

"Me either. It's strange how much I miss Malora."

"I know, me too. I can't wait to get back." When Elson frowned, it took a second for her to realize what she said. He didn't know she lived in Malora. "I—"

"Let's put our things up and get something to eat," he said.

Lanis was grateful he was letting her off the hook. They left their belongings in their room, along with Elson and Rose's weapons. Lanis kept her whip on and tightened it around her waist. She decided to keep her boot knife, also. She didn't expect trouble, but she needed to be prepared for anything. Being in Manight wouldn't make things easier; it would make them harder. Rose led them to a small vendor in a back corner and Elson bought them each a fried apple pie.

"You're right," Rose said, licking her fingers. "Apple pie will cure almost anything. I feel better already."

"See, I told you. On the way back we should get a few more," he said.

When the Castle came into view, it was a lot bigger than Lanis expected. It easily dwarfed the entire town of Malora. Tall stone walls surrounded it on all sides. She looked through the iron gates leading to the main entrance and couldn't help but be impressed. The grounds were immaculate. People were scattered everywhere inside the gates, setting up for the main part of the festival. The only visible way into the Castle was through the main gate. There had to be another way in. She couldn't enter through the gates.

"I don't see how you're going to get in without an invitation," Rose said. "The royal estate is probably the most protected place in Adearian."

"For our peace of mind, we have to rule out all possibilities," Elson said.

"We have to look," Lanis agreed. Once they left the marketplace, they entered a dense forest. They kept a discreet distance from the stone wall, following it to the cliff's edge. She stood by the edge, breathing in the warm evening air. Off in the distance, a ship headed into port. She stepped back when it dawned on her how far up they were. The Anlerm Sea surrounded the Castle on three sides. It would be nearly impossible for them not to see an attack coming. "Let's head back, get a good night's sleep, and figure something out in the morning. I'll take lead."

Rose smiled. "That sounds like the best plan I've heard in a while."

"I second that." Elson laughed.

Lanis spun around when his laughing abruptly stopped. They'd let their guard down and it was a costly mistake. One man held Elson by the throat, and another man pulled Rose close to his body. Lanis should have heard them approach. She stepped back and touched her whip when a woman stepped from between two trees and stood in front of the men. King Strunkot had been right, someone from her past. The same woman she saw earlier in the marketplace. The woman lifted her sword and smiled. Lanis instantly regretted not killing her years ago when she had the chance.

"From the look on your scarred face, I would say you remember me." She bounced the tip of the sword against her boot. "Do you remember this sword?" She lifted it up. "You should, considering it's the same one you killed my husband with." She took a step forward. "I told you I would find you and kill you." She pulled a piece of paper out of her pocket. "And look," she waved the paper around, "I'll even get a reward for killing you. A bonus." She threw the paper on the ground and started pacing. "I promised him I would avenge his death."

Lanis planted her feet and braced herself when the woman lifted the sword and ran at her. As she swung the sword, Lanis ducked, grabbed the arm that held the sword, and punched the woman in the stomach. The woman stumbled back and dropped the sword.

The woman screamed and ran at her, swinging her arms widely. Lanis caught her arms, twisted her around, and dragged her backward. Tightening her hold, she slammed the woman's head into a tree. She released her and let her body fall to the ground. When she stepped toward Elson and Rose, the men took a step back, dragging their captives with them.

"We want the relic," the man holding Rose said, running the tip of his knife up and down her throat like a lover's caress.

Lanis flinched as a trickle of blood ran down Rose's throat. These men couldn't possibly know about the stone the old women gave her. What else could they be talking about? She didn't have any other relic. What did they really want? They weren't working for the woman. That much was evident. What should have been an easy stroll ended up becoming a nightmare. Lanis had to detach herself from everything she was feeling. Emotions couldn't play a part in this. Things would end badly and from the looks in Elson and Rose's eyes, they knew it too.

She reached down, slipped the knife out of her boot, but never took her eyes off the bandits. They tightened their holds on Elson and Rose and took a step back. Another step back and they would all go over the edge. Elson started to struggle, clawing at the arm around his throat. Rose just stood there. She couldn't do anything with the cuff on her wrist. It made it impossible to fight back. When Elson bit the arm holding him, his captor loosened his grip, and they started throwing punches. Lanis felt a sense of dread when they both moved closer to the edge. She didn't hesitate when she threw her knife, crouched, and flicked her wrist. When her whip connected, she pulled, and knocked the bandit holding Rose off his feet. As if in slow motion, she watched him swing his arms and tumble backward. Lanis screamed when he grabbed Rose and they both fell over the edge. She scrambled to where they fell and looked down. She couldn't believe what she wasn't seeing. The bandit's body lay mangled on the rocks below, but Rose's body was nowhere to be seen. She turned around to look for Elson. Her knife was stuck in the other bandit's throat.

"Lanis." Elson stood, ran to her, and looked over the edge. "Where's Rose?"

"I don't know. They both fell over." She accepted the hand he held out and stood. "Rose's body should be down there."

"Maybe it fell in the water." But she could tell he didn't believe that.

Lanis shook her head and walked back to the woman. At least she could finish something she should have years ago and it would give her a small sense of accomplishment. She kicked the woman until she started to come around. When she moaned, Lanis picked her up and dragged her to the cliff's edge.

"Lanis, think about what you're doing," Elson said, but didn't move to stop her.

"Don't worry. I know exactly what I'm doing." She pushed the woman to the ground and stood over her.

"Please," the woman said, crawling to her knees. "Let me go."

"You mean like you let us go. Oh wait." Lanis laughed. "You didn't let us go. You were going to kill me and my friends." Lanis kicked her in the stomach and the woman doubled over.

"Please," she cried.

"You sound just like your husband right before I killed him." Lanis winked at her.

"You bitch," she spat.

"You couldn't care less about my friend's lives and I couldn't care less about yours. I should have done this four years ago." Lanis grabbed her and the woman clawed at her arms, leaving deep red marks.

"Wait," the woman screamed.

"Brace yourself. You're about to join your husband." Lanis smiled. "Tell him I said hello," she said, lifting her, and flinging her off the side. She watched with more satisfaction than she should have as the woman's body hit an outcrop, twisted, then landed in a heap on the ground next to the bandit's body. She walked over to the other bandit, pulled her knife, and rolled his body over the edge. "Rose couldn't have possibly landed in the water. I don't know where she is, but I'm sure she's not down there. She was full of surprises." She shrugged. "Maybe she had a few more. I'll tell you about the woman later. The short version is her husband is the one that gave me the scar, and I killed him. She vowed to avenge his death."

Elson was quiet, looking over the edge. "Good enough. Let's get out of here. Someone will have spotted the bodies by now and considering the number of guards around here, we need to go." When they entered the town square, she allowed herself to breathe. They followed along the stone wall and in no time, they were standing in front of the iron gates that would lead into the Castle. She watched the workers until her gaze fell on a woman surrounded by a group of people. She did a double take when she noticed the woman's necklace. She clutched her stomach and turned away.

"Lanis, you okay?"

"Yes." She stopped a man walking by. "Excuse me. Can you tell me who that woman standing in the center of the group is?"

He smiled and nodded. "Why, that's the Lady of the House, Lady Sara. She's been working non-stop to make sure the festival is a success." The pride in his voice was unmistakable.

Lanis rubbed her neck. "When did she get back?"

He frowned at her. "What do you mean? She comes out here every day about this time to work on the preparations. Why, I can't remember the last time she left the city."

"Thank you," Lanis said.

"What's wrong?" Elson asked, as they made their way to their room.

"Do you remember the riders that almost ran us over at the beginning of our trip? On the dirt road."

"You think that woman was one of them?" he said, pointing behind him. "You heard the man, she doesn't travel. How could she possibly have been there and now here? That's not possible." He got a strange look on his face. "What in the world would she have been doing there?"

"I don't know. I don't know about anything anymore." They were almost to their room when a cloaked figure brushed in front of her and placed a piece of paper in her hand. Lanis searched the marketplace, but the figure was gone. Vanished. Lanis squeezed her hand around the note and she followed Elson into their room. She slumped into a chair, laid her head back, and closed her eyes.

"Lanis," Elson said quietly.

"What?" She sat up and opened her eyes.

"Rose's things are gone."

"What?" She stood. "That's different."

"A little bit." He sat on the edge of the bed and ran his hand over his beard. "You think she's still alive?"

"At this point I wouldn't rule anything out." She laid the piece of paper on the table.

He pointed at it. "What's that?"

"Someone bumped into me on our way here and slid it into my hand."

"Open it," he said, standing beside her.

Only a few words were written.

Meet me at the West side of the estate as soon as possible.

"Not much there. Do you think this is why you're here?" Elson asked.

He looked as tired as she felt. "It has to be."

"Could be a trick."

"It could be, but I don't think it is. Besides, we've run into those before. I have a feeling I will be able to mark one thing off my list tonight."

Anya cried out, trying and failing to adjust her legs. After promising not to remove the sack from her head, her hands were tied in front of her. It was a welcome relief even though the pain in her shoulders intensified. Biting back a groan, she carefully leaned back against the wall and fought the urge not to fall asleep. After the first day, she realized they were putting something in her food to make her drowsy. If her calculations were correct, she'd been in this prison for six days, but sleep came so often, she wasn't sure about anything anymore. Which is what they wanted. Her faith, once rock steady, was being tested at every turn. No matter how many times she rinsed the sores on her feet and legs, she knew infection had set in. It didn't make any sense for the cuts to escalate to the state they were in. Every time a negative thought entered she mind, she pushed it as far back as she could, but that was also getting harder to do.

She sat up, every nerve in her body on alert, when the creaking of the door drew her attention. It wasn't dinnertime and she rarely got visitors. Nothing good ever came from an unannounced visit. Without a word, the heavy footsteps came closer to her, rough hands grabbing her arms, and dragging her off the bed. It took all she had not to fight back. The man dropped her on the floor, slipped his hands through her tied ones, and started dragging her out of the room. A scream ripped from her lips as her feet scraped the stone floor, breaking open the sores she had tried so hard to heal. She took even, shallow breaths, hoping the pain would subside when he stopped, and spoke to someone. Her body sagged of its own accord and was suspended in the air. If he dropped her, she wouldn't be able to get back up. After he stopped talking, he picked her up, and threw her over his shoulder. She lay limp against him and savored the pain subsiding in her feet. It was short lived when his steps slowed then stopped. The realization that this could be the end hit her full force and she forced her fears aside. Nia was with her. She bit back a cry when he patted her butt, grabbed her by the waist, and tossed her through the air. Her body jerked as it hit the mattress. Shock waves ran up her back and it felt like tiny pins were sticking into every available inch of her skin. She snapped her eyes shut as the sack was ripped from her head, not prepared for the blinding light that attacked her. If this was what death felt like, she wouldn't wish it on her worst enemies. Forcing herself to relax, even not knowing what awaited her, she let each breath come as it should. Within minutes, her breathing calmed, and she slowly opened her eyes. She squinted into the light until her eyes adjusted. A man she didn't recognize stood at the foot of her bed. His pressed black slacks and fitted red shirt screamed power. Whoever he was, he held a lot of influence. Letting her eyes wander around the room, she spotted Merek and the Jester standing near the corner.

"Take the binding off her wrists," the stranger said to a guard standing at the door.

Not a man to do the dirty work himself, just what she expected. She screamed, not expecting the pain that ran through her hands when the bindings were cut. She pounded her head back against the mattress, and counted backwards from ten, the way Lanis had taught her. She didn't want to, but she raised her hands to eye level. They were swollen, raw, and deep groves were cut into the skin where the bindings had been tied too tight. If she was alone, she would feel sorry for what she was going through, but she wasn't alone, and she would never allow these men to see her weak.

"What would the people of Malora think of you now?" Merek said.

She ignored him, listening to the stranger when he started talking instead.

"I am Dimitri, and I have finally come to a conclusion about your fate." He sat in a chair in the middle of the room. "I don't have such strong feelings for you as these two men seem to," he said, pointing at the Jester and Merek. "They are very passionate about what should be done, but my decision wasn't based on anything they want. Although my decision has undeniably made me an enemy, I don't feel you can be of any use to me. You know nothing of your Protector and I have found out new information about whom you sent the Prophecy with. My time would be better spent in Manight. And as for the Jester's suggestion." He shrugged. "I don't care what goes on in Malora and I don't need you for leverage. You don't have anything I want."

They couldn't know about Kaylynn. She struggled to sit up, and when she managed it, she caught Dimitri's eyes. Things weren't adding up. "Who are you?"

"I told you who I was."

She shook her head. "Who are you?"

He laughed and stood. "Let me properly introduce myself." He bowed. "I am Councilman Dimitri Ramus of the Queen's Court." He walked to the door. "By the time anyone finds you, you'll be long dead." He walked out, leaving her alone with Merek and the Jester. She would beg the Jester to kill her before she allowed Merek to lay a hand on her. Dimitri was the man she had sent Elson to kill and Merek had given her the information. The information had come from High Priest Lantor. It didn't make any sense that he would be involved in this, but at this point, nothing made sense. She had a feeling Dimitri didn't know he was being double-crossed. Nia did work in mysterious ways. Somehow, she didn't think Queen Abigail didn't know about his betrayal. Dimitri was a dead man and Merek— if Lanis didn't kill him, someone else would. He was too arrogant to live long outside of Malora. But the Jester was another matter, and one she didn't have an answer for.

Merek sat in the seat Dimitri vacated. "Look where we are now," he said, waving his hands in the air. "You don't seem like yourself, High Priestess." He snickered. "I just wanted to let you know that I will be the best High Priest Malora has ever seen. When your body is found, I will make it known that I am your successor. And," he said, standing, "I will find great comfort knowing the Prophecy will not be read."

That's what he wanted, to be High Priest. He had nerve; she would give him credit for that. In spite of the circumstances, she laughed. Sharp pains shot through her chest, but they were well worth the look on his face. "Do you think I am a fool? I took care of everything before I left Malora. I knew there was a chance I wouldn't be going back. I. Took. Care. Of. Everything. I know for a fact the Prophecy will be read." She chuckled. "I already have a successor in place. Even when you kill me, you will lose everything."

She recoiled from the hate in his eyes. He spit at the ground and inched closer to her, but stopped when the Jester held his hand up. "The only reason I'm not killing you is because he," he said, pointing at the

Jester, "asked to be the one who did and I have to say I will enjoy your death a lot more knowing how you will suffer." He stepped out of the room, leaving her alone with the Jester.

She smiled sadly at him. "Not our usual meeting place."

"No, High Priestess, it isn't." He knelt in front of her. "There has been a slight change of plans. Please don't get your hopes up. I cannot remove you from this place. I have sworn an oath not to. I do not go back on my word."

"I don't understand." She reached for him, but he stayed away from her touch. "I didn't think Rogues had an oath to anybody. You're powerful, just get me out," she pleaded. "I'm going to die here."

"No," he said, shaking his head. "I can't. When I took this assignment, I signed an oath to see it through. I can't go back on that now. But who do you think has been keeping you alive? I wouldn't, couldn't let them kill you." He spoke a few words and two buckets full of water and a basket with an assortment of breads, cheeses, and fruit appeared in the room. "This should keep you for a while. Please, listen carefully. I am going to enchant this room. What that means is no one will be able to enter and you won't be able to leave. You'll be safe."

Her insides started shaking and she grabbed his hand. She would die here. "How am I supposed to get out?" This was far worse than she ever expected.

"Listen." He clasped her hand between his. "You will get out of here. When I leave this place, I will inform the one person I know who will come." He shrugged. "It's all I can do. After this is done, I still have a life to lead. As much as I love you, I cannot get you out of here, but I am very good at what I do. There are ways around everything."

He couldn't possibly know about Lanis. "Who are you going to inform?"

He cocked his head. "Come on now, your love, of course. I had hoped that would be me, but the first time I saw you two together, I knew it would never happen. The look in your eyes." He shook his head. "It blew me away."

"You don't know anything." If he knew, what did others know?

"Yes, I do." He ran his hand down her check. "I am sorry for what you've been through, but Lanis will come for you, and may Nia help the people that stand in her way."

"She has her own oath to fulfill." She swiped at the tears falling down her cheeks. "She won't come until that's finished."

He laughed. "You think so? That's where she and I differ. My oaths are my livelihood. Lanis, on the other hand, would drop everything for you. You should see the way she looks at you."

"How do you know all this?"

"I get around. I hear things, see things." He stood. "The enchantment will last forever, but the food and water won't. Ration. Don't lose faith. And for the record," he said, stopping at the door. "That Protector of yours better hope Lanis finds him before I do. Hang in there. You'll be in Manight to read the Prophecy. That I am sure of."

At the click of the door, she almost lost all hope. All she had right now was faith, a few provisions, and Lanis. She never allowed her mind to linger on her. The pain of losing Lanis far outweighed the physical pain she was going through. Lanis would come for her. Deep down, she knew that. Lanis was her only salvation. She didn't know how she would get her out, but her one prayer would be that she could.

⁂

Lanis crossed her arms and stood her ground. "Elson, I don't have time for this. I am going alone."

"Think this through. You don't even know who the note is from." He threw up his hands and started to pace.

She blew out a breath and ran her hands through her hair. She knew he meant well. "We don't have the time to discuss this. I am grateful for you being here, but this is something I have to do. I know deep down this is why I am here." She patted him on the shoulder as she passed him and walked out of the room, closing the door behind her. He couldn't come, and they still didn't know what happened to Rose. Granted, it was odd, but something told her she wasn't dead; however, she had no clue where she could be. If magic hadn't saved her, she couldn't fathom what actually did. She walked through the marketplace, stopped at the edge of town, and waited. When the guards turned their backs to her, she entered the woods. Since the bodies were found, estate security was on high alert. She plastered herself to the nearest tree when two guards came her way. When they passed, she eased away, made her way to the fence wall, and leaned against it. Surprisingly, she wasn't scared, only nervous. After saying a silent prayer, she jerked her head up when someone grabbed her from behind and dragged her backward. Fighting free, she spun around to be confronted by the same person from earlier. It took her only a moment to realize she was on the other side of the wall. They were inside the Estate. "How?"

The cloaked figure dropped the hood back to reveal feminine features. Her hair was cut short with bangs sweeping her forehead. A series of small tattoos were lined up on her right cheek. "I'm Mattea." Her voice wasn't like anything Lanis had ever heard before.

"I'm Lanis."

She nodded. "I'm Veilshield and I was sent to fulfill an oath."

The Veilshield were shadow walkers. It was rumored they were assassins, but in Lanis's experience, rumors were just that, rumors. But now she knew they could walk through walls. It was a bit unsettling, but she could go with it. "Now I know how I'm going to get into the Castle, and I'm Ramden."

"We're not headed to the Castle." She shook her head. "I was wondering what part you would play." She turned to the Castle. "We don't have much time, follow close to me. Ready?"

"No."

"Good. Come on." They kept to the shadows, stopping occasionally when they saw movement ahead of them. It looked like they were headed to the Castle, but at the last moment Mattea took a sharp turn to the left. "Keep close," she whispered. It didn't take them long to reach another stone structure. Mattea reached back for her hand and Lanis clasped it. She led her beside a long wall and Lanis tensed when she wrapped her arms around her and walked backward. When they reached the other side, Mattea held a finger to her lips. Lanis nodded. They were in the shadows of some sort of stadium. She gasped, fighting the urge not to run into the arena when she spotted what everyone had gathered for.

A woman stood upright, suspended in the air in the middle of the arena. Her hands were tied above her head on a long beam that ran across the entire open area. Her feet barely touched the ground, her toes grasping for any bit of traction. From their vantage point, Lanis didn't know how the woman was still alive. Her clothes hung off her body in tattered rags, exposing her nakedness to everyone in the stands. Lanis clutched her whip as the woman's head fell forward and her body went limp, blood dripping onto the ground. No one deserved this kind of treatment.

Mattea whispered in her ear. "That is Princess Jalen."

The sudden impact of why she was called on this oath finally made sense. If her own people would do this to her, how could one of them save her? Besides, what could she have possibly done to deserve this type of treatment? Where were her guards? Lanis knew for a fact that Jalen had personal guards that were assigned to her from birth. She growled and stepped forward when the man beating Jalen cut the rope above her hands and her body fell to the ground. The crowd's shouts, once loud and boisterous, instantly quieted.

"Let's go," Mattea said, grasping her hand. "This way." They jogged in the shadows until they were a few feet from the door to the dungeon. Lanis watched a guard throw Jalen over his shoulder and walk toward them. She would kill them all if she had to. "Ready?"

She looked at Mattea. "Yes." This is why they chose her. When the guard walked past and shut the door, Mattea grabbed her and dragged her through the door and into a small opening in the wall. "Be quick. I can't help you from here. They have alarms in place to alert them to the presence of a Veilshield. I'll be waiting outside." Before Lanis could say anything, she was gone. She pushed back against the wall, took a deep breath, and blended. She could do this. This is what she was called for. Rounding a corner and staying plastered against the wall, she made her way down the hall. She had never been in a dungeon before and she didn't want to visit one again. The foul smell of decay mixed with the coppery taste of blood was unmistakable. Death lingered in the air.

She walked along the wall until she reached Jalen's cell. The disgust she felt for the guard grew two-fold when he knelt next to Jalen's body. She saw her chance as he turned away from her. She pushed off the wall and entered the cell, instantly blending with the wall. The cells were small. Barely big enough to fit four people. Three of the walls were stone while the one facing the hall was made of iron bars. Lanis now understood what Mattea was talking about. There were a number of holes in the walls and the ceiling to let light in. There weren't any shadows.

She cursed when the guard rubbed a hand down Jalen's check and told her she was getting what she deserved. Holding her blend, she waited until he shut the door and locked it behind him before approaching Jalen. When Jalen finally took a breath, Lanis pushed away from the wall, and crouched next to her body. Jalen's eyes flew open when Lanis touched her arm. "I'm getting you out of here, but I'm going to need your help. When I hear the guard come back, I'm going to lift you in my arms, and we're going to blend with the wall. Try to cooperate with me. I will not hurt you. I am Ramden."

"Okay," Jalen croaked. "I don't want to die in this cell." She started coughing, spraying blood all over the straw covered floor. Lanis pushed her panic down and looked around the cell for something she could use. Reaching in the corner, she picked up a plate and without thinking about her actions, she started banging it against the bars. It only took a moment to hear footsteps running down the hall. As fast as she could, she lifted Jalen in her arms and moved back against the wall. Struggling, but keeping a firm hold of her, she moved them next to the cell door and blended. A guard skidded to a halt outside the cell, panting heavily. She would have to act quickly. She would only get one chance. The guard's fingers fumbled with the key until the lock clicked and he flung the door open, entering the cell. He kicked the straw laden floor then ran back down the hall, shouting at the other guards. Eyeing the door opening, she tightened her hold and dragged Jalen across the hall, where she blended with the stone wall just as the guards ran back toward the cell.

Readjusting Jalen, she stayed along the cell wall until she reached the opening where Mattea had left her. It didn't take long before a guard opened the door, the same guard that had beaten Jalen. He slammed the door open, waved his hands in the air, and shouted at three other guards. Lanis burnt his image into her mind. If she had the good fortune of meeting him again, she would kill him. When he turned away from them, she took her chance, and slid out the open door. He swung back around, frowning at their exact position. He scrubbed his hands down his face and pulled the door shut behind him.

Lanis struggled, losing her grip on Jalen, when

Mattea waked out of the shadows next to them.

"Good grief," Lanis said, breaking her blend.

"That's amazing," Mattea said. "I'll take her from here." She easily took Jalen in her arms.

"Wait, how do I get out of here?"

Mattea shrugged. "I'm sure you'll figure something out," she said before disappearing. Lanis ran her hands through her hair. She'd pulled it off. After blending, she looked around until she saw a small opening on one the side of the stadium. Making her way there, she slipped out into the courtyard. She walked the same way Mattea had brought her before. Every time she caught a glimpse of a guard, she would blend, but the constant blending was draining her. She couldn't believe that it only took a matter of minutes to save someone it had taken almost two months to reach. All they had been through was over in an instant. She looked at the Castle and smiled, realizing that Anya was somewhere inside. She couldn't wait to see her. She jumped at the touch on her arm.

"Were you planning on staying here all night?" Mattea snickered.

"It was a possibility."

Mattea laughed. "Come on, I'll get you to the other side." Stepping out of the shadows, Lanis got her first good look at her. Her clothes were black, but she could still make out the blood that covered them. "You shouldn't stare. You have blood on your clothes too."

For the first time, Lanis noticed how blood soaked her shirt was. "Is she going to be all right?"

"I hope." She wrapped her arms around her, pulled her back into the shadows, and through the wall. "Good luck, Lanis."

Lanis tried to cover as much blood as she could,

but it was a wasted effort. Walking back through the woods, she entered the marketplace, thankful when no one looked her way. She stopped when she heard, then saw, a group of men laughing and drinking near one of the taverns.

Then she heard his voice. Her heart pounded and her entire body popped out in a cold sweat. She leaned against the wall to steady herself and to get her emotions under control. He shouldn't be here. He should be in the Castle with Anya. He shouldn't be here, not like this. With a new resolve, she walked along the sidewalk until she reached the group of men. Slipping her arms around his neck, she whispered in his ear. "I choose you." He stiffened and all the men hollered and slapped their mugs together. Lanis pulled him away from the group and through the marketplace until she reached her room.

He pulled away from her. "Please," he begged.

She pounded on the door and the instant it opened, she threw the man in. "Don't beg me, Ramuk. You're already a dead man."

Elson looked at the man then quickly dismissed him, bringing his gaze back to Lanis. "That better not be your blood," he said, eyeing her clothes.

"It's not, and my oath is done." Finally.

"If your oath was fulfilled, your bracelet would be gone."

She looked down at her wrist. "I don't have time to worry about that right now." He better have a good explanation for this. Anya had to be safe. Lanis slid her knife out of her boot. "Get in the chair," she said, addressing the man. "Now."

"Please don't kill me." Ramuk begged, standing up, and sitting in the chair she indicated. "Look. I…"

He ran his hands through his hair. "It all happened so fast."

"Lanis," Elson said. "What's going on and who is he?" He picked his sword up off the bed and joined her.

She couldn't tell him, could she? "Elson, please understand there is more going on here than you know. I'm not exactly who you think I am."

"Okay. Who is he?" he said, pointing his sword at the man.

"Listen, man, you have to help me. This is all a misunderstanding. Don't let her kill me."

Lanis ignored his pleas. Pathetic. "Where is she?" She had a sneaking suspicion by the way he was acting Anya wasn't in the Castle, or even in Manight.

He fell to his knees and started crying. "Please." He clung to her legs.

She pushed him away. "The last man that begged for his life I killed. Get up," she ground out.

"Lanis, who is he?" Elson asked.

"I'm only going to ask one more time. Where is she?"

"Fine. I'll answer your questions if you promise not to kill me," the man said.

She laid her knife on the desk, picked the man up, and threw him in the chair. She grabbed her knife and ran it along his throat. Deep enough to draw blood, but not kill. "Ramuk, you are in no position to negotiate with me. You will die, but if you don't answer my questions, I will kill you slowly, then find whatever family you have, and kill them too. Understand? I warned you that if anything happened to her, I would kill you."

He gulped several times and nodded franticly.

"We were ambushed on our way here. These men came out of nowhere and attacked the carriage." He gulped again and looked away. "I got scared and ran. I saw them drag her out of the carriage, but I kept running."

No. No. No. Not Anya. "Where is she now?"

"I don't know."

"You don't know," she spat. She held back the urge to kill him. "Where is the mask?"

He looked up sharply at her. "I threw it away. While I was running, I took it off and threw it."

"Lanis, what is he talking about? What woman and what mask?" Elson touched her arm. "After all we've been through. You can trust me," he pleaded.

Lanis couldn't believe what a coward this man was. "You knew the mask would have protected you. Idiot. You are the vilest person I have ever meet. You let someone drag your High Priestess away," she screamed.

"What?" Elson shouted. "Lanis, tell me what's going on."

Besides Anya, he was the one person she did trust. "Elson, I am High Priestess Anya's Protector. When I was called on this mission, I had to find someone to take my place temporarily. I chose him." She pointed at the man. "I made a rash decision. Anya didn't give me time." She ran her hands through her hair then turned back to the man. "Who took her?"

He shook his head. "I don't know who took her, but I know Merek was involved. I swear, that's all I know."

"You let someone kidnap our High Priestess," Elson said. "And you came here to what, have a good time while Goddess knows what's happening to her?"

"Yes," he squeaked out, looking between them

both.

Lanis walked behind him, pulled her knife across his throat, and pushed his body out of the chair, and onto the floor. Elson picked up his sword and ran it through the man's heart. He was breathing hard. "What now?" he said.

Lanis was numb. She couldn't believe something like this could happen. If she had never taken this oath, none of this would have happened. She should have never left her. "We find her."

"Okay," he said, cleaning the blood off his sword.

"You're okay with everything that just happened?" She slipped her knife back into her boot.

"I know you and I know you would have never brought him here unless you had a good reason." He spat on the man's body. "Worthless scum." Everything was quiet until Elson spoke again. "You're her Protector." She cringed when she heard a bit of awe in his voice.

"Yes, but I'm also just Lanis. We have to find her," she whispered, slumping in the chair.

He sat on the bed and crossed his arms. "Is that all you are?"

"What?" She kept her eyes on the dead body.

"The look on your face when he said she was taken. I've seen that look before. You don't have to tell me, but trust me when I say I understand."

"You can't tell anybody." She didn't know what would happen if others knew of her and Anya's relationship.

"I won't." They swung their heads toward the door when there was a knock on it. "I'll answer it," he said.

"No, I will." She braced herself and opened

the door. "What are you doing here?" People kept surprising her and not always for the better.

"I, my dear," the Jester said, walking in, and looking around the room. "I have come to help you." He only gave the body on the floor a brief glance before sitting down at the table.

"What could you possibly help me with?" Lanis said, shutting the door behind him.

He smiled, cocked his head, and crossed one leg over the other. "I know where Anya is."

About the Author

Born near Chicago, but raised in Southern Illinois, where she still lives, Shannon spends her free time writing. When she isn't writing, she enjoys binge watching fantasy, science fiction, or true crime shows.

You can contact Shannon at -

Website: smhfiction.com
Email: smh1981@live.com
Facebook: facebook.com/smharrisauthor